CAPPUCCINO DUSK

Kankana Basu is a writer, illustrator and journalist based in Mumbai. Her book of short stories *Vinegar Sunday* was published in 2004. *Cappuccino Dusk* is her first novel.

First published in India in 2009 by
HarperCollins *Publishers* India
a joint venture with
The India Today Group

ISBN: 978-81-7223-752-3

2 4 6 8 10 9 7 5 3

HarperCollins *Publishers*
A-53, Sector 57, NOIDA, Uttar Pradesh – 201301, India
77-85 Fulham Palace Road, London W6 8JB, United Kingdom
Hazelton Lanes, 55 Avenue Road, Suite 2900, Toronto, Ontario M5R 3L2
and 1995 Markham Road, Scarborough, Ontario M1B 5M8, Canada
25 Ryde Road, Pymble, Sydney, NSW 2073, Australia
31 View Road, Glenfield, Auckland 10, New Zealand
10 East 53rd Street, New York NY 10022, USA

Typeset in 11/14 Adobe Garamond
Starcompugraphics Private Limited, Delhi

Printed and bound at
Thomson Press (India) Ltd.

CAPPUCCINO DUSK

Kankana Basu

HarperCollins *Publishers* India
a joint venture with

New Delhi

for Sandip

Introduction

When the Banerjees shifted residence from Calcutta to Bombay, they made it a point to carry certain crucial items with them, much like the owl and the pussycat going off to sea with merely three vital items of belonging. Hugely popular with most of the residents of Calcutta, these items had an order of priority. They began, in their order of importance, with a dozen bottles of adult gripe water which went under the improbable sounding name of Aqua Ptychotis. This was guaranteed to tackle everything from peptic ulcers to mild indigestion, and though it left a trail of fire down the gut when swallowed, it also left the patient feeling one with the world and one's gastric juices. The second was a set of small green tubes of the scented antiseptic cream Boroline, fabled to alleviate everything from acne to melancholia with an awesome efficacy. The hauntingly delicate perfume had a soporific effect on the user and left him with shining skin and a benevolent disposition towards his fellow beings. The third was a collection of muslin mosquito nets of assorted sizes, grey from repeated washings with the hard water from Calcutta's taps but with their efficiency undiminished. They performed the incredible feat of letting in the breeze from the ceiling fans while holding back fiendish mosquitoes, guaranteeing the sleeper many hours of sweet, uninterrupted dreams.

Good digestion, sound sleep and a peaceful frame of mind taken care of and in proper sequential order, the Banerjees sallied forth for Bombay.

They did not travel by sea, of course, and definitely not by a pea green boat. They preferred to take the Gyaneshwari Express that started from Howrah at 9.30 p.m. It thundered through several states, condescending to halt at only the most important railway stations, devoured the miles and reached Bombay in seventy-two hours flat.

Besides being fast, the Gyaneshwari was sparklingly clean when it started from Howrah. It was known to have caterers plying soup, soft drinks, tea, coffee and cutlets at all hours of the journey. Pronoy Banerjee was deeply partial to chicken cutlets which tilted the decision in favour of the Gyaneshwari (over the slower and more plebeian Geetanjali). His wife, however, sniffed at the cutlets distrustfully, saying that they were sure to have been made from leftovers judging by the tiny chicken bones that stuck out, waiting to give the eater's dental equipment sharp little surprises. Coming from Ira Banerjee, such dampening remarks were a sure indication that she was feeling unsettled and dyspeptic (as she frequently did) and the others took no notice of her.

The Banerjees chose to travel in the three-tier compartment of an air-conditioned coach. A few hours into the journey, the floor, as was to be expected, was scattered with oil-stained, crumpled newspapers, empty packets of potato chips, human hair and dust. The children, four in number, were ordered to sit crosslegged on the bunks, their tender bodies at a safe height from such shocking pollution. With an air of dark determination, Ira Banerjee pulled out socks of all sizes from the bags for the eight little feet that needed extra protection. Going to the bathroom meant peeling off the socks to prevent them from getting wet and donning them again on returning. The whole exercise proved so very tedious that the children were asked to refrain from consuming fluids. Huge stainless steel boxes of food were carried for this important railway journey that was to change their lives forever. With children you had to play safe (Ira was heard telling her fellow passengers), as you never knew when there could be a delay. The presence of food in large quantities was always a considerable moral support in the most crippling of circumstances as it was sure to keep tempers, egos and bowels in order. The Banerjee family's journey by railway was fraught with action, emotion and drama, given the children's bickering and the parents' quick fixes. With the kind of commotion it generated, it vaguely resembled a new circus coming to town. The journey was undertaken at a time when Mumbai was still the breezy Bombay and Kolkata was still Calcutta, the latter pronounced crisply and smartly with the tongue hitting the palate audibly and the breath exhaled noisily while pronouncing the double 't's. Bombay was still a stretched city of seven islands officially belonging to the proud East Indian fisher folk who hadn't attained the dreaded 'protected class' status. They could be seen spreading their fishing nets for darning on the Mahim Causeway and lining the pavements with their upturned fishing boats. McDonald's and mobile phones had just about entered the city limits.

On entering the city's outskirts, the Banerjees found themselves staring out of the train windows with wonder and awe at the filthy slums that sported television antennae and other trappings of modern life. They saw bright cloth awnings strung with multicoloured lights in the hutments and spirited celebrations with loudspeakers blaring out the latest film songs.

This is faux poverty, thought Pronoy Banerjee disapprovingly, unlike West Bengal, where the poor are really poor.

As it happens with most new places, the first thing that the Banerjees noticed on disembarking from the train was the alien amalgam of smells. The smells of speed, petrol, concrete, night soil, fish, glamour, and the all-pervading saline whiff of the sea. The two little girls, Bonny and Mishti, stood gaping, transfixed by the hoardings, the neon lights, the noise and the activities of the busy railway station. Pronoy Banerjee, trying to handle an irate wife, four children hypnotized into temporary immobility and an overzealous porter who seemed to be keen on taking off with the luggage at the speed of light, felt a wave of nostalgia hit him in the midst of all the bustle. Nostalgia for the inherent shabbiness of Calcutta, for busty Bengali women in crumpled cotton saris, for the smell of the crackling paanch phodon that lurked elusively in the potato preparations served at street corners, for the sight of trams and for roadside tea that one sipped from little earthen pots smelling of rain and wet soil and which one smashed daintily after one finished one's tea.

Pronoy Banerjee looked at the city of Bombay with loathing and distrust.

1

Nineteen-year-old Siddharth Banerjee woke up to a smog-filled dawn. As usual, a hundred thoughts came crowding into his head the moment his eyes were open, but today just one out of all that cacophony stood out. He had been accepted at the prestigious Sir D.V. College of Architecture! His heart missed a beat with excitement at the thought. The Sir D.V. College of Architecture swam in his mind's eyes, with its majestic old stone facade and students who moved around the campus with portfolios and T-squares tucked under their arms. He had always dreamt of belonging to that select group of architecture students and now, with his admission confirmed and his term fees paid, Siddharth's dreams seemed to hold the exciting possibility of translating into reality.

He gazed out at the sooty skyline that split his bedroom window into two horizontal halves. Blackened chimneys rising from a line of cloth mills belched dark smoke into an already grey sky while the uneven jagged rooftops of the industrial sheds broke the smooth tenor of Bombay's horizon. A gleaming rivulet of chemical effluent wound its way through the cityscape and a faint whiff of sulphur trioxide hung in the air. It was not a pleasant view by any stretch but it excited Siddharth. This murky greyness would be his canvas as an architect, he thought exultantly. On graduating, he would rip the canvas to shreds and restructure, redesign and reconstruct the entire skyline.

Beyond recognition. Replace chaos, filth, unplanned growth and aesthetic bankruptcy with alignment, symphony, sound construction and flawless planning. He felt the heady rush of adrenalin in his veins as he visualized the future. He saw a horizon with tall, silver structures gleaming with chrome and glass that reflected unpolluted sunsets. He saw concrete kerbs giving way to roads and residential buildings with no dusty interruptions in between. In his mind's eye, he saw immaculate landscaped gardens that broke the monotony of construction with vibrant patches of green. He saw neatly allotted low-cost housing schemes that eradicated the presence of slums. He saw metal, glass, granite, precision, symmetry and splendour in place of soot, filth, crowding and pollution. He turned away from the window, humming a happy tune under his breath. It was time for his bath and he didn't want to be late on the first day of college. He had miles to walk on the pathway to dreams and he looked forward to taking his first step. He glanced out of the window one last time before heading for the bathroom. The smog outside was denser than usual but seemed to be shot with a strange kind of anticipation.

More than five years had passed since Pronoy Banerjee's death. A framed portrait of Pronoy (painted by an unknown artist) was beginning to gather fungus around the edges. The fresh marigold garlands that were changed daily in the first year following his death had given way to plastic flowers (that could be dunked in water for quick, easy cleaning) and these in turn had been replaced by a slim circlet of sandalwood shavings that filled the room with a muted scent and needed no cleaning. The late Mr Banerjee, bespectacled, benign and half-smiling, hung on the wall, and was slowly and comfortably fading into the distance over the years and showed every sign of dipping over the horizon like the setting sun. The earlier hushed tones had been dispensed with and the family now freely and frequently referred to him in their conversation. The loudness of their voices and the cheerful normalcy of their tones heralded the end of mourning. Pronoy Banerjee was remembered with a kind of absent-minded affection by his wife and children who never failed to put in an obituary in the newspapers on his death anniversary. No ghosts haunted A-502 Pushpa Milan, the abode of the Banerjees.

The death certificate cited myocardial infarction as the tongue twisting medical cause of death but Pronoy's family and friends knew it was otherwise: blocked arteries had nothing to do with the case. Pronoy had died pining for the green, pond-filled landscapes of West Bengal, the easy availability of pabda fish (unheard of in Bombay) and the hot, dusty smells of Calcutta trams. Pronoy Banerjee had been a sentimental man. And though nobody spoke about it (not wanting to cause undue embarrassment all around), everybody knew that Pronoy Banerjee, ex-editor and proprietor of the popular tabloid *Noon Voice*, had died of pure, undiluted homesickness.

Ira Banerjee, who had come to Bombay as a frumpy young 'homemaker', disgruntled at being uprooted from her beloved Calcutta, found herself morphing into a nearly unrecognizable person over the years of widowhood. From a gauche recluse perennially draped in cotton saris, with outlandish hairdos and conversant only in Bengali, she graduated to voiles and chiffons. She even sported sunglasses on sunny mornings (more a medical necessity than a fashion statement, her eldest daughter had told her sternly, presenting her with one of the latest models). She could now effectively refrain from saying 'ek tho', 'do tho' while shopping, the 'tho' bits coming out with the force of pistol shots as direct translation of the Bengali 'aekta', 'dooto'. Where earlier she was conditioned to weighing her days by the number of chores performed, she now learnt to use new units for measuring life and live by moments of pure uncomplicated happiness. It was a slow, painful process, but while earlier she would have said that a satisfactory day was one in which she laundered the curtains, cleaned out the cupboards and fried piles of that strenuously crafted coconut-filled sweet lobongo lotika, a few years down the line she looked upon a day of reading Tagore's poems as immensely fulfilling. A short, quality conversation with a friend on the phone (in the surreptitiously stolen moments during the lull after lunch), a rare moment of insight into the finer mysteries of life that often came to her on quiet, clear mornings left her feeling blissfully satiated. A snatch of an old favourite song heard over the din of housework and mundane things like a butterfly coming to perch on her son's T-shirt hung up to dry filled her with a delicious kind of pleasure. That cuisine and geographical demarcations need not be mutually exclusive but could merge seamlessly was another lesson that the city of Bombay taught her. A few years of happy osmosis had Ira Banerjee spiking the very Bengali shukto with peanuts like the Maharashtrians and substituting paati shaapta with dosas. Mustard fish was often served with McDonald's burgers and bhetki fry with bhature. Subject to her innovative culinary experimentations over the years, the Banerjee children learnt to respect and appreciate the merits of fusion cooking. Along with imbibing adventurous food habits, their Bengaliness dropped from them, as did their Calcutta accents, and they gradually started exhibiting a certain cosmopolitanism in their mannerisms, which they liked to describe to themselves as 'savvy'. Their Calcutta cousins begged to differ, often branding them as traitors to their caste and culture and referring to them as 'those insufferable Bombay snobs'. Slowly, over time, such remarks stopped mattering to the Banerjees and the city of Bombay engulfed them almost entirely.

A few years down the line, Ira realized that her children, like her, were changing. Maybe faster. She watched their metamorphosis with growing apprehension. Her older daughter Shraboni (Bonny for short) had grown from chubby adolescence to chubbier womanhood. A staunch feminist streak added to the hormonal confusion and gave her a battle-axe-like exterior. She was perpetually at war with the world and effectively frightened away all prospective suitors. Ira's younger son Siddharth's dreamy eyes reflected only mansions and cities and she quailed at the magnitude of his dreams. Her younger daughter Mishti (shortened from Sharmistha), Siddharth's twin and the baby of the family, was not very bright but as sweet as her nickname, and wanted only to look pretty and hook all the boys. Her uncomplicated goals and sunny disposition made her the undisputed darling of the family.

And there was Soumitro.

Som was a boy who had moved beyond his mother's powers of comprehension long ago. Losing his father in his late teens, being pitchforked into editorial duties before he had even learnt to think straight, taking charge of *Noon Voice* while tackling raging hormones and a world disintegrating around him had unusual repercussions on the eldest born. Slowly and inexorably, Som had withdrawn into himself. Into a dark, private space where nobody was allowed, not even his mother. Where hate, a sense of injustice and inadequacy bred and fermented like some poisonous wine. Som withdrew from the world around him.

To fester in private.

2

Bonny and Mishti awoke to a morning that seemed full of promise. The air smelt faintly of sulphur trioxide and the blue skies outside were blotted out by layers of smog. But the two sisters had enough sunny thoughts on their minds to counteract such environmental hazards. It was Mishti's first day at college. While her twin dreamt of building cities and castles, Mishti dreamt of having her face plastered on every large billboard in the city some day. Her love affair with Bombay had started the moment she stepped off the Gyaneshwari as a child and was bombarded by myriad glittering stimuli from all quarters. This fascination with Bombay had only grown over the years, making her breathless with anticipation at what the future might hold for a pretty girl with grace and charm. She wasn't very sure what exactly it was that she wanted from life but was certain about one thing: some day her face (mammoth-sized) was going to smile down at adoring pedestrians and motorists.

Mishti sat up in bed, glancing apprehensively at her elder sister. Bonny's temper and disposition had a tendency to fluctuate, but today Mishti noted thankfully, her sister seemed to have woken up in a cheerful frame of mind. Bonny rose, and as her regular routine dictated, examined herself critically from all angles in the mirror to check whether she had added any unwanted inches on her person in the night. Nipping her nightdress in at the waist with her fingers, she slowly did a three hundred and sixty degree turn before the mirror. Convinced that she was of the same dimensions as the night before, she started singing to herself in relief.

Bonny's entire adult life had been spent trying to battle the bulge in various zones of her body, though on the face of it she made a great show of being nonchalant and indifferent about her personal appearance. Only those closest to her knew that the devil-may-care attitude was a façade and that acne and cellulite caused her immense anguish.

Mishti padded down the passage to check whether the bathroom was empty. She was greeted by loud singing accompanied by the swish of water jets. Sid seemed to be having an early bath. Rubbing sleep from her eyes, she remembered that it was her twin's first day at college too. Mishti peered into the boys' room on her way back to her bedroom. It seemed dark and silent from the brief glimpse that the partially open door afforded, which meant that her elder brother was sleeping late after working on his crossword well into the night. Mishti tiptoed back to her room, not wanting to disturb Soumitro. Dada would be like a bear with a sore head if disturbed early in the morning.

A-502 Pushpa Milan was shabby but comfortable, done up in a style best described as eclectic. It was on the first floor of a fifteen-year-old ramshackle building flanked by newer, taller ones, and faced the vast sprawling slums that went by the grandiose name of Durga Nagar. Holding pride of place in the drawing room was a reclining chair in Burma teak that had once belonged to Pronoy Banerjee. It was now Soumitro's official property and nobody other than him dared sit in it. Soumitro liked the roomy comfort of the chair. Besides, the forty-five degree angle of the reclining chair aided his linguistic skills, and his crosswords when constructed lounging in the chair, emerged tough and mindboggling in their complexity. Soumitro belonged to that category of people whose mental agility was in inverse proportion to the angle of inclination of his body – he thought best when supine.

The drawing room was a riot of colours. Bonny liked to have lots of cushions around the place and cushions of every conceivable size, mauled shapeless in their playful childhood years, were strewn around in faded covers. A lone basil plant stood on the windowsill, sending a stray scented leaf wafting through the house on windy days. Ira Banerjee showed a preference for white after being widowed, and the walls of the house were painted a blinding white. Mishti loved all shades of pink, purple and fuchsia, while Siddharth preferred cool shades of blues and greens. Bonny, after extensive reading of Feng Shui and Vaastu books, proclaimed yellow-orange hues to be auspicious for their westerly flat and the result was a kaleidoscope of every possible tone in the room. Since Soumitro saw the world in shades of grey and had renounced all colour early in life, nobody bothered to ask him for his opinions on décor. A line of west-facing windows caught the evening sun. At a corner of the drawing room stood a mahogany study table that had been Pronoy Banerjee's prized possession. It was now burnished to a shine and kept ready for Siddharth's architectural work. A massive modern music system on a wall unit immediately proclaimed to visitors that the Banerjees were a music-loving lot.

Among the many things that the Banerjees took very seriously (besides music), tea and coffee headed the list. Two kinds of liquor were brewed every morning. While light Darjeeling leaf tea, especially Orange Pekoe, was preferred by Ira and Soumitro, the younger lot opted for the strong tea boiled with milk and sugar that was popularly termed 'gutter brand Bambaiyya tea'. Tea was sipped in complete silence, affording the beverage the respect it deserved. People passing under the building breathed in the early morning aroma appreciatively and were reminded of the mist-laden slopes of Assam and Darjeeling. In the evenings it was coffee for everybody and one could choose between espresso, cappuccino and filter coffee (the coffee beans being procured from Karnataka regularly). Mishti could whip up a mean espresso, whipping away at the coffee and sugar till her arm ached and her face turned pink with exertion, but the resultant cup of froth-laden beverage was a drink to die for, in the words of her elder brother Som (who was fairly stingy with compliments).

The minuscule kitchen at A-502 Pushpa Milan was a constant hub of activity. Gleaming stainless steel utensils banged against each other and the blaze of red tomatoes and fresh green coriander scattered on the windowsill at all hours created a splash of colour amidst the culinary chaos. Smells of cooking wafted in and out of the flats situated in the adjoining wings of the building, the windows being set at close angles to each other. While the vapours of vegetarian cooking from the Jains' kitchen next door came blowing into the Banerjees', oil fumes from fish being fried at A-502 Pushpa Milan blew into the strictly vegetarian household of the Jains. It was, as Bonny put it, 'a classic case of cosmic irony'.

In direct contrast to the noisy, colourful kitchen and drawing room, the two bedrooms down the corridor waited – dark, quiet, curtained and dreaming. The scent of incense sticks planted in every room in the mornings hung heavy and enigmatic throughout the day and low, old-fashioned ceiling fans groaned rhythmically on rusty joints. The teakwood beds were high, equipped with tall posts to hang mosquito nets, and the faded bedspreads sported exquisite cutwork embroidery. Both the bedspreads and the mosquito nets were treasured items from the Calcutta days. On entering either of the bedrooms, one got the feeling of having stepped back in time, and no matter how disturbed one's frame of mind on entering, peace and sleep came easily in such a room.

3

Soumitro Banerjee, editor and proprietor of the city tabloid *Noon Voice*, sat at his table with a sheet of blank paper before him. The paper had lain blank for quite a while now (in fact, since his arrival at the office early that morning) and was beginning to look a little wilted and dog-eared. With a savage gesture Soumitro swept the paper off his desk, crumpled it into a tight ball, and with unerring accuracy, flung it into the wastepaper basket placed close by.

As usual, no ideas were coming to him this morning.

Soumitro ran a tired hand through his thick unruly hair and glanced around the silent office of the *Noon Voice*. It was too early for anyone to be in as yet, though Beatrice D'Monte, the receptionist-cum-secretary, always an early bird, should be here any moment now – tapping noisily on pointed high heels and announcing her entry to the world, thought Soumitro in irritation and amusement. He couldn't afford to ever be angry with Beatrice. After all, what would he do without her? His survival as a muddle-headed editor depended wholly on her bracing efficiency.

Why, why, oh why did his late grandfather have to be such a brilliant novelist, thought Soumitro for the thousandth time in despair, letting out a long, audible groan into the silence of the empty office. Over the years, his entire clan of relatives (and there were too many of them, he thought grimly) had been waiting with bated breath for him to make his debut as a novelist. And he, Soumitro Banerjee, as he well knew, was no novelist. He could construct a mean crossword that would leave his readers stumped and stunned and which he regularly did for the weekend issues of the *Noon Voice*. Crosswords that challenged one's vocabulary and general knowledge, left readers in ecstasy and despair, often tearing their hair in frustration – qualities that were the undeniable selling point of the tabloid. Sales escalated amazingly during the weekend and Soumitro modestly admitted to the fact that maybe his much awaited weekly crossword (along with the astrological predictions) was one of the reasons for such an inexplicable jump in Sunday sales.

But all said and done, novelist he was not. He had inherited his grandfather's linguistic genes all right, but had missed out on the genius altogether. He did not have story plots coming tearing at him like wild stallions in the night, dragging him willy-nilly to their fruition in his waking hours. And neither did words spill out of him with searing accuracy as in the case of his grandfather. Ideas did not gush forth at all times – rich, abundant and original, begging to be put down on paper. He was a good editor, no doubt, ruthless with punctuation and rigid with grammar. But novelist, he told himself for the hundredth time, he was not. He had his grandfather's famous aquiline nose and wiry physique, but the gift for creative writing had eluded his chromosomes completely. But how did one explain this to those imbeciles across the Hooghly, waiting for the eldest grandson of the late Shankar Deb Banerjee to write his masterpiece? Not only was this book nowhere in sight, it was unlikely to get written in the next few years judging by the way things were going.

Soumitro felt a surge of hysteria rise within him and a sudden, wild urge to laugh long and hard at the grim humour of the situation. I'm not like Dadu, he wanted to scream at everybody. Dadu was different. I do not have a passionate love affair with words like my grandfather, nor does my imagination stretch, bend, warp and leap in a million directions like his. All he felt for words, Soumitro realized in a sudden moment of insight, was an ambiguous half-hearted affection, the kind one felt for roses or newborn babies. I'm more like a butcher, he thought in resignation, I can chop, mince, lacerate, stab, wound, mutilate and pulverize an article to the required shape, length and word count. Subeditors and reporters at his office trembled with fear and reverence in his presence as he was well aware, having built up a reputation as a formidable editor. But creative writing was just not his cup of tea. But how did one explain such intricate literary technicalities to elderly relatives expecting 'little Som' to write his bestseller?

There was nothing remotely 'little' about Soumitro Banerjee. He was over six feet tall with a thick, dark beard and bushy eyebrows which concealed most of his features. The eyes were striking: intense, tortured, bleak and haunted, angst and a hundred nightmares shifting continuously behind dark irises. There was an air of suppressed turbulence about Soumitro and most of his juniors preferred to address their remarks to his chin or his collar instead of looking into those terrifying eyes.

The morning wore on at *Noon Voice*. Soumitro felt the usual black waves of depression beginning to wash over him. He glanced around the shabby office distractedly. He had inherited the tabloid by default when his eldest uncle, the proprietor, and his father, the first editor of *Noon Voice*, had died within a few months of each other, leaving a young and reluctant Soumitro holding the baby, so to speak. He still remembered with horror his early traumatic years as a rookie journalist struggling to keep the paper afloat. Thank god he had managed to survive, and so had the paper. Definitely not wildly popular, but it had, over the years, attained a moderate degree of success and a loyal readership. Enough for him to support his family comfortably, send the twins to expensive colleges and even think of getting Bonny married shortly. Filial and fraternal duties of the premature sort could be depressing at times, and they particularly seemed so on this dreary morning. Soumitro thought longingly of his father's dainty little bar back home.

Though generous to a fault with other things, the late Pronoy Banerjee had been extremely possessive of his snazzy little bar. Bottles of Scotch whisky, liqueurs, and dry and sweet wines stood at attention in the mirror-inlaid bar with soft concealed lighting and a strong locking arrangement. After his death, there was no one to really bother and the fused bulbs remained unchanged while the mirrors gathered dust. Ira Banerjee, running short of cabinet space, took to storing bottles of antacid and antiseptic lotions in the bar, slowly but surely turning it into a medicine chest of sorts.

Pronoy Banerjee had always taken great care to keep the bar locked, a habit that had puzzled the young Soumitro deeply.

'Who do you think is going to pinch your booze, Baba? Ma, me or the twins?' he had asked perplexed.

His father had laughed uproariously, giving him a tight hug and a conspiratorial wink.

'You never know, you never know, even the walls are thirsty these days,' he had answered mysteriously, wagging a playful finger at the bewildered Soumitro.

After his father's death, on a rainy night of deep despair, the young Soumitro had opened the bar and taken his first swig of alcohol and made a discovery. That the stuff tasted foul at first shot but its properties were magical. It could make a person forget, expand and cope. And above all, carry on with the demands made by life. The bar remained perennially unlocked after that and if Ira Banerjee noticed the levels in the bottles dipping steadily and new bottles appearing in place of the antacids, she wisely held her tongue. A drop or two of alcohol taken once in a while served as a good bronchodilator, she told herself, and a growing boy could do with a bit occasionally. And if Soumitro's words slurred and his limbs faltered on certain dark nights, she conveniently looked the other way.

4

The *Noon Voice* office was on the first floor of a predominantly residential quiet bylane of Bandra. Barely 750 square feet in floor space, the office was split into tiny cubicles by low wooden partitions. The staff could see each other clearly over the waist-high partitions, lending the entire office an air of camaraderie and openness. The furniture was cheap and the décor shabby. As editor, Soumitro gave himself no special perks, sitting in a cramped, ill-lit cubicle like the others, with an untidy mound of papers before him. Soumitro's curt exterior hid a rare magnanimity of nature as the staff well knew, and just about anyone and everyone was welcome to walk into the office of the modest city tabloid. It provided a great platform for beginners to do their internship – a place where they could gain experience, hone their skills and move on to better prospects. And Soumitro bore no grudge at being used thus, merely urging his employees to move ahead in life. All kinds of talents were welcome at *Noon Voice* and all kinds of deviations accepted. People with all kinds of beliefs, ideologies, sexual orientations, intelligence quotients and talents drifted around the place. Writers, poets, artists, cartoonists, heterosexuals, metrosexuals, Marxists, morons, atheists walked in and out over the years. They left considerably enriched and enlightened after their stint at the tabloid, and no matter which end of the globe they landed up at later, they always remembered their Bombay days at *Noon Voice* with a special feeling of gratitude and affection for the moody editor. And the newspaper office continued to remain open to all, provided one could put up with the editor's perpetual surliness. If a visitor walking into the office found the inmates a bunch of weird birds, he refrained from making any remarks. For the taciturn editor, the brilliant cartoonist and the astringent weekly columnist churned out an immensely readable and popular newspaper, year after year.

The staff of *Noon Voice* consisted of two fledgling reporters, Parthasarathy Sharma and Joshua Abraham, Maltesh Roy the cartoonist, CoKen the weekly columnist, Pankaj Bhatt the subeditor, Ashish Surve the accountant, and Ganesh Murthy the peon. Ganesh, the betel leaf chewing, politically savvy peon had bullied Pronoy into having his meals in time while playing catch-as-catch-can with the young Soumitro on his weekly visits to the office. Years later, he continued with his bullying tactics with the present editor, whom he still saw in his mind's eye as a naughty little boy in shorts. The two rookie reporters who had been recruited recently seemed more intent on avoiding him than confronting him with their stories, thought Soumitro with bitter amusement, while Pankaj Bhatt the subeditor, who had been longest at *Noon Voice*, seemed to be getting more overbearing and obnoxious by the day. But he was good at his work, Soumitro had to concede grudgingly, and invaluable to the newspaper. Soumitro found himself looking forward to the weekly columnist Kenneth Strange's visit. He came in just once a week, operating from home at other times, but made his presence felt in that one short visit.

The wall clock struck ten and Beatrice D'Monte entered the office on a wave of strong perfume and to the sound of clicking heels. She took up her position at the reception desk. There was about her an air of cool efficiency and authority. Her crisp no-nonsense appearance made age a rather superficial factor and she could be anything from twenty-five to fifty years of age. She wore tight skirts that skimmed her knees and emphasized her endomorphic physique. Her bosom was a challenge to the laws of physics, with each breast facing a rival direction. The entire staff of *Noon Voice* puzzled endlessly about how Beatrice managed to get her breasts into such impossibly pointed shapes, how they seemed to point northeast and northwest simultaneously and how they seemed to be made of concrete rather than flesh. They were too tactful (and scared of Soumitro) to voice their doubts in public but they sprang out of the way in alarm when Beatrice came bearing down with her bosom pointed at them with a sense of purpose, determination and sheer force, resembling the *Titanic*'s prow in shape and intent. Her thin limbs came as something of an anticlimax after the bombastic effect of her bust and hips.

Beatrice's whole demeanour was militant and she was, thought Soumitro gratefully, the greatest asset of *Noon Voice*, acting as a one-woman security force and line of defence to the editor. She had no patience with mediocrity and could smell anything fake a mile away. She was ruthless with time-wasting small-time actors and starlets seeking instant celebrity and shooed them out before they could get anywhere near the editor.

5

His first meeting with Malto the cartoonist was etched vividly in Soumitro's mind even though years had passed after the event. The memories could still make him smile. It had been a rainy kind of day, remembered Soumitro, and he had been lounging in his chair after everybody had left. As was his habit, he had been dozing fitfully. The office had been dark and gloomy, with the wooden furniture gleaming in the light of a sole lamp, and the bright crimson floor rugs providing the only splashes of colour. Suddenly, as he watched from the corners of his sleep-laden eyes, one of the rugs seemed to shake itself and come heading straight at him. Soumitro had jerked awake from his stupor, his thoughts jangling together in a startled flurry of wakefulness. On reaching the lit-up area, the rug transformed itself into a young man who stood before him with downcast eyes and bent head. He held out a battered-looking portfolio.

'I'm Maltesh Roy, an illustrator and cartoonist. I'm looking for a job,' said the rug.

It moves! It talks! It sketches! Soumitro thought in wonder, staring at the shaggy young man before him. It was providence indeed! They badly needed an artist at *Noon Voice*, the present one having just accepted an offer from a rival tabloid.

'Sit down, sit down. Here, let me look at your work,' Soumitro gestured to the bearded young artist, whose matted hair hung down to his shoulders and whose crimson T-shirt had obviously seen cleaner days. Soumitro switched on a table lamp.

The next minute he felt his breath catch in his throat. The sketches lying before him were done in charcoal. The strokes were swift, clean, minimal and brilliant, capturing the essence of the subjects (some of them well-known personalities) without being malicious or judgmental. In a strange and subtle manner, the artist's pencil seemed to suppress all that was superficial in his subjects and highlight the deeply human. The overall effect was simply stunning.

Soumitro looked up and met the artist's eyes. Lonely, bleak eyes that were now anxiously waiting for an answer.

'You'll do,' said Soumitro trying to contain the excitement in his voice. 'You'll do fine. Why don't you come over first thing tomorrow morning? We'll settle the money and other things?'

And then suddenly, a tiny fawn-coloured head with two glittering little eyes had peeped out from the artist's breast pocket, giving Soumitro the second fright of the evening.

'I'm sorry,' Maltesh had mumbled in apology, trying to push the little creature back into his pocket. 'That's my pet gecko. Goes everywhere with me.'

'Oh, I see.' Soumitro's voice was carefully noncommittal as he started scrutinizing Maltesh's sketches once again.

'Do you have many of such... er... friends?' he asked cautiously, looking up from the sketches.

'Only a guinea pig and a goldfish. Archimedes the goldfish stays in a jam jar at home and is taken out only on special occasions. Julius the gecko and Brutus the guinea pig travel everywhere with me. They are rather insecure little creatures,' explained Maltesh seriously.

'Yes, yes,' Soumitro suddenly seemed to find himself short of words. He continued to gaze at the brilliance of the charcoal sketches before him. They seemed almost hypnotic in their intensity. Such illustrations were just what were needed for the page two corner of *Noon Voice*.

'Your pets have interesting names. Archimedes, Julius, Brutus.'

'Besides art, I loved history and physics in school.'

'I see,' Soumitro said. 'Anyway, you're most welcome to get your friends to office, Maltesh. Only make sure nobody steps on them!'

Soumitro smiled magnanimously. The two men, so alike in height and appearance, stood up and shook hands. Each of them felt a strange connection with the other. It was, as they were to realize much later, one lonely man instinctively recognizing another.

6

Dibyendu Ganguly and Mustafa Saifee watched the Banerjees descend from a taxi, groaning under the weight of luggage. They had no idea how deeply their lives would be entwined someday. Dibyendu and Mustafa's angles of perception differed drastically. While Mustafa watched the drama unfolding from his posh thirteenth storey penthouse facing Pushpa Milan, Dibyendu watched the proceedings from his first floor balcony at an angle of forty-five degrees to Pushpa Milan's entrance. He had to lean out and crane his neck to get a satisfactory view, and in the process, found his nostrils assailed by an assortment of smells, both pleasant and unpleasant, rising from the Durga Nagar slums. Mustafa's gaze took in the travel-worn passengers, ill at ease in a new city, and came to rest interestedly on Siddharth Banerjee, who appeared to be roughly the same age as himself. He felt a spark of excitement quickening the blood in his veins. A boy around the same age was an easy passport to entering a new home. And who knew what exciting possibilities lay in the future with new friends made?

Dibyendu's mouth was pulled down at the corners with disapproval as he watched the scene. A confirmed bachelor, he had enjoyed years of blissful freedom in Bombay, unhindered by dozens of relatives trying to feed him, mother him and get him married to every eligible female in the vicinity (as was the habit of his Calcutta relatives). And now Ira Mashi and Pronoy

Meshomoshai had to arrive with their brood. And to reside in the very next building, if you please! Could life get more tragic, thought Dibyendu, in disgust. He hoped with all his heart that Ira Mashi (whom he had met only a couple of times) did not belong to the category of women with a tendency to smother bachelor nephews. He'd shift his residence if that was the case, he thought rebelliously, go away to Goregaon, Kandivli or even distant Dahisar. Dibyendu groaned with displeasure. The Banerjees were well aware of his existence in Bombay and he'd have to make that perfunctory visit in a day or two.

Dibyendu belonged to a Shaivite cult, which was another topic of hot debate in the family. His ascetic, celibate life was a matter of concern to relatives, and frowned upon darkly. He was considered something of an oddity. Relatives were convinced that a man in his early thirties sans girlfriends, affairs, vile addictions or a steamy past was not to be trusted. Dibyendu was thankful to be posted out of Calcutta where he could steer clear of family interference, and hopping all over the country on postings suited his lonesome existence admirably. But now these infernal Banerjees had arrived to threaten his peace of mind, leaving him feeling vexed, unsettled and utterly helpless in the hands of fate.

Mustafa strolled back into his house. There was no point hanging around in the balcony as the new family, after a brief haggling session with the cab driver, had moved indoors – bedding, baggage, boxes and all. Mustafa's footsteps echoed on the expensive marble of the floor. The house stretched before him, exquisitely furnished, gleaming, lonely and forlorn. The furniture was of pure leather, and the artefacts priceless. Mustafa threw himself down on a sofa and glared at the chandelier overhead. Aziz, the cook, would come in any moment and start wheedling and coaxing him to eat some dinner. He might eat, or he might not, thought Mustafa, making his up mind to harass the devoted old servant with a show of habitual non-cooperation. Aziz would whip up his favourite caramel pudding in all probability, setting it into apple-shaped moulds. There would be some dal gosht, which Aziz specialized in, but Mustafa felt curiously indifferent towards food this evening. He wondered what the new family across the street was doing for dinner. The mother looked like she might be a good cook. How wonderful to have a mother who cooked, thought Mustafa wistfully. How wonderful to have a mother who cared. How wonderful to have a mother. Period.

Mustafa's father, a busy industrialist, had moved to Bahrain with his new young wife. Mustafa and Nazneen had never taken to each other and it seemed a good idea for Nazneen to accompany her globetrotting husband on his business jaunts. A rather neat way of evading a pesky stepson with a difficult, uncooperative disposition and a knack for scathing sarcasm. When Altaf Saifee decided to settle in Bahrain while his son continued with his architectural studies in Bombay, there were unanimous and audible sighs of relief all around. Short meetings with definite endings were fairly tolerable for both Nazneen and Mustafa; anything more than that was a strain on the nervous system. He never could curb his awfully timed jokes in the presence of his stepmother, thought Mustafa wryly, and Nazneen sadly lacked (among many other things) a sense of humour. Once again Mustafa glanced at the first floor flat at Pushpa Milan. Lights showed at the windows. The new family looked just his type. He'd barge into the house someday soon on some pretext or the other and make friends with them. They'd be thrilled to meet him, of course. After all wasn't his charm known to be simply irresistible?

Mustafa gazed around at his immaculate home with its distinctive designer décor. He had a sudden yearning for the noise, laughter, warmth and the shabby untidiness that he could glimpse through the windows of the houses around. He glanced at his wrist watch (an expensive gift from his stepmother, probably for staying out of her hair) and noted that the time was close to nine o' clock. The college canteen would be closed at this hour. Mustafa was invariably the first person in and the last person out of the canteen of the Sir D.V. College of Architecture. Often he had to be shooed away at closing time by the good-natured owner and waiters. They were fiercely protective about the lonely, angel-faced boy who lounged around the canteen all day long (using a row of plastic chairs to form a sofa of sorts) and sipped ginger tea interminably. And who believed in entertaining all visitors to the canteen with the most outrageous brand of poetry. Famous as he was for being something of a juvenile seer, freshers and juniors never failed to walk up and pay their respects to Mustafa, who rewarded them with blessings from a delicate, languid hand and a few choice lines of Ghalib's poetry. And just like the rules and principles of architecture that were ingrained in the students over the years at college, the essence of Mustafa Saifee, the omnipresent, omniscient poet supreme with a unique philosophy towards life became a vital ingredient of campus culture. With a popularity that made him almost iconic in nature, Mustafa emerged as a force to reckon with by both students and professors alike.

The canteen, with its loud clanging of cheap steel utensils, the angry hiss of hot oil as samosas and vadas were fried to a crisp, tea fumes and the incessant chatter of students, seemed to have a soporific effect on Mustafa, often lulling him into a deep sleep. The professors, who had given up on Mustafa's academic progress, viewed his chronic absence from class with a resigned tolerance. The thought of passing out of such a benevolent institution filled Mustafa with a cold dread, the future looming grey, menacing, lonely and shapeless. And though eloquent with predicting other people's lives, Mustafa chose not to look too far into his own future. With single-minded determination Mustafa succeeded in failing his exams year after year, thereby ensuring for himself many more happy years in the campus. The professors, mostly a humane lot, read between the lines. Bending rules by discreet inches and keeping in mind the hefty donations that Altaf Saifee made to the college regularly, the faculty of architecture accepted Mustafa Saifee as something of a heritage piece. To be protected, cherished and retained.

7

Dibyendu Ganguly settled down comfortably into the Banerjees' household in what seemed like a matter of weeks. His initial fears, he realized, had been completely unfounded. Not only was Ira Mashi one of those wonderfully unobtrusive women who firmly believed in the 'live and let live' policy but also his second cousins were proving to be fairly entertaining. Mishti was a delight, with her scatterbrained friendly ways, and he watched with awe her experiments with various kinds of beauty therapy. On some days she lay back on the sofa with mashed bananas plastered on her face and on some others it was a concoction of honey, lime and fresh cream.

'If you're feeling hungry, you could take a quick lick of your face pack. A two-in-one deal,' Siddharth told his twin.

All he got in answer to his suggestion was an angry grunt as talking would disturb the delicate balance of the face pack. Mishti chose to keep her eyes shut tight on these occasions and replied to conversation merely in sign language, using her fingers.

Dibyendu heartily approved of the friendly bickering between siblings that went on all day long at A-502 Pushpa Milan, never having had a taste of such things, as an only child. He felt a deep respect for his cousin Soumitro's wizardry with antonyms and synonyms (never having had a flair for languages) and he enthusiastically approved of Siddharth's dreams of watching the sun rise over futuristic colonies in the city someday.

Of all his relatives, he liked plump, bubbly Bonny the best. Dibyendu had always had a horror of women who wore designer clothes, exuded clouds of expensive perfume and spoke in high-pitched nasal voices with fake NRI accents. Already tall and bulky, he seemed to suddenly gain further height and girth in the presence of such women, becoming bull-like and blundering, with his hands and feet ballooning clumsily. He invariably fumbled, dropped his glasses, sent a chair crashing in his nervousness and ran into painful grammatical obstacles in his speech with his respiration becoming heavy, noisy and erratic. But Bonny, he thought with approval and affection, was different. Just his kind of person. She did not threaten his peace of mind by dressing up, choosing to keep all her distracting zones covered discreetly with loose-fitting clothes. And neither did she come charging at him with her breasts thrust out, waving her femininity like a red flag (like some of these modern young women). Nor did she simper, blush or go overboard with make-up. There was a clean heartiness to her androgynous manner, and gender – her breeziness seemed to suggest – was as inconsequential as boiled potatoes or aubergines. Soumitro, Siddharth, Bonny and Mishti, who found themselves going into shock on being introduced to their portly 'Ooiimen pharrsstt, ooiimen pharrsstt!' bellowing second cousin with his dated mannerisms, snapped out of their temporary state of paralysis soon enough. Benuda, they realized, was only a harmless god-fearing individual with a marked fondness for the blue god of destruction. A staunch feminist at heart, 'Women first, women first' was a motto he advocated with zeal, shouting it out loud and clear at every possible public place. His grammar and pronunciation were a highly personalized and convoluted affair which often left the Banerjees slightly baffled, but except for Mishti's unfortunate tendency to dissolve into giggles, they chose to ignore such trivial aspects of his persona.

A-502 Pushpa Milan was steadily proving to be a popular haunt, with friends and relatives trooping in regularly for coffee in the evenings. The shy, retiring artist Maltesh, who spoke in monosyllables and who often accompanied Soumitro home, was fast becoming a favourite semi-permanent fixture, as was the Anglo-Indian columnist CoKen. The evenings were a cacophony of voices as the decibel level rose argumentatively over music and coffee.

Dibyendu stole surreptitious glances at CoKen this Tuesday evening, trying to figure him out. Kenneth Strange, with the fair skin of his English ancestors, lived up to his name in Dibyendu's eyes. He wore his blond hair long, gathering it into a neat ponytail with coloured rubber bands. He had the startled-looking light eyes so common in Englishmen and he lined these thickly with kohl in an attempt to look more exotic and oriental. Kenneth was known to have an aversion to being addressed as a firang or gora and could speak and write excellent Hindi. A cocaine addict, Kenneth wrote a weekly political column for *Noon Voice*. Most of the time, the pieces ranged from the mediocre to the atrocious – three hundred words of vitriol passing for language, topped by a bleary-eyed mug shot. But under the influence of cocaine (snorted once a month), his columns took on the touch of genius. Brilliantly worded observations rendered with incisive clarity resulted in the Saturday edition being completely sold out. Such once-in-a-month flashes of brilliance more than made up for his non-performance at other times and Kenneth Strange remained a much valued writer at *Noon Voice*. So vital was his role in periodically lifting *Noon Voice* out of the quagmires of mediocrity that Soumitro clung on to him despite frequent differences of opinions of the political kind. And so admiring was everybody of his simulated genius and its connection to cocaine that the staff of *Noon Voice* rechristened him CoKen with all the solemnity of a church baptism.

Every evening threw up a new subject for discussion at A-502 Pushpa Milan and the topic for this evening was the unnatural lifestyle led by Bengali widows. Bonny was holding forth vociferously.

'Why don't you eat fish, Ma?' Bonny turned on her mother exasperatedly. 'You could do with some proteins at this age.'

Ira Banerjee looked flustered at this sudden attack on her.

'I... er... ummm... Bengali widows are not expected to eat onions, garlic, fish...'

'Utter bunkum!' exclaimed Bonny angrily. 'Rules made centuries ago by chauvinistic Brahmin men who wanted to cut costs on food...'

'Hush, Bonny,' said Ira nervously.

'... and who feared that the female libido would go leaping around the place, threatening their peace of mind. And bodies, onions and garlic being aphrodisiacs,' finished Bonny triumphantly.

Ira Banerjee looked horrified and distraught at the direction the conversation was taking.

'Yeah, Aunty,' said CoKen, joining in the argument enthusiastically. 'Why don't you just bite into a nice, juicy chicken burger? Should I get you one from McDonald's?'

Ira found herself suddenly bereft of speech. She belonged to the genteel post-Partition era where discussions of these types were considered to be in extremely bad taste. And one did not question social norms at her age, one merely went with the flow. Less unsettling for everyone around. But she could neither explain all this to outsiders nor put the matter properly into words, being a rather inarticulate sort.

'Leave Ma alone. She is fine the way she is,' said Soumitro curtly, walking into the room. In his mind's eye, he had a sudden, horrific vision of his widowed mother wearing blindingly bright saris and engaging in a spirited tug-of-war with a leg of chicken. He blanched at the picture.

'Bonny, kindly chuck your skewed opinions into the nearest dustbin,' he added repressively, 'and behave.'

CoKen looked at his colleague in amazement. Really, he thought in disapproval, sometimes SB seemed like a complete throwback to the dark ages.

'Yes, Bonny, that's no way for a Bengali girl to speak,' said Ira plaintively, finding an unexpected ally in her eldest son.

'Bengali girls don't talk like this and Bengali girls don't talk like that! Bengali girls don't do this and Bengali girls don't do that! What *are* Bengali girls ideally supposed to do, may I ask?' said Bonny irritably.

'Well...' Ira cleared her throat, not very sure of the answer. 'For one, Bengali girls don't scream at their elders and they don't swear. They don't challenge tradition unnecessarily or try and behave like men.'

'That's the spirit! That was great for starters, Ma,' said Soumitro approvingly. 'Bengali girls don't smirk at prospective grooms, throw Karl Marx at them or wear clothes fit for the circus. And Bengali girls are supposed to be good cooks, for god's sake! Bonny, the omelette you gave me yesterday tasted like blotting paper. And, most importantly, Bengali girls of marriageable age lose WEIGHT!'

'Hmphhhh!'snorted Bonny disrespectfully.

'And Bengali girls,' continued Soumitro in a soft, suave tone, 'never make vulgar sounds like "Hmphhhh!"'

The bickering continued. Dibyendu leaned back in his chair, a feeling of bliss washing over him. This was what life was all about.

'Wahan kaun hai tera, musafir, jayega kahan...' sang S.D. Burman in a nasal twang, providing a melodious backdrop to the conversation. The liquid gold of the setting sun seemed to lend the evening a strange incandescence. Dibyendu's eyes touched upon every face in the room. Siddharth was bent low over his desk, Rotring pen in hand, drawing endless lines with exquisite precision. Oblivious to the conversation around, he hummed under his breath while he worked, matching notes with the song. Bonny and Soumitro's half-hearted argument with CoKen as referee was beginning to peter out as Ira cleared the centre table for coffee, her expression impassive. Maltesh the artist, fondly nicknamed Malto, had drifted into the room sometime. He sat lost in thought, Julius curled up in his lap. Wary of frightening the shy artist, who was known to have an aversion to conversation, everybody avoided looking at him directly or asking him any personal questions. Conversation of the general kind flowed over Maltesh like warm, viscous honey and he was left with the comfortable option of choosing to be either participant or audience.

Mishti was brewing coffee in the kitchen. The aroma of cappuccino, voices raised in conversation and loud laughter from the Banerjees' house on the first floor floated down to the tired pedestrians hurrying below. They smiled. The usual din at A-502 Pushpa Milan, they thought indulgently. That meant all was well with the world.

8

The Dinshaw Vacha College of Architecture was situated amidst a sprawling campus right in the heart of the city. The college building sported a Gothic style of architecture, giving it an effect that was both gracious and timeless. Lines of casuarina trees planted around the campus whispered in the sea breeze all day long. Their heads were bowed low as they buffered the college from the sounds of the busy streets around. There was a dark, dreamy air to the campus atmosphere and a brooding silence hung over the long corridors flanked at regular intervals by ornate stone columns. Stairways with intricate spirals rose from every corner of the building, and though the pitter-patter of energetic young feet broke the silence at certain hours of the day, echoes of a bygone era and resonances of the colonial days hung heavy around the place.

Over the years, in an attempt to add a dash of colour to the sombre landscape, a series of zealous principals had added patches of lawn and flowerbeds which were regularly planted with bright seasonal flowers. When these bloomed, the campus took on a bright, cheery air and looked inviting. Stone lattices at the ends of the corridors on each floor let sunlight in, and it seemed as though one could almost touch the golden beams. But it was all an illusion, as the architecture students well knew. Illumination could never be trapped. Or touched.

The classrooms were huge, with high ceilings that had wooden beams running along the entire length. Old-fashioned, long-stemmed ceiling fans whirred slowly and noisily through the day. Pigeons roosting in the alcoves flew in and out of the classrooms all the time, beating their wings. It wasn't unusual for a student to labour for hours over an assignment, only to be rewarded with fresh pigeon droppings on the paper. Once in a while, a confused bird flew into the blades of a fan and then the students got splattered with fresh, warm blood.

Gargoyle-shaped fountains in various states of disrepair were strewn across the college grounds. While a few gushed crystal-clear water, others trickled half-heartedly, and yet others ran totally dry. Neglect and pride, chaos and method, beauty and unsightliness, hope and weariness balanced each other out at the Sir D.V. College of Architecture. While hundreds of students stepped in every year charged with enthusiasm and zeal, an older lot of students and ageing professors stalled their energies effectively, yanking them down to ground reality.

All except Professor Anant Deshmukh.

Anant Deshmukh ran caressing fingers over the cold stone railings on the first floor as he walked to class. He knew and loved every inch and corner of the college, rather in the manner of a man who recognizes a lover's contours with his eyes shut. His feelings for the old stone building came very close to being those of a lover. Even after years of teaching, he could still feel an aching possessiveness and a thrilling pride for the Sir D.V. College of Architecture. He knew, with his eyes shut, the view that each stone corridor afforded and he could tell which floor he was on by merely touching the walls and columns. He knew the patterns of the carvings on the stone and could identify the smell of ammonia emanating from the third floor toilets from his room on the fifth floor, and he never failed to reprimand the janitors for stinting on the phenyl. He could sense the throbbing excitement that pulsed through the students a fortnight before the college festival. He exulted when a trophy was won and anguished over a lost intercollegiate competition. Professor Anant Deshmukh's hands, now old and gnarled, had taught faultless architectural rendering to batches of students over decades. They now shook. With age and apprehension.

For the last few years, Professor Deshmukh had slept little and woken up to uneasy dawns. There was in his ears the perennial rumble of distant thunder. An ominous warning. Of failure. Of destruction. Of the death of dreams that had been painstakingly built over the years.

Professor Deshmukh was deeply worried about the future of the Sir D.V. College of Architecture. Born to a Communist father and a mother who hailed from the princely family of Solapur, Anant Deshmukh sincerely believed in uplifting the backward classes and the equal sharing of wealth. On the other hand he also believed in the supremacy of the aristocracy. He believed in taking education to the oppressed classes, but he was of the opinion that the aristocracy too had its uses. Awards could rarely be won by the grandchildren of tribals who still thought in units of sticks and stones. Sometimes, he thought ruefully, one needed the aristocracy, with their global exposure, arrogance and polish, to give a fresh thrust to ideas.

For the last ten years, the college had suffered deeply due to the blinkered, orthodox thinking of the present principal, Professor Dilip Dongre. In Professor Deshmukh's eyes, the college had suffered from nepotism in its worst form, with an abnormally large number of seats being allocated to the friends, relatives and offspring of the principal, his sycophants and the trustees of the college. The final year results had dived abysmally, pushing the status of the college from number one in the city to grade B in the last few years. Professor Deshmukh had bled silently for his beloved college. The climax of his grief had been reached when the highly coveted Ralph Correa Intercollegiate Award for Excellence in Architecture (monopolized by the Sir D.V. College of Architecture for years) had slipped out of the hands of the college, never to come back till date. The majestic Gothic building of the college continued to stand proud and mighty but the walls, Anant Deshmukh knew, had hollow insides.

Glancing down over the banister of the stairs, Professor Deshmukh saw a slight figure hurrying to make it to class in time. He smiled, his eyes tender. For the first time in years, he felt a sense of hope and his heart warmed at the sight of first year student Siddharth Banerjee coming panting up the stairs. If ever there was a chance for the college to salvage its lost pride, it lay in Siddharth Banerjee. The boy was like a burning flame on a dark night, thought Deshmukh, feeling positively poetic with excitement. He had proved his mettle in the very first examination with his quick grasp of architectural principles. His crystal-clear concepts, his blending of technology with flawless aesthetics, put him head and shoulders above the rest of the class. But apart from all these traits, Siddharth Banerjee revealed something that no one at the college had had for years. He had vision. And courage. Courage to dream big dreams and vision to sculpt new horizons. He had the calibre and originality to move out of the crippling mesh of jaded design norms and rise above the murky sea of mediocrity. If only there wasn't a student called Medha Dongre on the scene, thought Professor Deshmukh, groaning in despair.

Professor Deshmukh quailed at the thought of the principal's daughter, Medha Dongre, who was Siddharth Banerjee's classmate. She was unimaginative, unexceptional, unoriginal, meticulous in her work and timid. In short, she possessed all the prerequisites desirable in this college, thought Anant Deshmukh grimly. She challenged no clichés and broke no new ground with her ideas. She was safe and dependable, the perfect candidate for all the scholarships in the coming years which could either make or break an architect's career. She possessed the right domicile certificate and the right genes. She was, by birth, geography and IQ the most suitable candidate to be backed and promoted in the formidable competition that lay ahead. Professor Deshmukh felt his heart twist with bitterness at the injustice of the situation. He suddenly felt a deep, paternal urge to protect Siddharth from the unfair grinding mechanism at work in the bowels of the college. A wild, passionate resolve took hold of him, to nurture his precious sapling till it grew roots, shoots and branches and was ready to take on the world.

Professor Deshmukh and Siddharth Banerjee reached the doorway of the classroom almost simultaneously. Siddharth Banerjee was the undoubted choice of messiah for the sinking college, thought Professor Deshmukh, glancing at the boy and feeling just a little theatrical. Placing an affectionate arm on the shoulder of his protégé, Professor Anant Deshmukh walked into the waiting classroom, beaming from ear to ear.

9

Call for prayers rose from the minaret situated in the middle of the Durga Nagar slums. The minaret was at a distance of a hundred yards from the Banerjees' balcony. It was a slim, swan-like projection, reaching for the skies from the sea of shoddy asbestos hutment roofs. It sported the usual little green flag with the moon and the star and emitted long, haunting calls to prayer. They reminded Siddharth of the vast stretches of arid desert across which the Prophet had travelled centuries ago to spread the message of Islam.

The evening congregation for coffee at A-502 Pushpa Milan was steadily increasing in strength, the latest addition being Mustafa Saifee from the tall building across the road. Mustafa, who had been toying with the idea of befriending the Banerjees for a long time, found his task simplified when he ran into Siddharth in the corridors of the Sir D.V. College of Architecture.

'Hey!' Mustafa accosted Siddharth delightedly. 'Aren't you the new kid in town? I'm Mustafa Saifee, your neighbour back home and senior in this college.'

'I'm not strictly new, been around a while. I'm Siddharth Banerjee, first year Arch.' Siddharth took the proffered hand, staring at the dazzlingly handsome boy before him.

'Oh, you're considered new till you get yourself a thick domicile certificate, pal. Anyway, just telling you that I'm the spiritual guide around the place. If you have any problems of the emotional, psychological or existential kind, look no further. Just come to Uncle Mustu. I specialize in Sufism, Zen philosophy and the poetry of Ghalib, T.S. Eliot and Yevtushenko.' He bowed low, then added as an afterthought, 'Any problems other than architectural ones, that is.' With an ironic salute, he moved away. 'Who, or rather, *what* was that?' asked Siddharth in a stunned voice after a few moments.

'Oh, that's Mustafa, the in-house joker. Take no notice of him. He's been around the college for hundreds of years, says my elder brother. From the time of Moses, I think,' replied his classmate Xavier Fernandes as the two of them walked through the lawns.

'But how could he do that?' asked Siddharth, mystified. 'This is just a five year degree course.'

'He has managed to fail repeatedly, that's how.'

'MANAGED to fail?'

'Yep. He has mastered the advanced art of failing repeatedly. Once in a while he passes, though, but such occasions are rare. He goes into terrible depression on passing and it takes the efforts of the entire college to pull him back into good humour again.'

They had reached the gates of the college and Xavier turned to look at Siddharth.

'For various complex reasons that you won't be able to grasp right now, Mustafa is considered a permanent state-of-the-art fixture of this college. Understand that, Sid. Like those columns you see out there, those gargoyles and these casuarina trees,' said Xavier conclusively, his expression ironic.

Siddharth felt completely baffled. Here he was, rearing to finish his studies, get his graduation degree and get cracking on the city's skyline, and there was someone who wanted to fail repeatedly and preferred canteens to classrooms! He shook his head in perplexity.

'Next time he fails, he may be thrown out of college, though,' said Xavier darkly. 'After all, you are allowed to fail only a certain number of times by the university.'

When Mustafa drifted into A-502 Pushpa Milan one evening, like a lost autumn leaf, there were mixed reactions to the newcomer. Siddharth felt a thrill of excitement at seeing the most controversial student of his college strolling into his sitting room. Mishti, who was on her way out, exchanged the briefest of greetings and Bonny, who was momentarily distracted by the sound of his name, recovered soon enough to give him a rousing welcome. Fortunately or unfortunately, Soumitro was missing.

Mustafa smiled in a seraphic fashion at everyone. His first meeting with Dibyendu Ganguly fell under the tricky category, though, and it was a long time before relations smoothened out between the two men.

'Mustafa, my cousin Dibyendu,' said Siddharth by way of introduction.

Mustafa held out a limp, fair hand.

'How's you, dude?' he asked laconically.

Dibyendu froze, his ready smile vanishing into thin air. Nobody, in the thirty odd years of his life, had ever had the audacity to address him as 'dude', nor did he approve of the wilful mutilation of the English language.

'My health is bheri phine, thank you,' said Dibyendu stiffly.

'Oooff! The gentleman is touchy! How marvellous! I thought this endangered species was already extinct,' said Mustafa admiringly.

There was a moment of silence as Dibyendu slowly turned a rich shade of purple. He controlled himself with an effort and walked away, putting as much distance between him and the new visitor as possible.

Dusk was falling. It was, as Bonny called it, Ma's Florence Nightingale hour. As if on cue, Ira Banerjee wafted into the twilit room, holding a puja thali with a burning lamp in her hands. The lights had still not been switched on and Ira, treading slowly in her white sari, lit up the room with the flame of her lamp. She looked across at Mustafa over the glow of the flickering flame and for both of them, it was a classic case of love at first sight. Ira saw a lonely boy hiding behind sarcasm and bravado and waiting to be mothered. Mustafa saw a woman whose eyes smiled tenderly even though her mouth was stern.

Holding a protective palm over the flame, Ira walked over to Mustafa and held out a handful of prosad. Sugar crystals had melted over the coconut shavings, creating a viscous mess.

'Ma,' hissed Bonny. 'What are you *doing*? Don't give him prosad. He's an "M".'

But Mustafa accepted the prosad meekly enough, popping it quickly into his mouth. Ira bent low. Holding his wrist gently, she turned up his palm and wiped his sticky hand with her pallu. He breathed in the amalgam of smells emanating from her body. He could identify camphor, incense and eau de cologne. There was something else that was elusive, alien and very, very Bengali.

Suddenly he had the most extraordinary feeling of having come home.

10

It was noticed by all that Soumitro Banerjee went through life in a perpetually foul mood. The degree of foulness varied from day to day but chronic foulness, it was widely accepted, was a way of life with good old Som. Some said it was the early demise of his father, some others attributed it to an obese sister who was a disaster in the matrimonial market, and yet some others put it down to his allergy to women and Muslims. Whatever it was, his neighbours in the Durga Nagar area were used to the young man looking through them glassily on certain days, shopkeepers were used to his curt monosyllabic demands for a lone cigarette (which he lit with the shopkeeper's matches) and the staff at *Noon Voice* regularly felt his scorching gaze burn holes in their bodies. But everybody who knew Soumitro had a deep abiding affection for him and chose to take as little notice as possible of his dark and disconcerting mood swings.

The only person who could connect overtly with Soumitro and whom he talked to without inhibitions was Maltesh and Soumitro was often seen placing an affectionate arm across the artist's shoulders while passing by. Maltesh would look up from his sketches and smile his rare charming smile. Soumitro showed a courteous respect for Maltesh's pets besides, allowing the guinea pig to sniff his socks and the gecko to cuddle up on his keyboard.

The reasons for Soumitro's antipathy towards Muslims and women were slightly hazy to everybody but it probably had a lot to do with his grandmother's stories of rape, pillage, mayhem, murders, feuds and the bloodbath that followed in the days after the Partition. Muslims were not to be trusted, she had whispered into his baby ears in a sinister tone, not even the panwalla, the egg-seller or the biryani-maker down the road. They possessed a warped, fanatical, unreasonable psyche that could erupt into violence at the slightest provocation. They were not men, they were beasts, she had whispered. They were relics of a pagan, illogical, bloodthirsty civilization with treachery and treason encoded in their chromosomes. And they ate Hindu children for Friday breakfast. Little Soumitro had listened avidly, with his eyes popping out of his head, and his toddler brain was programmed to a language of hate and revenge forever. To even use the taboo words 'Muslim', 'Mussalman' or 'Mohammedan' was sacrilege, his grandmother whispered into his ears conspiratorially, and the code letter for the enemy in future was to be 'M'.

Things like logic and rationality subsequently got into a convoluted mess in Soumitro's growing years. His virulent anti-women stance was also something of a mystery. His family and relatives suspected that it probably arose from having seen a favourite cousin shoot himself in the head at the age of twenty-six on being jilted a day before his wedding. The cousin, whom the teenaged Soumitro had adored, had been of an extremely thoughtful kind. Deeply apologetic about what he was doing, he had shot himself on his birthday, thereby making it convenient for his family to celebrate his birth and death anniversaries on the same day. July remained a dreaded month for Soumitro who found himself swamped by dark, rainy memories of an unforgettable death.

Slowly, over the years, Soumitro struck off all 'M's and women from his life and the staff of *Noon Voice* remained predominantly male (except for Beatrice D'Monte) and devoid of Muslims. Women were not allowed to get anywhere near Soumitro. Ma, Bonny and Mishti were okay. They were family and not women for goodness' sake, he told himself, and the human computer Beatrice D'Monte, god bless her Roman Catholic soul, was just Beatrice, tight skirt, boobs and all. Soumitro now trod a narrow, insulated corridor of safety. Life had given him a raw deal by snatching away his father at such an early age, and by some twisted, irrational logic, he held Muslims and womankind responsible for his fate. Somewhere at the back of his mind, he guessed that his grandmother had spiked her stories with spice, corkscrewing the truth beyond all recognition and presenting a comfortably one-sided view of past events. Her maligning of the Muslims and glorifying of the Hindus as martyred saints did not ring strictly true to his adult mind, but the tiny open-mouthed Soumitro still lurked inside the towering adult. He was itching to hate somebody and no amount of growing up was going to change that.

Equipped with abundant hatred, Soumitro went through life charged with venom. Women! They were the root cause of all evil, as the case of his beloved cousin Mintuda clearly proved. Holocausts, avalanches, tsunamis, fathers dying before time, cousins shooting themselves in the head, teenage angst, acne, literary inadequacies, crosswords that didn't match up and other disasters happened entirely due to women. They were not to be trusted at any cost. He knew that for a fact.

Over the years, Ira Banerjee watched with distress her elder son's childish leanings crystallize into full-blown prejudice. She feared to think which direction such enormous quantities of misguided emotion could take him some day. But she was too gentle and ineffectual a mother to tackle such tidal waves of emotion. She could only hope that some day he would meet a sweet girl who'd purge him of all that hate.

Everybody was glued to their desks, busy putting finishing touches to their stories before they went to print, Thursdays being busy days at *Noon Voice*. Soumitro leaned back in his chair, his thoughts dwelling on his brother in his first week of college at the other end of the city. He could barely believe that his kid brother, who had come to be more like a son, was actually training to be an architect! If all went well, Sid would graduate in a couple of years from now. Knowing his calibre, he was sure to be snapped up in the campus placement scheme and then the sky would be the limit for this talented youngster. Soumitro sighed, feeling a warm sense of satisfaction course through him. At least one filial duty had been taken care of properly, he told his absentee father, looking upwards. Now to get Bonny married. The next minute Soumitro had let out a groan of despair. Who in this wide world would ever marry his baby elephant-like sister? With her strident feminist views and her cutting sarcasm? He did not have much to offer the bride in the way of material assets either. Soumitro glanced around the office dejectedly. He had a lot of expenses looming ahead. The office needed new furniture, ceiling fans and new blinds. They were hopelessly understaffed, besides. He looked up at Pankaj Bhatt scowling at his computer at the next table.

'Bhatt, we need to recruit some new subs. Some smart young graduates with a flair for writing. Handle it, will you? I'm leaving for Cal tomorrow, should be back in a week.'

'Sure. By the way, boss, could we do something about these creepy-crawlies around the place? They're getting on my nerves.'

Soumitro sighed.

'That blasted lizard got into my pants yesterday and wriggled all the way up to my knee,' Pankaj's voice rose peevishly.

'Good thing it didn't go any further,' Soumitro laughed, trying to ease the situation, but there was no answering smile from Pankaj, only a grim silence.

Soumitro sighed once more. This was an old problem rearing its head again.

'You can't separate Malto from his reptilian relatives, Pankaj. They are an extension of his personality. He needs the tactile security these creatures provide. He's such a lonely man, can't you see?' Soumitro tried to explain patiently.

But Pankaj Bhatt obviously didn't see.

'I suggest we get a new cartoonist then,' he snapped irritably.

Being the oldest employee at *Noon Voice* often gave him a sense of exaggerated importance.

'There wouldn't be another Malto even if we scoured the entire world. He stays and so do his pets,' Soumitro snapped back, equally abrasive.

Once in a blue moon, thought Soumitro with distaste, came that rare occasion when he needed to show just who was boss around the place. And this was one such occasion. He stomped out of the office with long, angry strides. Though he did not need to assert his authority too often, the rare occasions when he had to do so left him feeling drained and depressed. His feet dragged as he walked to the nearest bus stop.

11

Soumitro arrived home to find an exquisitely good-looking boy lounging gracefully on the sitting room sofa. He stopped short. His irritation with Pankaj Bhatt and all the shoving encountered in the overcrowded bus vanished, with surprise replacing irritation. Siddharth sprang to his feet at the sight of his elder brother and Bonny held her breath.

'Dada,' fumbled Siddharth nervously, trying not to appear defensive, 'this is my friend from college, Mustafa Saifee.'

Soumitro froze in his tracks. He stared at Mustafa for a long moment. Then turned on his heels and slammed out of the house without a word.

'He didn't like me? He didn't like *me*?' asked Mustafa, dumbfounded. Such an idea seemed inconceivable to him. Siddharth coughed apologetically and Bonny rushed into speech.

'No, no, no. It's nothing like that,' she said in a consoling tone.

But Mustafa still looked perplexed.

'It's just his peptic ulcers playing up. They do that. Often,' said Bonny, blurting out the first thing that came to her mind.

'Ah, that's it then. Very bad thing, peptic ulcers. Best to sip chilled milk at regular intervals throughout the day,' said Mustafa knowledgeably.

'For god's sake, why peptic ulcers Didi?' groaned Siddharth after Mustafa had left. 'Couldn't you think of anything better?'

'That's the only thing I could think of at the spur of the moment. Besides, would you rather I came clean and told him about Dada's crazy religious prejudices?' demanded Bonny.

Siddharth was silent. He could see tricky times ahead.

Siddharth Banerjee was on a steep learning curve. It had only been in the last few years that he had truly begun to savour the essence of the city of Bombay. In a young, breathlessly enthusiastic manner. In school, while in Calcutta, he had been used to reading about ponds and greenery and the poets and patriots of West Bengal, with Bengali being the third language. In Bombay, he read Marathi and studied about the indomitable Shivaji, about forts on rocky, hostile mountains and the use of iguanas in warfare. Awestruck, he learnt about Maharashtrian women who draped their saris tight like breeches, rode to battle with their men and raised sons to bloodthirsty, revengeful adulthood. It all seemed a far cry from the intellectual men and weepy, sentimental women of Bengal.

While in Calcutta, it was considered perfectly okay to dust yourself white with scented talcum powder, have impassioned political views, wear outlandish clothes and argue yourself hoarse at roadside cafes; in Bombay, he learnt, things were different. You were streetsmart, tech savvy, wore hip clothes and were at all times bored, world-weary and apolitical. You remained unfazed in the face of communal riots, earthquakes, deluges and D grades in assignments. You took an occasional pull at your best friend's fag and tried just a bit of marijuana on the side, but mainly remained focussed on building cities and citadels. While in Calcutta you could plaster your hair with scented oil, in Bombay it was grunge. You never wore your emotions on your sleeve and remained understated in dress, behaviour and ideology. You said one thing when you meant quite another and the operative word in this city was 'cool'. You pronounced it c-o-o-ooool, with the tip of the tongue kissing the inner mouth diagonally upwards while one's voice drooped down to a husky baritone. Profundity was frowned upon but a good stock of obscene jokes helped. You lived life in the fast lane. Even if the speed killed you.

An imaginary skyline hovered in Siddharth's thoughts at all times as he learnt the fundamentals of architecture. Tall, silvery skyscrapers lined this skyline, their glass panes catching the light of the sun. Immaculate, broad roads led to clean kerbs, which in turn led to aesthetically designed residential and office areas. Brilliantly coloured landscaped gardens planned all over the city broke the grey monotony of asphalt. A sleek, futuristic city with the timeless look of structured minimalism. Metal, glass, concrete and planned greenery. Siddharth shivered with delightful anticipation at the mental picture. He could barely wait to get that graduation certificate in his hands.

12

Mishti was having boyfriend problems. Three affairs (in quick succession) had proved to be short-lived; the fourth one was showing all the distressing symptoms of a premature demise.

'It's lovely to fall in love,' Mishti announced to the evening congregation, 'but far lovelier when you fall out of it.'

There was a sympathetic murmur all around.

'That reminds me,' said Soumitro looking up from his crossword-making activities. 'Could you guys give me a single-word cryptic clue for "love"?'

'Bliss,' breathed Mishti.

'Mirage,' said Siddharth.

'Prayer,' said Dibyendu forcefully.

'Bullshit,' said Mustafa.

'Okay. Will do. Thanks.' Soumitro bent down to his task again, expression abstracted.

He avoided looking at Mustafa directly or addressing any remarks at him. If the others around noticed the drift of things they chose to ignore it.

'This is the fourth aborted love affair. I feel sorry for poor Mishti. She is going through such heartache,' whispered Bonny to Dibyendu, glancing at her younger sister's downcast face.

'ANTACID!' roared Dibyendu. 'Give her liquid antacid. Quickest remedy for heartburn.'

'The problem is *heartache* not *heartburn*, O great Brahmin,' Mustafa informed him gently.

Dibyendu gave him a look of pure dislike.

'The problem with boys,' sighed Mishti following her own train of thought, 'is that they are either too possessive or two-timing. Nobody with the perfect balance.' She sighed disconsolately, appearing totally disillusioned with the male species.

'That reminds me of the famous lines of Ghalib,' said Mustafa. He cleared his throat noisily and quoted:

Kabhi kisi ko mukammal jahan nahin milta
Kahin zameen to kahin aasman nahin milta

'Which translated for you, ignorant child, is,' Mustafa paused and looked at Mishti:

Even if you do manage to get the bread and butter in life
You rarely get the marmalade.

Siddharth looked up from his drawing board, a doubtful expression on his face.

'Are you sure that's quite the right interpretation, Mustu?' he asked suspiciously.

'Oh, very close to it, very close to it,' said Mustafa airily.

Everybody in the room except Mustafa and Soumitro was sitting around cutting sponge. The task had been designated to them by Siddharth. It would eventually find its way to the lawns of the model house that he had to submit for his term assignment. Extra pairs of scissors had been brought in from the neighbours for the task. On completion, the finely chopped sponge would be dipped in a mug of bright green paint and then spread out to dry on sheets of newspaper. Family and friends would be advised to watch their step and keep off the grass. There would inevitably be a lot of hopping and skipping as people picked their way with caution. When dry, the sponge would be uniformly sprinkled on a thermocol sheet smeared with glue to form emerald lawns of the little model house. Siddharth would then place minuscule lounging chairs and garden umbrellas as the final touch.

The sponge was being collected on a sheet of newspaper spread in the centre of the room. Julius the gecko dived into the sponge pile merrily, burrowing frantically into the heap and then twisting himself playfully.

'What about you Mustu? Don't you have models to make in the senior year?' Bonny looked up at Mustafa enquiringly.

'ME?' Mustafa seemed scandalized at the question. 'I've risen above such trivial matters in life. I merely contemplate the spiritual intricacies of town planning. I don't dirty my fingers with menial tasks any more.'

There was a chorus of exaggerated coughing all around but Mustafa appeared unfazed. Dibyendu, who had got his thick fingers stuck in the handles of a pair of scissors, had to be assisted out of his predicament by Bonny.

'Tell me, Sharmistha, what are the requirements for an ideal boyfriend?' enquired Mustafa.

Mishti promptly dropped her scissors and leaned back, looking contemplative.

'Well,' she began. 'My requirements are fairly simple. He should have a mind of his own but be ever willing to bend it to my bidding. He should be manly and macho but definitely not in love with his own biceps. He should be violently non-vegetarian as I hate the sight of vegetables. He should be good-looking but not overpoweringly and sickeningly so. He should be chivalrous yet not old-fashioned, sentimental but not mawkish. His mother, if the relationship is to proceed, should preferably be two-dimensional and framed on the wall with a garland around her. He could drink a little but never get sozzled. And he should never, never look at any other girl. And I mean never.'

'Phew!' exhaled Mustafa looking heavenwards. 'Allah! All this for a trivial thing called love!'

'Be quiet!' bellowed Dibyendu, standing up suddenly and waving his red, sore fingers agitatedly. 'Lobh is NOT tribhial. Lobh and lobh alone makes the world go round and round and round and...'

'Stop! I'm already beginning to feel dizzy!' protested Mustafa.

'Lobh,' continued Dibyendu in a thunderous voice, 'is celestial glue that is bhinding two SOULS phorebher...'

'Yech! I think I'm going to puke,' muttered Mustafa into Siddharth's ears, gagging.

'Each heart bheating against OTHER, each in thoughts of ANOTHER. All day, all night, two bodies bhut ONE SOUL!' The last word came out with the vigour of a cannonball. A long stunned silence followed.

'What's with your cousin's grammar?' whispered Mustafa quite audibly into Siddharth's ear.

'Sshhh!' hissed Siddharth.

Benuda's language was a very delicate topic in the family and not to be discussed with outsiders. It had, over the years, evolved in a unique and individualistic fashion, rather like the evolution of the animal forms in the isolated continent of Australia. Dibyendu's spoken language was characterized by loud bellowing to indicate important words and noisy breathing to imply exclamation marks. A sudden dip in volume with husky undertones denoted subtle things like commas and semicolons. Dibyendu harboured a contemptuous disregard for superfluous things such as conjunctions and prepositions, and in times of stress, did away with them from his vocabulary altogether. With tiny colloquial additions gathered over the years of rural postings, the language that emerged often left the most sympathetic of listeners confused, but was undoubtedly unique, colourful and dramatic. It possessed immense vitality and was rich with obtuse implications lurking under the acoustic aspects but had very little to do with the Queen's English. But one couldn't very well say all this to Mustafa, thought Siddharth uncomfortably.

'Oh, Benuda gets a little emotional sometimes and this affects his language,' he said instead.

Everybody stopped cutting sponge and waited respectfully for Dibyendu's respiration to get back to normal after his sterling oratory.

'How are your peptic ulcers?' Mustafa turned around and asked Soumitro.

'Peptic ulcers? Mine?'

Siddharth hurriedly knocked a T-square off his table. It landed on the floor with a deafening crash, making everyone jump.

'Mind your equipment, brat. I can't afford anything new till next March,' Soumitro told his younger brother wryly.

The matter of peptic ulcers seemed to fade into the distance and Siddharth heaved a sigh of relief.

'Why, what about your Diwali bonus, Dada?' Siddharth asked his brother innocently.

'We're holding back the bonus for now,' said Soumitro, his voice grim. 'These are tight times at *Noon Voice*. Go easy on the movies and clothes, girls.'

Mustafa leaned forward animatedly. He loved to hear talks about the intricacies of home finance. The painfully stretched, scrounging, depressing talks of middle class finances thrilled him in some strange manner. They gave such a warm, magical touch to the little pleasures of life. When one splurged on movies but held back on buying music, when one sacrificed the monthly restaurant dinner to buy a good book. He thought of his father's vast fortunes and business ventures that were spread around the globe and multiplying steadily. His sweeping economics could never offer such wonderfully special moments to his only son. Mustafa's pocket money alone, as he well knew, could easily fund the entire monthly household expense of the Banerjees. He felt a twinge of guilt followed by a wave of affection for the warm family that had adopted him so very unconditionally. He had a sudden, intense urge to do something lofty, heroic and significant for Ira Aunty, but wasn't quite sure what that could be.

Soumitro stood up abruptly, nodding to everybody (except Mustafa) in farewell.

'Sorry to leave in the middle of this hugely stimulating discussion but I've got to go. Crossword goes to print tonight.'

He left, Maltesh in tow, his crossword papers clutched tightly under his arm. The doorbell rang within minutes of their departure and Bonny rose to answer it. It was the postman, holding out a sky blue inland letter.

'Do people still send handwritten letters in these days of emails and mobile phones?' asked Siddharth wonderingly.

'Certain people I know do,' said Ira tersely, a worried expression on her face.

'Who is it from, Ma?' Siddharth enquired casually, looking up from his job of chopping sponge.

Ira slit the letter with urgent fingers and her anxious eyes scanned the contents. She turned the letter a complete three hundred and sixty degrees in stages, squinting at the minute writing that crawled along the sides. The writer of the letter had obviously believed in utilizing every millimetre of space available. The next minute the letter had fallen from Ira's nerveless hands as she stared ashen-faced at the company. The letter drifted away, settling to a halt under the dining table.

'It's Thamma! Your grandmother. She is coming here. Today! Anytime now. The letter got delayed in the post,' her words came out in a panic-stricken whisper.

There was pandemonium in the room. Siddharth started collecting his precious sponge like a madman, shoving them into a polythene bag. Mishti tore around trying to plump up the cushions and arrange them into a semblance of order and symmetry.

'Thamma! Coming here? To Bombay? Good god!' Bonny exclaimed, sounding thunderstruck.

'What will we do with Mustu?' wailed Siddharth, shaking like a leaf.

'Who is this Tumma person and what's with all the chaos?' asked Mustafa perplexed.

'The Bengali term for one's paternal grandmother is "Thakurma". It generally gets shortened to "Thamma" by lisping little grandchildren,' explained Mishti.

'So that's great news. Why is the idea of this Tommy coming here creating such a ruckus?'

'Because... because... by the way, Tommy sounds like a dog,' said Siddharth.

'We'll have to call Mustu by some other name. Mohit, Mohan, Mihir, Madan, Mahesh anything. Yes, Mahesh sounds okay,' said Bonny decisively.

'You see, Mustu,' began Mishti. 'Thamma actually had to escape from Dhaka to Calcutta during the Partition and she was only an adolescent at that time. And you know what that means. So we'll have to call you Mahesh.'

Mustafa stood up affronted. He was going to be renamed some ghastly Hindu name just because somebody's infernal grandmother had attained puberty while crossing the national border. And that too, decades ago. What kind of idiocy was this? He stood up bristling indignantly.

'Now look here...' he began, his tone belligerent.

'Too late!' shouted Siddharth from the window. 'She's here!'

There was an ominous sounding scrunch of brakes from the road below. A noisy argument, clearly audible at A-502 Pushpa Milan, followed.

'What! Chaarsho taka for an hour's drive from the station? Hothobhaga! Mook poda! Scoundrel! Take that and that and be off if you know what is good for you!' screamed a shrill, shrewish voice.

There was a loud, agitated swish of a car accelerating as if the driver was in a tearing hurry to be gone. Bonny turned away from the window from which she had been watching the scene. Her expression was grim as she faced Mustafa squarely. She knew she had only a few minutes before her formidable grandmother sailed in. This was just not the moment for politeness or tact.

'Mustu,' she began before swallowing hard, 'MY GRANDMOTHER HATES MUSLIMS.'

There. She had said it. Pronounced the words loudly and clearly, pausing in between words to emphasize the implications. Heartbreaking, cruel words that she had never thought she would utter someday in this unladylike manner. Bonny turned away, suddenly feeling close to tears. An imperious tap-tapping of feet sounded on the stairs outside and the front door flew open.

'Ki re, tora kothay?' a loud, shrill war cry-like greeting rang through the house. The elderly woman who stood at the doorway was barely five feet tall. But what she lacked in inches, she more than made up for in sheer presence. Her snapping black eyes gleamed behind spectacles and she wore a crisp white cotton sari draped in the traditional Bengali way. A bunch of keys hung from the ends of the anchol tossed over her right shoulder. Her lips were stained crimson with betel leaf juice and her mouth worked incessantly. She had the air of a bantamweight boxing champion preparing to defend his title. Behind her stood a harried-looking coolie whom she had abducted shamelessly from the railway station. He was bent low under the weight of luggage which seemed adequate for a small army. Good god, thought Siddharth in dismay, is she migrating to Bombay or something?

Mustafa watched in awe and wonder as the Banerjees rushed to touch the old lady's feet simultaneously, nearly falling over each other in their haste. Brushing a hand over each individual head while murmuring customized blessings took up some time and it was a couple of minutes before the old lady saw Mustafa.

'And who is this handsome young man?' she asked interestedly. 'Come here. Sit next to me.' She took up a position on the sofa and patted it invitingly. Mustafa went forward and meekly took a seat beside her. Bonny, Mishti and Siddharth stood frozen and white-faced.

'And who are you son? Siddharth's friend?' she asked.

Mustafa leaned back on the sofa with languid grace. Through half-closed eyes he shot a sly glance at Siddharth and his two sisters. He then schooled his face into an expression of limpid, angelic innocence.

'Who am I?' he said in a soft dreamy voice. 'Does anyone ever know the answer to that question? With forefathers who rode over deserts and oases, I pray facing west. I go without food and water for weeks in the presence of the sun at certain parts of the year and see form in the formless. Ultimately, who am I?'

Shreya Banerjee slowly lowered her glasses and looked at Mustafa over their rims. Her gaze was long and thoughtful. She seemed totally unperturbed by the young man's impertinence.

'Dear me! A visionary,' was all she said calmly. 'I see that I'm going to have fun here.'

13

Dibyendu Ganguly stood at his balcony in his night clothes. His elbows rested on the wooden railings and his chin was cupped in his palms.

There was something fascinating about squalor.

He couldn't quite put his finger on it but he could stand and watch the hutments below for hours on end. Young women with lean brown limbs bathed openly besides gutters at this morning hour, the droplets of water catching the pink-gold of the rising sun. The sun rays winked, gleamed and shifted on the surface of the bath water held in low-priced shiny, aluminium buckets. Soaping was a delicate business, wherein a rich lather had to be built up for a satisfactory bath, yet the wet sari had to be strategically prevented from slipping off the body. It was a tricky operation, requiring immense dexterity and skill. There was nothing voyeuristic about Dibyendu's gaze, merely immense admiration for the spunky women who lived in the Durga Nagar slums, tackling odds every moment of their lives. These same women, he knew, would emerge from the slums shortly, dressed in cheap nylon saris and carrying roomy Rexene handbags. Where did they go, wondered Dibyendu with a kind of vague concern, what did they do for a living? What kinds of worlds did they inhabit all day long? Posh flats to be dusted and cleaned, spoilt rich kids to be looked after or beer to be poured into the glasses of thirsty, leering men at bars? Were they domestic workers, masseuses, bar girls, sex workers, terrorists? What did they carry in those mysterious big handbags? Mirrors, combs, compacts, condoms, a change of clothes, knives, RDX?

With the women out of the way the menfolk of Durga Nagar came into their own. They got down to some serious mid-morning gambling while country-made hooch flowed from glass to glass in generous quantities. A couple of noisy squabbles were sure to follow, as Dibyendu well knew, after which the men would sleep off their hangovers in rope charpais, snoring loudly with their mouths open. By evening they were fresh, revived and ready to beat the women again. On days when the men were truly exhausted with the day's gambling activities, they demanded fried fish with the evening drinks. Dibyendu marvelled at the way the women met all demands, however unfair and unreasonable, with a kind of stoic acceptance, and his feet itched to deliver a couple of well-aimed kicks at the collective posteriors of the men of Durga Nagar.

Children played on the roadside, their limbs caked with mud. While the younger ones made do with sticks and pebbles, the older and more enterprising ones had an impressive array of discarded plastic toys to choose from. A hierarchy existed among the urchins, with the head honcho choosing the biggest and the brightest toys. Once in a while, a child could be seen leaving for the municipal school close by, self-conscious and stiff in his school uniform. But such heartening sights were few in number. Tea simmered in the open on little brass stoves while the older women roasted rotis on tavas set on open flames barely inches away from the traffic on the road.

There was something about squalor all right, thought Dibyendu. It attracted him, repelled him, fascinated him, hypnotized him and held him a helpless captive. There was an element of selfishness to the attraction as he well knew. The filth and chaos of Durga Nagar highlighted the clean, spartan orderliness of his own bachelor existence. The abject poverty he saw below set into relief the comfort of his own well-kept flat. The gloating pity he felt for the wretched conditions of the slumdwellers somehow elevated his modest achievements in life, giving a vital edge to his existence, where every little joy seemed like a major bonus from the powers above.

The slums were a great leveller, thought Dibyendu. Penthouses, one-bedroom-kitchen flats and chawls uniformly flattened to the same altitude by the presence of the sprawling slums around. One's drawing room could flaunt crystal and onyx but the view outside would continue to show squatters lined up for their morning ablutions. And all the perfumes of the world, thought Dibyendu philosophically, could not drown out the smells of garbage and night soil. It was, he agreed to himself, hugely chastening to have slums around.

He sighed and straightened from his comfortable crouched position. It was getting to be time for his bath. He'd wear his pistachio green shirt today to the Banerjees'. Bonny loved the colour green. The corners of his mouth turned up happily at the thought of Bonny. He would be meeting her grandmother, Shreya Dida, after years. He felt a sense of anticipation coursing through his veins at the thought of the coming evening.

Ira Banerjee and her mother-in-law sat working in companionable silence at A-502 Pushpa Milan. They made an interesting pair. Ira, with her vacuous, short-sighted gaze, her tall, willowy figure, her scanty hair revealing bits of her scalp and bundled into an untidy knot, and the short, snappy Shreya with her irrepressible dry wit. There were no surprises for guessing who led and who followed and looking at them, older generations of Steinbeck readers were reminded of Lennie and George, while the middle generation of comic book readers were reminded of Big Moose and Midge. While the woolly-headed Ira Banerjee did not strictly fall under the 'Duh' category (a term popularized by Siddharth), she was not exactly genius material either. She was best described by her eldest son who was in the habit of telling people (with characteristic disrespect): 'Oh my mother? She's spaced out.'

The tragedy of Ira's thinning hair had occurred in her childhood, when bleary-eyed with sleep, she had smeared her scalp with photography lotion, mistaking it for hair oil. Clumps of hair had parted company, leaving her with a handful of loyal remnants and by the time she was twenty, Ira looked about forty years old. Her eyes were the most notable things about her. They lay concealed behind spectacles, but on the rare occasions when people saw her without them, they were struck by the eloquence of her eyes. They held trapped within them the untimely death of a spouse, loneliness, depression, malnutrition and anaemia. Ira did not speak much and when she did she invariably said something that was totally unconnected with the topic being discussed.

Shreya Banerjee hailed from an era which had seen the departure of the British. An era full of dark deeds and polite phrases. Psyched by the men in the family, Shreya and her sisters had learnt to hate the British with their entire being.

But in their treacherous women's hearts they coveted the perfumes, the cosmetics and the lingerie that the white women brought with them. On quiet afternoons when the men were away, they stealthily learnt about sheer stockings and rouge, while some kindly ivory-skinned woman taught them how to bake cakes and cut wafer-thin cucumber sandwiches. Shreya and her contemporaries slowly found themselves turning away from the overpowering fragrances of attar and sandalwood and embracing light, floral English scents like lavender, dandelion and hyacinth.

While fish was considered auspicious in their Bengali zamindar home and mutton feisty, poultry (introduced by the gora sahibs) was severely frowned upon. Eggs were boiled and chicken roasted furtively in outhouses or in servants' quarters. A strange, skewed hybrid mentality emerged which rejected the colonists but embraced the finer things that they had brought with them. Patriots could die a dozen a day but tea suddenly came in silver services accompanied by cakes and sandwiches. A generation emerged, which was a strange amalgamation of contradictory beliefs, where special chairs and crockery were contemptuously reserved for Muslim and British visitors while baking and biryani-making techniques were ferreted out with stealth and cunning from these tainted categories of people. Shreya, a typical product of her generation, had read Bankim Chandra Chatterjee along with Somerset Maugham. She could steam hilsa in freshly ground mustard and toss pancakes in golden syrup. Articulate and sociable, she could hold forth on any topic from soccer to the Kamasutra.

'I'm glad Bonny and Mishti have opted for the arts stream, Ira. It suits girls to choose arts subjects,' said Shreya.

'Bonny has finished with her graduation studies, Ma. She is doing a correspondence course in mass communication.'

'That's good,' replied Shreya. 'She can keep you company at home. And besides, with all these oversexed boys around, girls are better off at home.'

'Oh, I don't think Bonny stands in any danger from the boys. In fact my sympathies are with any boy who comes in contact with her,' said Ira with a twinkle in her eye.

Her mother-in-law threw back her head and laughed uproariously. She was sitting crosslegged on the sofa with the centre table pulled close. A pile of betel nuts lay on the table and she cracked these, one at a time, with a dainty silver nutcracker.

Ira, who had graduated from the traditional foot vegetable-cutter, the bonti, now wielded a knife. She sat at the dining table with her elbows resting elegantly on the sides, chopping French beans. Bonny walked into the room with her usual heavy tread and Ira looked up at her smiling.

'Your grandmother was just saying that it is a very good thing both you girls have opted for arts subjects.'

Bonny stopped mid-track, a militant gleam coming into her eyes. She seemed to take on an invisible coat of arms, shield and lance. From a dowdy Bengali woman on the wrong side of twenty-five, she seemed to metamorphose into Xena the Warrior Princess.

'What exactly do you mean by that, Thamma? Explain yourself,' her voice rang out, crisp and steely.

Shreya Banerjee looked up and quailed at the forbidding expression on her granddaughter's face. She was a courageous woman who had travelled the length and breadth of the country alone on various teerth yatras after her husband's death. She was known to have bullied porters, thrashed cheating auto rickshaw drivers and even slapped a ticket checker who had dared to get fresh with a lady passenger. But when her eldest granddaughter got that public prosecutor's expression on her face, even the indomitable Shreya shivered in her slippers.

'All I meant was,' she began in a flustered, placating voice, 'that history, geography, sociology and literature are such *comfortable* subjects. You can study them under the ceiling fan. Now engineering, chemistry, microbiology – such hot, smelly, messy subjects, don't you think? Terrible for a girl's skin and hair.'

Bonny took a deep breath and raised herself to her full height, which wasn't much really, being a mere five feet two inches.

'Know this, ladies,' she began in a thunderous voice. 'Knowledge has no gender, though men would have us believe otherwise. And anyone who refutes this fact deserves to be beheaded. History shows us that women seeking knowledge have always been persecuted. You've heard of witches being burnt at the stake, have you ever heard of wizards being burnt? Women writers have taken on male pseudonyms, has it ever been the other way round? Thamma, I'm sorry to say that you are a blot on the feminist movement! I'm utterly ashamed of you.'

Shreya Banerjee dropped her nutcracker with alacrity and rose hurriedly, gathering up the folds of her sari with trembling hands.

'I think it's time for my puja,' she said in a quivering voice and beat a hasty retreat from the room.

Bonny followed hot on her heels, breathing fire.

'Phew!' breathed Ira into the suddenly silent room.

14

'I don't need men in my life. I'm in a very happy state of homoeostasis without them,' announced Bonny at Sunday breakfast.

There was a flurry of agitation all around with reactions to the statement varying diversely.

'Bravo!' cried Mustafa with his mouth full of toast.

He had invited himself for breakfast and was still in his night clothes.

'Good for you, Didi! Way to go!' cheered Mishti.

'Though I must say that men have their uses at times,' she added thoughtfully a moment later.

Her twin gave her a dark glare from across the table.

'Selfish girl!' said Shreya severely. 'You seem bent on blocking your elder brother's prospects of settling down to matrimony.'

Mishti looked horrified at the idea.

'No matter what, I pledge not to marry,' she declared in a tone of tragic sacrifice, 'till Dada and Didi get settled.'

'You're too young to be thinking of marriage, baby,' Soumitro told her mockingly, 'hardly out of your diapers.'

Mustafa leaned towards his friend.

'Watch out, Sid,' he whispered warningly, 'at this rate you'll miss the matrimonial bus altogether.'

'I've decided,' repeated Bonny in a louder, firmer voice over the buzz of conversation, 'that I really don't need a man.'

She had been waiting for Soumitro to get back from Calcutta before she made herself clear on this point. More than anything else she wanted to put an end to the endless charade of meeting prospective grooms.

'That kind of talk won't get you anywhere, Bonny,' said Soumitro severely. 'A boy will be coming to see you this evening, in fact. His father had spoken to me just before I left for Cal. Sounds promising. An MBA from XLRI and a good job with an MNC. Slather on the war paint and wear something nice, Bonny. Not one of your usual tent-like shirts. Sid, organize some soft drinks and snacks, will you? I'll come back early from work.'

Soumitro rose from the breakfast table, glancing at his watch. At the front door he turned to Siddharth who had followed him across the room.

'And see that the Muslim brat is not around in the evening when they arrive. He has an uncanny knack of saying the wrong thing at the wrong time,' hissed Soumitro venomously.

His face then brightened.

'Get Benuda to come over though, I could do with some moral support.'

The Banerjees' house gleamed and shone. Mishti, who always did a spirited job of cleaning up when visitors were expected, had worked herself to the bone polishing the brass and scrubbing the floors. The room glistened and glittered while fresh flowers in vases brightened every corner.

As was her usual habit, Bonny whistled gaily as she dressed for the evening. She felt completely detached and unmoved by the event that lay ahead of her. Such meetings were getting to be rather tedious and repetitive of late, with an average of four boys coming to see her every month. The prospective grooms and their families always left in a strange hurry, sending their message of rejection in an evasive manner on the telephone. There was by now a kind of predictability to the sequence, thought Bonny, who felt completely unconcerned about the results. Besides, she thought cheerfully, Benuda was coming today to lend her moral support. She adjusted a plum-coloured dupatta over her ample bosom and applied a generous coat of lipstick to her full lips. Her expression was icy and her body language aggressive. She could feel sarcasm and a sense of challenge bristling within her. She looked and felt rather like a knight preparing for battle.

'Bonny,' her mother announced, peeping in at the doorway, 'they've arrived.'

Bonny turned away from the mirror and started for the sitting room in an unhurried manner. At the door of the bedroom, she turned to her mother.

'If the boy behaves himself, get the samosas out. Or else it will have to be just tea and biscuits. And we can have the samosas for breakfast tomorrow.'

'I don't think that will seem quite proper,' said Ira agitatedly. 'After all they've come all the way from Cuffe Parade.'

'They could come from Timbuctoo for all I care,' snapped Bonny, brushing past her mother.

At the entrance of the drawing room she turned.

'We can't be so in-in-inhospitable...' protested Ira, stuttering in her nervousness.

Bonny gave her mother a long, cold stare.

'You will do as I say, Ma,' she said in a voice that brooked no argument.

Parting the curtains, she sailed in.

There was an odd restlessness in Dibyendu this evening. The Banerjees' drawing room felt cramped, with the prospective bridegroom and his family taking up every inch of space. Soumitro, playing proxy for his deceased father, was doing all the talking from the prospective bride's end. Bonny ambled in and out of the room nonchalantly at intervals. She walked towards the kitchen now, on her way to organize some soft drinks for the guests. Voices were raised as stilted conversation sounded from the drawing room. Dibyendu prowled around the house, hands deep in pockets. He found that he could hardly bear to be in the same room as the prospective groom. He felt irritable, moody and out of sync with all that was happening around him. He looked up at a sudden thumping sound. It was Bonny coming down the corridor with a tray laden with glasses of orange juice. Dibyendu halted and stared. It was the first time he was seeing Bonny dressed up and his heart suddenly missed a beat. She looked ripe, fruity and delicious.

Bonny – utterly beautiful!

He stared at her wordlessly from behind the curtains, his mouth not quite shut. His pulse seemed to gallop wildly while his heart did queer things. Oblivious to his presence, she passed within inches of him and entered the drawing room.

Dibyendu followed her on feet that were strangely reluctant. There was a lull in the conversation as the glasses of orange juice were handed around. The conversation then revived shakily, skittering edgily past mundane subjects like the prospective bride's hobbies, educational qualifications and the expenses of living in a city like Bombay. The boy's father eyed the furniture dubiously. Not much to be expected here in terms of material gains, his manner seemed to suggest, and the girl was no beauty either. Dibyendu, watching him, felt a sickening kind of anger beginning to well up within him. It suddenly threatened to erupt overtly in some kind of violent act and he rose hastily. Unnoticed by the others, he slipped out of the room.

The prospective groom sat, brushed and self-conscious and reeking of some exotic scent. He seems to have poured the entire contents of a perfume bottle over himself, thought Bonny caustically. The boy looked at Bonny furtively over the rim of his glass. Their eyes met for a fraction of a second before his gaze started moving down Bonny's person on a more interesting mission. It came to rest on her breasts, where it dwelt for a few seconds with a kind of lascivious fascination. Tearing itself away reluctantly, it travelled southwards again, to the interesting region of her thighs. Bonny watched the progress of his eyes with a kind of clinical detachment. She was, by now, used to men holding entire conversations with her bust line and her pelvic region.

'No,' she addressed herself silently to the groom, totally without any kind of rancour, 'no samosas for you, my lecherous friend.'

She walked out of the room. Mishti was coming down the passage to meet the guests. She was dressed simply in a pale pink salwar-kameez, her idea being to look presentable without overshadowing her sister. The glances of the two sisters met for a nanosecond. Mishti's gaze was hopeful and enquiring while Bonny's was coldly discouraging.

'Caution,' she muttered warningly as they passed each other, 'lecher ahead.'

Mishti's steps faltered. They veered to the right almost of their own accord, taking her to the side entrance of the house where Benuda hovered, looking strangely disturbed and uncertain. Sidestepping him nimbly, she tripped down the stairs and was out on the pavement in a minute. She inhaled deeply. How wonderfully fresh was the air outside, she thought. Relief washed over her as she breathed in the friendly sights, sounds and smells of a busy city at dusk. The house was filled with strange undercurrents this evening which were beyond her comprehension. Best to be out on the pavement till the guests departed, she thought.

Bonny entered the kitchen where her mother was brewing tea for the visitors.

'Marie biscuits,' she announced without preamble.

'But…' protested her mother, looking horrified.

'Marie biscuits,' repeated Bonny a shade louder.

'We can't serve just biscuits with tea!' wailed Ira, glancing wretchedly at the elaborate array of snacks laid out.

'MARIE BISCUITS!' thundered Bonny in a voice loaded with venom.

She swung around and left the room. Ira Banerjee sighed. Another proposal had bitten the dust as far as she could see. She set about switching menus with the air of a martyr. There was an ominous click of finality as the refrigerator door shut on the samosas, kachoris and rosogollas and a crackle of foil as she unwrapped biscuits. Slowly, with an air of utter defeat, she started placing the biscuits in concentric circles on a bone china dinner plate with a pretty blue pattern. There was an air of resignation to her actions. It was no use arguing with her elder daughter as she well knew. Some girls, she muttered darkly to the mute biscuits, were their own *worst* enemies.

15

The house was silent. The prospective groom and his family had departed with inexplicable haste after tea, without even bothering to exchange contact details with Soumitro.

Mishti had vanished into thin air, and so had Soumitro, it seemed. Ira and her mother-in-law were closeted for the evening puja and very soon the conch shell would be blown thrice, the sound diffusing into the twilight. Lamps would be lit before the deities and the house would be suffused with the scent of incense.

Dibyendu lay back on the sofa, gazing unseeingly out of the window. Storm clouds were gathering in the sky, sparking the evening with flashes of purple. His mood was sombre. There was an inexplicable turmoil raging within him. Why had the sight of the prospective groom sitting smugly and eyeing Bonny in that lewd manner roused him to such a fury?

Some strange chemistry had been at work of late, he had to admit. Though he felt it in his heart and sinews, it was not fully understood or acknowledged, even to himself. He craved to see Bonny these days with a degree of intensity that was almost frightening. He yearned to hear her boisterous laugh and listen to her firebrand feminist views. When she walked past him trailing the fragrance of lavender water and with her dupatta brushing against him accidentally, he felt parts of him hardening in a way that was most unsuitable for an ascetic. Such things had never happened to him before in all these years of celibate living and he felt deeply disturbed.

He tried to erase all thoughts of the groom's nauseating face from his mind. Given half a chance, he would have wrung that creep's neck like a chicken, he thought viciously. And with a great deal of pleasure. He schooled his face into an expression of calm unconcern with an effort. Bonny would be coming in with the tea any moment and in no way should he betray the true state of his feelings.

Bonny watched the water in the pan come to a boil and tossed the tea leaves in with a practiced flick of the wrist. She glanced out of the window. A cloudburst seemed imminent. Flashes of violet fire split the sky, followed by rumbling thunder. The intervals between the flashes and the rumble were slowly dwindling. The storm was moving in.

A cool, wet wind sprang up suddenly and somewhere a window banged hard. Bonny breathed in deeply. Tea fumes mixed with the scent of wet earth to form a delightful combination. She simply loved thunderstorms! Her mood was slightly less effervescent than usual though. The evening had been a crashing disaster, she had to admit, however grudgingly. There was not the remotest possibility of the prospective groom or his father ever getting back to them. This would be the thirteenth or the fourteenth boy who had rejected her. She had it all written down in serial order in a Bridget Jones-like diary. She would tear up the diary and consign the pieces to flames, she thought angrily. Incinerate all uncomfortable memories of failed matrimonial meetings. Or else dunk the diary into the Arabian Sea on her next visit to Juhu beach and relegate all taunts to her self-esteem to the hungry waves.

Suddenly she felt the delicious splash of cold raindrops on her face. The rain had arrived! She shut the window on the tempest raging outside, reminded of some old, favourite lines from Shakespeare.

But this rough magic
I here abjure and, when I have required
Some heavenly music, which even now I do

She quoted softly, straining steaming hot liquid into two tea cups:

To work mine end upon senses that
This airy charm is for I'll break my staff
Bury it certain fathoms in the earth
And deeper than did ever plummet sound
I'll drown my book

Picking up the tray, Bonny walked towards the sitting room. The house was dark in the storm. She padded on soundless feet and pushed open the drawing room door gently with her foot. She stood poised at the doorway, tray balanced delicately in her hands. A streak of purple lightning cleaved the sky, followed closely by another. The lightning lit up the shabby room for a few seconds, touching each object with a strange radiance. Dibyendu lay on the sofa, his eyes shut and his limbs spread out carelessly. A lock of his hair fell over his forehead. The buttons at his neck were open, revealing the thick, black hair on his chest. His arms rippled with muscles in the half-light of the storm and his taut thighs bulged. Suddenly and unexpectedly, he appeared virile and handsome.

And very, very desirable.

Bonny felt her breath catch in her throat. She stood shocked, frozen into complete immobility.

A crack of thunder exploded into the silence. Dibyendu jumped up. Knocking down a stool in the semidarkness he made his way to the light switch. There was a soft click in the darkness and sensible orange light from a 100-watt bulb flooded the room. In the mundane light of the electric bulb, Dibyendu, to Bonny's stunned eyes, once again appeared the kindly, bumbling cousin whom she adored. She stumbled into the room on unsteady feet and set down the tea tray shakily. Her hand trembled as she handed Dibyendu his tea, the trembling creating a muted soft rattle of china. What had happened to her for a few crazy moments, she thought frightened. What tricks had the lightning played on her? She stared at the rainwashed evening outside the window, her thoughts in turmoil. What kind of mischief was afoot this evening? What rough magic?

16

The house lay dark and silent. A full moon high up in the sky tenderly bathed shabby Durga Nagar in silver. Bonny stood uncertain in the dark corridor, dressed in only her cotton nightgown. Sleep eluded her.

A faint tinkle sounded somewhere and she started. Dada was at the bar! And why not, she thought, feeling a nauseous wave of guilt and failure wash over her. She had failed him. Yet again. It was inevitable, thought Bonny in resignation, that he should be at the bar tonight.

Her bare feet made no sound as she made her way to the drawing room. The room was lit dimly by a small table lamp, as if Soumitro preferred shadows to illumination this night. He looked up at his sister as she entered, his bloodshot eyes accusing. In the dim light of the table lamp she looked plumper and dowdier than ever, with the unbecoming floral nightdress doing all the wrong things to her complexion and shape.

'What are you drinking, Dada?' Bonny asked tremulously.

'What do you think this is? Milk?' Soumitro held up his glass to the light swirling the amber contents within.

There was a moment of silence.

'It wasn't my fault that the boy turned out to be such a creep,' began Bonny defensively.

'It never is. God! I wish I were dead,' groaned Soumitro.

Bonny looked down at her hands thoughtfully for a few moments, as if debating what to say next.

'I'll marry one of those jerks if it makes you happy,' she said, sighing with the air of one making a supreme sacrifice.

'Christ! You make me sick!' exploded Soumitro.

'But let me tell you,' said Bonny on a stronger note, her usual spirited self raising its head, 'that I have never believed in the traditional institution of marriage. And love doesn't always have to be consummated by doing a ring-a-ring-of-roses around a sacred pyre. Nor by hopping into the nuptial bed with a marriage certificate pasted on the wall making everything comfortably legitimate.

'Love could be magical, nebulous, undeclared and sometimes for a person considered improper by social mores. But that doesn't make it any less intense. And just because it cannot be acknowledged, it doesn't cease to exist. It is there all right. Solid, inescapable, tangible.'

Soumitro's mouth fell open and he stared at his sister as if she had gone stark raving mad. What on earth was she talking about, he thought in astonishment. He could hardly believe that the dowdy hippopotamus who had always posed as a model of virtue was actually lecturing him about sublime love! His brandy-fuddled brain teetered at the edge of sanity and he rushed out of the room in a drunken stupor.

Soumitro woke up with a hangover the next morning. His head felt heavy and throbbed painfully.

'Take the day off, Som. Stay in bed,' advised his mother gently.

'Stay *here?* In this loony bin? I'll only feel worse if I do that!' answered Soumitro.

Pulling on some presentable clothes, he strode to the front door.

His chin was dark with a day's stubble.

'But, Dada,' protested Mishti from the dining table, 'your breakfast…?'

'Oh, blow breakfast!'

He marched out of the front door, slamming it with a bang that nearly shook the entire building.

Soumitro marched up to the *Noon Voice* office an hour later, his expression darker than usual. His limbs felt leaden and his mood rotten. He wondered how he would get through the entire day. The office stretched out before him, an orderly, inviting refuge from the problems back home. He sighed with relief as he slid into his chair, the cosy, familiar cubicle closing around him protectively. He wouldn't stress himself any further trying to write his bestseller today, he decided. Wrong day for that. He'd meet Malto and discuss the day's cartoon instead. He rose from his chair to look for Malto. Ganesh the peon greeted him cheerfully in passing but got only a scowl in return.

And then Soumitro stopped dead in his tracks. An attractive young girl sat typing at the table at the rear of the office, just behind his cubicle. A sense of cold disbelief washed over him. Who the hell was this? The office was open to no woman other than Beatrice D'Monte, his antipathy towards women being a well-known fact at *Noon Voice*. And to some people outside *Noon Voice* as well. He strode over to Beatrice's desk with giant strides.

'Who is this creature and what is she doing here?' demanded Soumitro in a tone of suppressed fury.

Beatrice looked up frowning. She was busy drying freshly applied nail polish by waving her hands in slow, swaying, semicircular movements. She hated being disturbed at this early hour at office and generally unleashed disapproval upon anyone who dared do so. It didn't matter whether it was Ganesh the peon or Soumitro the editor. She looked at Soumitro coldly now.

'That's Malati Iyer, the new subeditor,' she said shortly.

'What? And who, may I know, had the gall to appoint her?' Beatrice frowned.

'I thought you had asked Pankaj Bhatt to recruit some new subeditors.'

'But a GIRL?' Soumitro nearly choked on the word.

Beatrice frowned once more.

'Did you specify the gender before leaving for Calcutta?' she asked.

She was right of course and the fact only served to incense Soumitro further.

'Well, get her out,' he snapped, 'and fast.'

'I can't do that!' Beatrice sounded scandalized. 'She has just been given her appointment letter.'

Soumitro felt a slow, helpless rage beginning to creep up from his toes towards his already throbbing head. He had the uncomfortable conviction that he was going to explode like a time bomb any minute.

Malati Iyer sat typing a story with single-minded concentration. It was the first time she was writing for a newspaper and she looked forward to the experience. The tip of her pink tongue stuck out as it always did when she was concentrating hard and a frown furrowed her pretty brow. Straight dark hair fell to her shoulders. Julius the lizard slithered up the table leg and settled down comfortably next to her computer.

'Hi there!' Malati looked up from her typing to address the gecko cheerfully. 'Nice morning, what?'

Malati had completed a week at *Noon Voice*, and being of a friendly disposition, was already on first name terms with everybody.

'He's not bothering you, I hope?' Maltesh enquired from the next table.

'Not at all,' said Malati with a straight face. 'I've always found lizards to be hugely stimulating company.'

Maltesh threw back his head and laughed softly. Malati was a good sport to be sure, he thought happily, unlike some other people in the office. He cast a glance of intense dislike in the direction of Pankaj Bhatt's cubicle. Beatrice came tapping along looking harassed and stopped by Malati's desk.

'Malati, the editor is back in town and would like to see you now, please,' she said.

Malati jumped to her feet, dropping the papers in her excitement. She had been waiting to meet the famous editor whose crossword-making skills she had heard about so much. Beatrice's eyes met those of Maltesh's. She arched her eyebrows and pulled a discouraging face from behind Malati's back. Maltesh coughed.

'Malati,' he said, his voice very kindly and avuncular, 'SB is actually a very nice guy at heart. Always remember that. Only circumstances make him behave the way he does.'

Malati looked at him in utter perplexity. His words did not seem to make any kind of sense to her. But she had no time to clarify matters as Beatrice was already tugging at her arm.

'Come along,' said Beatrice briskly.

She gave the younger girl a swift woman-to-woman look.

'Keep your wits about you, girl, and don't lose your nerve.'

With that bit of advice and a hand at the small of her back, she gave Malati a gentle shove, propelling her into the cubicle of the editor. Turning on her heels, Beatrice vanished.

Soumitro sat scowling at a sheet of paper. It was, Malati noticed (standing on the tips of her toes and peeping shamelessly), her biodata. The editor sat glaring at it for a while. He obviously did not believe in making eye contact with the new recruit.

'Where have you worked before this?' he growled.

'I did a short stint with a lifestyle magazine…' began Malati enthusiastically.

'We have no need for such fripperies at *Noon Voice*,' cut in Soumitro coldly. 'We only deal in hard news.'

Malati took a deep breath and continued.

'Subsequently, I went on to work with a women's magazine…'

Soumitro's face turned thunderous.

'We do not, I repeat, DO NOT carry women-centric pieces in our paper.'

Malati felt her inner good cheer slowly beginning to vanish. What ailed the man and what was his exact problem in life, she wondered furiously. And why couldn't he look at her directly in the eye and follow the basic rules of politeness?

'I have to tell you that I do not encourage rookie reporters with a Page 3 slant of mind at *Noon Voice*,' began Soumitro icily when Pankaj Bhatt, Parthasarathy Sharma and CoKen came bounding into the cubicle.

'Hey SB!' Pankaj greeted Soumitro enthusiastically. 'You're back! You've met Malati, I see. She's cute, isn't she? By the way, CoKen, Parth and I have been brainstorming in your absence. We've decided that what *Noon Voice* needs is a big dose of multivitamins in the face of so much competition. What we badly need out here are lifestyle and health supplements, women and kid-friendly pieces, loads of sexy celeb pics and oodles of Page 3 gossip.'

There was a long, uncomfortable silence after which the interview with Malati Iyer seemed to end with unexpected abruptness on the editor's side.

17

Mishti was in a dilemma. She did not know whether to paint her nails cherry red or frosted gold. Everybody sat around in respectful silence while she wavered between the two choices, trying to come to a decision. The household of the Banerjees ran on democratic lines, with issues involving politics, literature, sports, religion, cuisine and cosmetics being given equal and undivided attention and respect. Mishti's predicament was shared in a spirit of empathy by everyone around, no topic being considered too small or too trivial for collective contemplation.

'I'm sure red would look prettier,' said Shreya Banerjee.

'On the contrary red is considered passé, gold, silver and bronze being the "in" metallic shades,' Bonny contradicted her grandmother.

Soumitro shuddered.

'Paint your talons blue, green, orange if you wish, but for god's sake stop making such an issue of it, women,' he said in a disgusted tone.

Shreya ignored her eldest grandson and turned to look at her eldest granddaughter instead.

'*You* could do with a nice haircut, Bonny. And maybe a manicure and pedicure too...?' Shreya suggested gently.

'Me?' Bonny sounded horrified. 'Are you kidding? I've haven't seen the inside of a beauty parlour to date. And besides, are you suggesting I doll up for those morons who come looking for a bride, Thamma?'

Shreya gave a long sigh of resignation.

'Why is it that things are not working out for you, I wonder?'
'It's because she is fat!' said Soumitro from the other end of the room.

'I'm NOT fat,' stated Bonny with a great deal of dignity. 'I'm healthy. And besides, there are no fat people in the world, merely generously endowed ones. *Readers' Digest* says so.'

'Ha!' snorted Soumitro.

'You are such a nice person, Bonny. Everybody says so,' said Shreya consolingly.

'Who's everybody? I'd like to know,' asked Soumitro, feigning interest.

Shreya ignored him.

'You have your good nature showing clearly on your face,' she told Bonny encouragingly.

Bonny looked downcast.

'When people say you're nice, Thamma, they invariably mean you're dumb,' she said in a disconsolate note.

'Dumb?'

'Oh, not mute dumb. But dumb. As in stupid, imbecile, moron, mentally unevolved.'

'Oh, I see,' said Shreya doubtfully, though she did not see at all.

'When people say you're nice,' explained Bonny patiently, 'they generally mean that you're a little deficient in the IQ department and can be easily taken for a ride.'

'Oh, I see,' said Shreya again, rather inadequately.

She took a deep, thoughtful breath.

'I'm afraid I'm slightly out of sync with the present way of thinking,' she said, making one of her rare admissions to a personal shortcoming. 'But in my days when they said a girl was nice they generally meant that a girl was nice.'

'I'm afraid those days went out with the pterodactyls and the sabre-toothed tigers, Thamma,' said Bonny coldly.

Soumitro looked up from his papers and gave Bonny a long, hard glare from across the room. It wasn't often that he got distracted from the absorbing business of constructing crosswords but today was an exception. He gave his sister's topography a lengthy, clinical, brotherly analysis. His gaze was deeply exasperated. Bonny's Tropic of Cancer and equatorial regions were not too bad, he conceded grudgingly, but things went really haywire around the Tropic of Capricorn, it had to be admitted. She was the perfect pear-shaped endomorph. Only not a regular pear, thought Soumitro, but one of those freak gigantic ones that were generally displayed at fruit and vegetable exhibitions.

'Why don't you go on a diet, Bonny?' he asked her irritably.

'I tried,' said Bonny coldly, 'but I had hallucinations of gulab jamuns and nearly bit the postman from hunger.'

Her grandmother looked horrified.

'Don't ever, *ever* diet, Bonny!' she said worriedly.

Soumitro rose. Tossing his crossword papers aside he came over to Bonny and Shreya's end of the room. Pulling up a chair, he whipped it around briskly and sat down astride the reversed chair. His arms rested on the back of the chair and his expression was unusually attentive.

'Tell me Bonny,' he said, his tone both conversational and interested 'what kind of girls get snapped up quickly in the marriage market?'

Bonny thought for a bit.

'Oh, girls who are lean, mean and foxy. And who look at men in a hungry, predatory kind of manner.'

'And you?' Soumitro's prompted gently.

'Ah, me. I'm afraid I find most boys ludicrous to say the least and I can barely keep myself from smirking at them. And my expression when I look at them, I fear, is very, very vegetarian.'

'That won't do. That won't do at all,' said Soumitro sternly, shaking his head in disapproval. 'You must learn to look more carnivorous, Bonny.'

'I guess I must,' agreed Bonny in a forlorn voice.

Ira, who had just walked into the room, looked scandalized.

'This is a most improper conversation between a brother and a sister…' she began agitatedly.

'You could try thinking of things like meat burgers and fried chicken when you look at the prospective groom. It might help in getting the right expression,' advised Soumitro, interrupting his mother rudely. 'And go on a rigid diet for a week before the meeting.'

'Superimpose the fried chicken on the groom's mug in your mind's eye when you look at him,' said Shreya enthusiastically, getting into the spirit of things.

'And wear a low neckline. Show some cleavage,' said Soumitro.

'This is absolutely the most shocking kind of advice…' Ira sounded even more agitated than before.

Nobody took the slightest notice of her.

'And go sleeveless! You've got such nice shapely arms, Bonny,' said Shreya, practically gleaming with perspiration and excitement now.

Soumitro snapped his fingers in the air conclusively.

'A crash diet, lots of exposed flesh and a predatory expression. Voila! We'll have you married off in no time at all!'

He did an enthusiastic high five with his grandmother.

'This is the most scandalous, improper conversation for a middle class Bengali home,' declared Ira in a voice shaking with emotion.

As usual, nobody took the slightest notice of her. Mishti looked up from a long, serious contemplation of her toes.

'I think I'll paint my nails silver,' she proclaimed to the world.

18

Dibyendu Ganguly had an aversion to posh places. Places that had plush furniture, designer décor, smells of air conditioning and crystal planted at dangerous locations always brought upon him a sense of nausea, suffocation and a cold foreboding. Maybe it was because he knew for certain that he was going to knock off one of those crystal vases with his elbow or step on some oddly positioned artefact. Or maybe it arose out of his deep disapproval of any kind of excessive luxury that his Shaivite leanings did not sanction.

Dibyendu liked to think of himself as part-Buddhist, pledged to follow the middle path in all walks of life. He was proud of his ability to be morally upright at all times. Drunkards roused him to a fury as did drug addicts, wastrels and male chauvinists who engaged in boorish behaviour with women (whom he revered). However, flirtatious women and home-breakers roused him to a murderous wrath. Dibyendu liked his world washed clean, starched and ironed out to perfection. To reinforce this delicate cosmic balance, he wore the Brahmin's sacred thread across his body at all times and never forgot to chant the Gayatri Mantra at dawn and dusk, even on the busiest of days. Deviations of any kind and in anybody disturbed him greatly.

Religion had come knocking rather unexpectedly at Dibyendu's door at the age of twelve. Accompanying his father to the Ramakrishna Mission at Belur, sitting alongside people in deep, silent meditation, inhaling the scents of incense and introspection had been his first brush with inner silence. Lord Shiva, with his spectacular persona, seemed the best candidate to pin all his burgeoning religious fervour on.

'You made a wise choice in selecting Shiva out of the phalanx of gods and goddesses,' Mustafa told him approvingly. 'He is a hip blue, he is violent yet calm, he is generous with gifts and blessings, not unduly hung up on personal hygiene, smokes pot, inhabits crematoriums and keeps dodgy friends. In short, he is uber cool. Just my kind of a guy.'

While Dibyendu did not approve of Mustafa's unfortunate choice of words, he agreed with the general drift of Mustafa's thoughts. Shiva *was* truly cool.

Dibyendu leaned back, feeling happy and expansive. His glance roved around the Banerjees' house. He loved the hearty normalcy at A-502 Pushpa Milan. The whining of the noisy old ceiling fans, the scattered messy warmth of the drawing room and the superb meals served in homely stainless steel tableware without much fuss or fanfare appealed to him. The family ate with their fingers in traditional Bengali style and Dibyendu did likewise. He never could de-bone fish with a fork, anyway, though he occasionally made unsuccessful attempts to do so in fancy restaurants.

The Banerjees' home had such a welcoming air about it, he thought warmly, and any place which had Bonny... His thoughts ground to a halt as he felt suffused with a delicious kind of excitement. He blushed. He determinedly turned all thoughts towards the blue god who was his saviour in times of crisis. Over the years, whenever thoughts (which he chose to define as 'non-vegetarian') came uninvited to his mind, Dibyendu had a time-tested method of dispelling them effectively. Shutting his eyes tight and concentrating on a point between his eyebrows and in line with the axis of nose, he visualized Lord Shiva. Lord Shiva, in all his glory, with the Ganga flowing down his matted tresses and serpents doing a salsa around his neck (as Mustafa liked to put it). Lord Shiva, surrounded by a slowly revolving cosmos that reverberated with the echoing sounds of 'Aummmm...' Holding this picture steadily in his mind for about five minutes produced an effect that was miraculously soothing. On opening his eyes, he invariably found that he could effectively steer his mind clear of bikini-clad women, cravings for hot, spicy food, a wild urge to head the Indian cricket team and other such delusions of grandeur. A few private moments spent with Lord Shiva got his mind into a state of enviable equilibrium, the kind supposedly produced by the drugs Prozac and Alzolam (as his colleagues in office often informed him). He felt drowsy, drained and devoid of worldly aspirations, with his libido under strict control. Purged of all enticements, he felt at one with the cosmos.

Till temptation struck again.

Of late, he had this pressing urge to explain his Shaivite philosophy to the Banerjees. And to Bonny, in particular. His chance came now when the atmosphere seemed warm and conducive to any kind of discussion. As usual, heavy breathing played an important role in the vital speech that was coming up. Noisy, ragged breathing generally accentuated the seriousness of the topic while a silky accent with the breath held back indicated sarcasm. Dibyendu, it had to be said (as Mustafa repeated a dozen times) had a very *speaking* voice. He inhaled deeply now.

'I'm not one of those PHANATICALLY religious people, you know,' he began earnestly.

'We know,' said Mustafa.

Dibyendu gave him a brief glare and continued.

'Selph-denial gives me a kind of high that cannot be compared with any other intoxicant,' Dibyendu admitted, trying to explain the complex spiritual workings of his mind.

'BHUT,' the next word shot out forcefully, 'I NEBHER force asceticism down anybody's throat. I'm pretty libheral about the morals of others. I'm tolerant and sympathetic, you understand?' Here he looked imploringly at Bonny.

'I'm not a phanatic or a religious autocrat, only...' He paused, searching around for a more suitable word.

'Rabid?' supplied Mustafa helpfully.

Dibyendu uttered a sound like a car suddenly going into reverse gear.

'Mustu!' said Bonny warningly. 'Lay off! Stop baiting the poor man.'

'*My* philosophy in life,' interrupted Mustu, obviously thinking that it was high time that he spoke 'is based on...'

'Nobody is remotely interested in knowing it, let me assure you,' said Soumitro in a nasty voice, looking up from his papers.

'My philosophy in life is based on an old Dev Anand number which goes,' continued Mustafa grandly, as if Soumitro had not spoken:

Main zindagi ka saath nibhata chala gaya
Har fikr ko dhuyen mein udata chala gaya
Barbadiyon ka soz manana fizool tha
Barbadiyon ka jashn manata chala gaya

He paused a while for effect.

'Which translated for you Hindi-challenged heathens from Midnapur is,' he continued:

I walk in tandem with life blowing worries into the air,
Like smoke from a Charminar cigarette.

He made a mock sucking sound, puffing hard on an imaginary cigarette and went on:

It was pointless crying over spilt milk
So I whipped the milk into a soufflé of celebration.

'Mustu!' said Siddharth in a tone of despair. 'I really don't think you're much of an interpreter. And why Charminar for god's sake? Couldn't you think of anything better? Marlboro? Dunhill?'

'It's because I believe in all things Indian especially in the matter of cigarettes. I'm a true patriot.'

'I'm sure Sahir Ludhianvi would do a somersault in his grave if he heard your interpretation of his lines,' Siddharth told him.

'On the contrary, he'd be delighted to have an interpreter of such vision. One who sees the soul of poetry and not mere superficial things like words.'

'If anybody says that poetry is removed from words, he needs a head transplant. And fast,' said Soumitro in a dangerous kind of voice, addressing his remark to no one in particular.

The weather at A-502 Pushpa Milan seemed to be running to turbulence again and Siddharth hastened to smooth out matters.

'You were saying Benuda…?' he turned to Dibyendu.

'Yes. In my mind, at all times I dwell on the blue god Shiva, who is my greatest anchor,' said Dibyendu, relieved to get the conversation back to spirituality once again.

Mustafa turned on him aggressively.

'Do you know what the famous courtesan Chitralekha told the priest? She said,' he declared:

Sansaar se bhage phirte ho
Bhagwan ko tum kya paoge
In logon ko bhi apna na sake
Un logon mein bhi pachtaoge

There was a wild clamour of voices as everybody frantically tried to drown out any further onslaughts of poetry from Mustafa. He waited for the din to subside and then calmly continued:

Stop doing the 100 metres flat race against the world, pal
You'll never nab god that way
If you can't get chummy with your brethren down here
You bet you're going to be sorry up there, man.

There was complete silence, broken only by the sound of Dibyendu's temporary respiratory distress.

'I'd leave such sentiments to the courtesans, thank you,' he said stiffly.

Shreya Banerjee walked into the room on discussions holy. She looked fresh and rested and smelt like a garden. She was leaving for her daily puja at the Ram temple around the corner. Dressed in a dazzling white cotton sari, she held a gleaming brass plate full of puja paraphernalia: joss sticks, a conch shell, camphor, sugar crystals, a whole coconut, a bunch of green grass and a little copper urn of raw milk. Brilliant orange marigold flowers and deep red hibiscus lay in colourful abandon on the plate, along with twigs of three-leaf bel patti.

Shreya was in the habit of bathing a second time in the evenings. The evening bath was a quick affair while the early morning one followed an elaborate ritualistic procedure. The morning bath was preceded by a stream of warm coconut oil being poured on the top of the head and gently slapping it down with a flat palm till the oil rivulets travelled swiftly down the hair shafts. The cool trickling was immensely satisfying and standing on the balcony at dawn, Shreya prolonged the entire oiling operation till the Durga Nagar slums below started waking up. The bath water had to be just right as very hot water resulted in dry, dehydrated skin and too cold water meant the sniffles. When she emerged from her bath liberally dusted with talcum powder she looked like a ghoul with chalk-white skin and her hair hanging in damp strands. But a minute at the dressing table with comb and cold cream transformed her completely.

Smiling at the gathered company genially, Shreya stood poised to leave for the temple. Mustafa watched her, a thoughtful expression on his face.

She infuriated him.

The manner in which she sat cracking betel nuts, her expression serene and blissful and her whole persona embodying peace, calm and a smug satisfaction with life roused him to an irrational fury. Mustafa disapproved of such permanent calm. A static state of bliss was unnatural and unhealthy, according to him. Human existence, for centuries had been destined to have periodic upheavals. It was good for the system, forcing one to restructure and rethink one's parameters and perspectives and so very necessary for physical and mental growth, in Mustafa's eyes. Reinventing oneself constantly was imperative to human existence.

He watched Shreya head for the door with her daughter-in-law and granddaughters fussing over her as she got ready to step out. Mustafa's eyes narrowed speculatively. Every situation in life needed an opposition. Unanimous consent was a strictly unhealthy trend. At a very young age and with a great deal of zeal, Mustafa had appointed himself leader of the opposition in any and every kind of situation. He sincerely believed that he had come into the world for the sole purpose of keeping situations and individuals from becoming stagnant and predictable. He could switch sides with amazing speed and dexterity, leaving both parties dumbfounded, but on general principle he tried to make it a point to be on the side of the minority or the underdog.

Siddharth's grandmother was stepping out of the door now, her puja thali held at chest level. Mustafa stood up with an air of purpose. He had a job in hand. The old lady had no business looking so self-righteous and important, he thought disapprovingly. He would have to do something about it. And fast. Take the pomposity out of the pious, so to speak. He knew exactly what it was that he was going to do. His real name hung tantalizingly between them. Mustafa Ali Saifee.

Shreya trod on the dusty pavement on bare feet, her puja plate held firmly in her right hand. She recited Lord Krishna's name a hundred and eight times in her mind, keeping count of the chant on the fingers of her left hand. The mission was fraught with hazards as she had to keep her thali intact, the count of her chant accurate and prevent her sari from touching the filth on the road. She also had to dodge passers-by, so that no mangy dogs, menstruating women or non-Brahmins touched her en route to the temple, and was relieved to reach its entrance unpolluted. Transferring her thali to her left hand, she touched the threshold of the temple with a devout forefinger and lifted her right leg to step in when someone tapped her on the shoulder from behind. She stood in a ridiculous pose, with one leg raised, for a surprised moment and then turned around irritated. Mustafa stood grinning at her.

'Morning, Tummy,' he said breezily. 'Thought I'd give you company.'

Shreya snorted crossly and raised her leg again to cross the threshold when Mustafa touched her on the arm affectionately.

'One should never lie in holy places,' he said conversationally. 'And my name is neither Mahesh nor Mihir as they told you.'

He took a deep breath to emphasize the words that were to follow.

'My name is Mustafa Ali Saifee and I'm a BOHRA MUSLIM,' he said, belting out the last two words with unnecessary force.

There was a moment of stunned silence. And then Shreya gave a little shriek, her hands flying up to her face in shock. The puja thali went flying from her hands, the marigold and hibiscus blossoms rising high up in a colourful floral fountain. The copper urn dashed into the stone wall, sending a cascade of raw milk down the temple walls.

Shreya Banerjee was sick and bedridden for nearly a week. Her temperature fluctuated between 100 and 101 degree Fahrenheit for days, refusing to drop to a normal 98.6. Conversation was hushed at A-502 Pushpa Milan and the Banerjees tiptoed while going about their day-to-day activities. Ira walked into her mother-in-law's room on day six with a glass of barley water in her hand. Setting it on the table she stealthily walked over to the window. The curtains had remained drawn for the last few days and it was high time the room got some sunlight and fresh air, thought Ira resolutely. She tugged the curtains open and warm morning sunshine poured into the stale room. Bird cries and street sounds floated in from the outside and the drone of cricket commentary sounded in the background. But there was no response from the huddled figure on the bed. Ira sighed. Pulling up a chair, she sat down next to the bed, running a gentle hand across her mother-in-law's feet.

'I know what he did was unpardonable, Ma. But Mustafa is not a bad sort at heart. There is absolutely no harm or malice in him,' she said.

There was no response.

'It's just that he has a slightly misguided sense of fun,' continued Ira heroically. 'He may not be a Hindu or a Bengali or a Brahmin but he is such a sweet boy. In fact there are times when I feel much closer to him than to any of my own children.'

She paused. There was movement from the shrouded figure at last. The figure sat up in bed, wrestled with the tangled bedclothes and finally threw them off with a violent gesture. Shreya was pale, dishevelled and her hair a matted mess. She looked like an ageing witch at the witching hour and all she needed, thought Ira, was a long broom and a wand.

'You think I'm angry with Mustafa?' she demanded shrilly. 'Why, I simply *adore* that boy. He has more spunk in him than five generations of anaemic Banerjees. And I may hate Muslims in general but I have nothing against them individually.'

She pointed a finger at the barley water and shuddered.

'And take that horrendous stuff away from me, woman. My allergy is abating and I'm going to breakfast on luchi and alu dum.'

Ira stared at her mother-in-law. Ma liked Mustu! She adored him! She approved of him! Grabbing the glass of barley water, she skipped out of the room to organize an elaborate fried breakfast for the invalid. Her limbs felt light and her heart sang many tunes as she reached for the baby potatoes and the pressure cooker.

19

Maltesh Roy sat sketching. Evening sounds echoed from the street below while loud vociferous voices rose in argument around him at A-502 Pushpa Milan. Maltesh was building up his collection of portraits and he intended to sketch each member of the Banerjee family in turn before going on to sketch their cousin and friends. Mishti was the muse of the moment. She sat with her chin propped prettily in her hands and her hair spilling over her shoulders.

Portraits were Maltesh's forte. He barely looked at his subjects while working. It was almost as if he had permanently stored the subjects' features, appearance and expressions deep in the recesses of his mind. His hand danced like a puppet as he sketched, making quick, clever strokes. He was partial to Nataraj 4B pencils which he had been using from his schooldays, but sometimes, while rendering eyes, he chose to use charcoal sticks. The finished work of art invariably left viewers breathless with admiration and the subject vaguely disturbed. For Maltesh Roy captured not just the face, features and hair of a person on paper but every secret and every nuance lurking within his subject. He drew his inspiration from voices, word choices, seemingly casual gestures and the tone of laughter. It was as if his eyes could see the entire psyche of his subject. Though most people loved the reticent artist, some others (like Pankaj

Bhatt at *Noon Voice*) were left feeling uncomfortable and naked in his presence.

'Tell us something about yourself, Malto,' said Mishti.

She was the only person who could get away with personal questions owing to her innocent girlish charm (a fact that she used to full advantage). The others, who had been arguing noisily about the dismal state of hockey in India, fell silent. A deep curiosity about the shy artist lurked in everyone, though it was never expressed.

'Yeah, Malto,' said Mustafa enthusiastically, 'give it to us.'

Siddharth looked at his friend curiously. Mustafa, he noticed, never ever poked fun at Malto. Almost as if the tall artist with the thick, wild hair, bleak eyes and uncertain manners touched a strange chord in Mustafa. A kind of secret code of understanding lay between the two bipolar personalities, a pact of silence. Each of them seemed to recognize the misery that lay behind the carefully constructed facades that they wore.

Maltesh looked up from his sketching briefly. He was slightly red at being the cynosure of all eyes but quite composed otherwise.

'There is nothing much to tell, really,' said Maltesh, sounding almost apologetic. 'I grew up in Kodaikanal. I was a boarder at the St Joseph's High School for Boys.'

I was passed from one reluctant relative to another in my childhood, like some grim bizarre game of passing the parcel. And then dumped unceremoniously on the gentle nuns and padres, he thought silently.

'What was Kodai like?' asked Mishti.

Kodai was heaven, especially after living with hostile relatives. How do I explain it? The mist over the treetops, the morning air laden with the scents of wildflowers, wild, wonderful things growing underfoot, the smell of flora and fauna at their healthiest, Maltesh wanted to say.

'Kodai was lovely,' he said aloud, briefly.

'Tell us about your hobbies, Malto,' invited Bonny.

I saw serpents moult out of their skins, watched a million caterpillars burst forth as butterflies, saved hundreds of larvae from being eaten up by predators and aided chrysalis whenever I could. I watched eagles spiral out of ravines and soar away with the wind in their wings, he remembered with aching pleasure.

'I did a lot of nature study,' he said aloud.

'You've always had a way with animals, Maltesh?' Ira's voice was gentle.

Maltesh thought of the way injured birds had instinctively perched on his shoulder, fluttering for help, while abandoned baby squirrels had snuggled into his vest looking for warmth. Snakes, even on the few occasions that he had nearly stepped on them, steered clear of his path, while scorpions and centipedes lurking under stones kept their stings under check and chose to ignore his prying fingers and toes. Very early in life, he discovered the strange healing touch that he had with animals and an inexplicable affinity for all creatures big and small. Animals, likewise, drawn to him irresistibly, seemed to instinctively recognize him as a healer and protector.

'Yes.' said Maltesh softly, 'I seem to have a way with animals.'

And a complete inability to connect with humans, he thought.

He went back to his sketching, head bent low, but his thoughts were very far away.

Foxgloves growing next to gurgling streams, he thought, morning mist in my hair and beard. The smell of eucalyptus on mountain slopes and lonely jaunts over the mountains looking for mushrooms to be cooked for dinner at the convent. Chewing on deliciously sour clover leaves that grew in shady glens and standing for hours at the lakeside to watch kingfishers, ducks and fish. Soaking in the silences of the woods and hating the tourist season when the annual boat race attracted swarms of vistors and rendered the fish, the ducks and the birds miserable.

If he narrowed his eyes, he had learnt, and deliberately unfocussed his vision, he could see a myriad activities of little creatures in the trees, which were otherwise invisible. It was a trick taught to him by the kindly Father Noronha who was a nature lover himself. It was a practice that was to carry through into his adult years – deliberately blur vision to target on the important things in life. The padres had been very kind, teaching him all the right codes of conduct for an upright existence, even reading the New Testament aloud in the nights. But had they really equipped him for the whole messy business of living?

Nostalgia washed over Maltesh. It all seemed so very far away now. He felt a deep twist of longing within him. A yearning for another time, another place, now probably lost completely to his past and destined to exist only in memory. His friends in the room watched him surreptitiously. His words had been stark and brief but his tortured eyes told many other tales. Tales that they might never get to know.

The doorbell jangled, startling everybody. The door opened to reveal Bonny with a stranger in tow. The woman was roughly in her late thirties and looked frail and frightened. She was clad in a crumpled sari of an indeterminate colour.

'Hi, everybody! This is Bubla Basu from Halfway House across the street. Bubla, my family and other animals,' said Bonny by way of introduction.

Everybody looked up attentively. It was not often that Bonny got a friend home. Dibyendu, ever chivalrous, rushed to pull out a chair for the newcomer while Mustafa hurriedly adjusted the window blinds so that warm sunlight poured over the visitor without getting in her eyes. She looked up at him with a pathetically intense expression of gratitude, as if it had been a long while since anyone had taken any kind of trouble over her.

'Thank you,' Bubla muttered in a tremulous voice, looking at Mustafa shyly. 'You're very kind.'

'Oh, I am,' agreed Mustafa readily, 'I'm extremely kind. Believe me I'm so very kind that I surprise myself at times.'

Bubla looked nervous, not quite sure how to react to this statement and dropped her purse in her agitation. It fell open to reveal pitifully few contents – a crumpled kerchief, some loose coins and an asthmatic's inhaler.

'Mustafa!' said Bonny in a warning tone. 'That will be quite enough!'

'You live in Halfway House? That's the building around the corner that is being renovated, isn't it?' asked Soumitro conversationally.

'Yes. The electrical wiring is being changed and water proofing done. I live with my elder brother and his family on the second floor,' Bubla spoke softly and haltingly.

'Your brother has twin daughters, doesn't he? I've seen them cycling around the place,' Dibyendu joined in the conversation.

'Yes. Nina and Tina. They turned ten last month.'

For a split second Bubla's wan face became animated. It was clear that she loved her little nieces very much.

Siddharth walked into the room, T-square tucked under his arm, and looked enquiringly at the visitor.

'Wecome to the DNFSA, Sid,' said Mustafa in a loud whisper.

'What's the DNFSA?' Siddharth whispered back.

'The Durga Nagar Frustrated Spintsers' Association,' said Mustafa in a louder whisper.

'Hush, both of you,' snapped Mishti, sounding annoyed.

Conversation veered to general topics like the state of plumbing in the Durga Nagar area and the rise of the number of hawkers on the street below. Bubla got up to leave a short while later, smiling timidly all around.

'Don't hesitate to drop in, Bubla,' said Mustafa magnanimously, as if he owned the place. 'Think of this house as your own.'

Bubla smiled and left, leaving behind an elusive fragrance of musk. There was a brief silence in the room. Everybody felt curiously disturbed.

'Nice girl, that. But I believe the brother and sis-in-law are stinkers,' said Soumitro.

'Yeah. The brother, I've heard, is the usual invertebrate Bengali husband, completely spineless. And the boudi, I believe, is the reincarnation of Lalita Pawar,' said Mishti.

'Bubla's parents died within a few months of each other, a few years ago,' Bonny informed her mother and grandmother. 'And Bubla never got married, owing to her chronic asthma.'

'Tragic,' said Shreya.

'We MUST make her happhiness, take under our WHING,' said Dibyendu, losing grammar but gaining volume in his excitement.

'She needs some ghee, butter and sweets forced into her. She is far too thin,' said Shreya, whose burning ambition was to fatten up the malnourished populace of the city.

Another lame duck waddles into A-502 Pushpa Milan, thought Soumitro in resignation.

'We must do all we can to make Bubla happy,' stated Mustafa in firm tones.

'By the way Mustu,' said Bonny disapprovingly, 'don't you think you should be calling Bubla "didi" or "aunty" or something? After all, she is almost twice your age.'

'Didi! Aunty! Me? Good god! Are you out of your mind, Bon Bon?' Mustafa sounded horrified at the idea.

'I'm afraid I've risen above the petty parameters in life such as age, gender, social status, height, shape, size, caste, creed, race, etc.' Mustafa, explained himself further. 'Why, I even call my dad and my stepmom by their first names! I see merely the spirit, the essential ether in a person, you get me? And the spirit, as we all know, is ageless.'

But Bonny seemed completely unimpressed by such exalted glimpses of spiritual altitude.

'Well, whatever it is,' she snapped, glaring at Mustafa, 'she is going to be a regular visitor now and I simply will NOT have Bubla being addressed as "Boobs"!'

20

Soumitro sat twiddling his pen restively. A sheet of paper lay before him, blank and painfully white. He glanced out of the window next to his table. The city of Bombay stretched before him, hot, dusty and busy, all its grandeur and squalor condensed into the ten feet by five feet frame of the *Noon Voice* window.

As usual, no ideas were coming to him. Day after day, month after month and year after year he had waited for literary inspiration to visit him and all he had got in return for his efforts were nine-lettered synonyms and thirteen-lettered antonyms that flitted through his mind irrepressibly. Syntactic thoughts haunted his waking hours while alliterations stalked his dreams. His crosswords got more complex and confounding by the day, but he was nowhere nearer to writing his debut novel.

It was all Mustafa's fault, he fumed unreasonably, and that of that infernal subeditor Malati Iyer. As if it wasn't bad enough that the Muslims had invaded his home turf, now women were laying siege to his office. How could he ever get that novel written when his doom was being carefully planned by cunning conspirators? He thought of his grandmother with a feeling of helpless rage welling up within him. The old woman seemed inordinately fond of the Muslim brat these days, gushing over him and feeding him the choicest Bengali delicacies all the time. And after all the childhood brainwashing she had subjected him to against the treacherous 'M's. Talk about crossing sides, thought Soumitro venomously, one couldn't even trust one's flesh and blood these days!

He had deliberately and childishly shifted his desk to face the window so that he had his back turned to Malati Iyer. The sight of her freshly scrubbed pretty face roused him to an irrational anger and he preferred to face a blank grey wall (that came spotted with bird droppings) instead. He made it a point to speak to Malati only when absolutely necessary and restricted his speech to short biting comments. Everything about her irritated him, her classy dress sense, her innate poise and her flawlessly written stories which he couldn't blow holes into even if he tried. He attempted to rile her at every available opportunity and hoped that, fed up with his boorishness, she would hand in her resignation very soon.

Malati Iyer sat typing down the office, her pearly white teeth gritted tight in anger. She banged hard at the keyboard trying to think of ten painful ways in which one could kill an editor. Would pouring boiling oil over the victim in a gradual trickle be more pleasurable to watch or slow poisoning, she wondered. No method of murder could be too painful or too brutal for the likes of Soumitro Banerjee, she muttered to herself in a murderous rage. She wished she could get her hands on a nice, big meat chopper, the kind used by Jack the Ripper.

In the last few months, the editor had succeeded in making her feel half-dressed, incompetent, frivolous and scatterbrained. She seethed in anger at the memory of the perpetual high-handed arrogance that Soumitro displayed in his dealings with her. Malati, who possessed a very healthy self-esteem and a well-nourished ego, found herself floundering in the editor's presence and struggling for poise for the first time.

Maltesh watched Malati's mercurial changes of expressions with interest. She was getting Som all wrong, he thought with regret and concern, and through no fault of hers. Maltesh's recent efforts to talk some sense into his friend (in this matter) had met with a blank wall of resistance. Maltesh sighed. He'd take Malati over to A-502 Pushpa Milan some day soon and let her see Som in a new light with his family.

Malati rose and walked over to Soumitro's desk, holding her chin high and proud.

'I'm doing a profile on Sonia Singh,' she said, naming an upcoming starlet, 'she's sure to be in the news soon.'

'Are you trying to say that news follows you?' Soumitro's voice was incredulous.

'I am not *trying* to say it, I *am* saying it,' stated Malati, with supreme confidence. 'Anyone I write about makes headlines in a fortnight.'

It was uncanny but true, thought Soumitro uneasily a moment later. Every personality and celebrity Malati chose to write about landed in the news in a fortnight's time. It was most unusual and interesting. The bimbo, thought Soumitro uncomfortably, was getting to be pretty vital to *Noon Voice*, almost an asset. Her sensational pieces on the double lives led by celebrities had sent the sales of *Noon Voice* skyrocketing recently. So much for his plans for dislodging her on grounds of incompetence, he thought, feeling defeated. Once again, he got his usual hunted feeling – of being handpicked for persecution by fate.

Time dragged on at the *Noon Voice* office as it always did on Wednesday mornings. Every head was bent to work. Soumitro gazed out of the window unseeingly. He felt the usual grey weariness beginning to weigh down on him. He felt unusually introspective this morning and realized that he had stopped feeling solid, pure and clear emotions long back. All his feelings, after his father's death, came in a diffused manner, as if he was looking at life through a pair of smoky glasses. His family life and educational quotient were nothing to complain about but in love and literature his god had failed. A deep, swamping indifference permeated his entire being. Nothing in the world mattered, he told himself, just nothing at all. All of life was a mirage. Somewhere in the pit of his intellect he knew that he was carefully building up a defence mechanism to deal with any kind of future hurt. Erecting a strong barricade always helped and nihilism, as he realized very early in life, was a very safe shield to equip oneself with, particularly when the reality around came crumbling down ever so often.

But now, he thought furiously, this audacious new girl had got his carefully constructed equanimity all rattled. He hated the sight of her face yet longed to hear the sound of her voice. He hoped against hope that she would throw in her resignation and yet palpitated with concern if she was absent for even a day. What was wrong with him? He believed in instant coffee, instant noodles and instant sex (the sad kind that one bought off pavements on dark, lonely evenings). But instant love was an idea that he just did not buy. No sir, no way, he told himself cynically. It went against all logic and all the laws of physics, chemistry and biology. Yes, physics did say something about unlike poles attracting and biology text books were full of chapters on pheromones and other things. Chemistry between the sexes was written about ad nauseam in the magazines. But love? Love per se was humbug. Pure, unadulterated bullcrap. Love was an idea that he, Soumitro Banerjee just did not buy.

Never. He would stick to his theory that women were double-crossing, hypocritical, scheming creatures (his grandmother being a case in point), unworthy of affection or trust. And no chit of a subeditor was going to cause any revolutionary resurrection of the softer emotions in him. Never ever.

21

For about twenty minutes every evening Durga Nagar came alive. The gold-orange of the setting sun washed the slums lovingly, igniting the cheap asbestos roofs and the grey roadside puddles and turning them to liquid gold. A strange magic seemed to weave through the narrow dirt tracks, making every urchin, drunkard and whore look beautiful momentarily. All that was ugly and dirty seemed to take on an illusion of beauty, symmetry and style.

Ira Banerjee dumped all housework at this time of the day to stand at the window and watch the sun set over Durga Nagar. Sometimes, one of her children gave her company, and the latest of her companions was her mother-in-law Shreya. The sun turned a deep, fiery crimson when it edged towards the horizon, gaining size in degrees, and there was a long, collective sigh when it finally vanished behind the ragged skyline of the city.

'Coffee time!' sang out Mishti.

It was the cappuccino hour. The door was left ajar for the line of visitors who were expected to troop in shortly. Dibyendu came in first, followed closely by Mustafa and Bubla. Shreya turned away from the window, having watched the last smouldering sliver of sun fade.

'I think I'll leave you youngsters and go and read some Ram Katha now,' she told the assembled people.

There was a murmur of protest all around as Shreya rated very high on the popularity charts and was a valuable participant in the evening discussions.

'RAM?' Bonny snorted derisively, 'What do you want to read about Ram for, Thamma?'

'What do you mean, Bon Bon?' Mustafa sounded offended. 'Ram is the ultimate model of human virtues. Even to read about him is as good as a benediction.'

'RAM? Pshaww!' said Bonny in a tone of disgust.

'Now Bonny, that's no way to talk…' Ira began her usual plaintive refrain.

'Ram was the ultimate model of truth, uprightness and integrity with an awesome amount of duty sense,' interrupted Mustafa who considered himself an authority on Indian mythology.

'Like hell he was! Ram? Are you out of your mind? Ram was a wimp who played to the galleries and had as much spine as a bowl of caramel custard!' said Bonny.

'Here!' said Mishti angrily, looked up from filing her toenails, 'Who said anything against caramel custard? It's my favourite dessert. Be warned!'

'Bonny! Mishti!' Ira sounded as if she was gagging.

'He abandoned his wife when she was pregnant with twins, eventually ditched his devoted brother Laxman who accompanied him through vanvas and did not care a hoot about separating him from his wife for fourteen years when he took him along to the forests…' continued Bonny.

'Bonny, this kind of talk is sacrilege and will not be tolerated in a middle class Bengali…' Ira sounded desperate.

Bonny ignored her.

'... Ram was the biggest and earliest politician in Indian history, who knew how to pander to the vote banks brilliantly. And like all politicians, his public life was spectacular and his private life a disaster!' she concluded.

Soumitro walked in to find that the drawing room had split into two distinct camps, with Ira and Mustafa in the pro-Ram team and Bonny holding the fort for the anti-Ram camp. Mishti was a little unsure about matters but instinctively sided with her elder sister while Dibyendu, who found his heart and head at loggerheads suddenly, maintained a stoic silence. From time to time, he muttered 'Shiv, Shiv, Shiv' under his breath. Everybody appealed to Shreya who looked horrified at being appointed sudden referee for a satisfactory end to the argument. She gathered up her sari pleats with urgent fingers and started heading for her bedroom. At the doorway she turned.

'Ram was the epitome of duty, selflessness and valour,' she said in a trembling voice, 'but it is a fact that he would never win brownie points with the feminists.' Turning away with alacrity, she fled. A cacophony of voices sounded as the argument resumed with force after her departure.

There was a sudden, surprised lull in the argument as Maltesh walked into the room with a pretty young girl hanging on to his arm. Malto had a girlfriend? The idea seemed amazing. Soumitro's eyebrows rose wordlessly as his sardonic eyes met Maltesh's helpless ones across the room.

'This is Malati Iyer, our new subeditor at *Noon Voice*,' Maltesh introduced the newcomer to the assembled company.

'Dada!' shrieked Mishti in delighted tones. 'You've appointed a GIRL!' Soumitro looked thunderous and his glance at Malati was scorching. He went back to making crosswords, turning his back to the room, denouncing all ties with the rest of the group.

'Sit down Malati, and tell us something about yourself,' Ira smiled kindly at the girl.

Coffee was done with and everybody was feeling relaxed and expansive. Bonny sat on the windowsill, swinging her legs. The evening sunlight spilled over her, lighting her plump figure up in a blaze of gold. Dibyendu watched her, his expression besotted, worshipping and faintly idiotic. He seemed oblivious to the conversation around him.

Malati bounced up and down on the sofa, looking like an energetic little terrier. Tucking one leg under her, she made herself supremely comfortable.

'I'm sixteen, footloose, fancy-free and all applications for the post of boyfriend are acceptable,' she announced.

There was a startled silence all around and she burst into peals of laughter.

'Just kidding, folks. I picked up that line from a retro movie – Katherine Hepburn, I think.'

Her expression sobered.

'I'm twenty-six and a Tamilian Brahmin. I did my schooling and college in Delhi. I have a postgraduation in English literature and I've come down to Bombay to make a career for myself,' she said.

Bubla gazed out of the window at the murky Bombay skies. Her expression was dreamy and faraway. How would my introduction run, I wonder, she asked herself.

Name: Bubla Basu.

Description: Colourless, shapeless and aimless.

Qualifications: Chronically asthmatic.

Maltesh inspected his feet with a thoughtful expression. His toenails needed clipping. He pondered over his antecedents.

Name: Maltesh Roy.

Religion: Unknown.

Parentage: Uncertain.

Claim to fame: Affinity with animals.

'I live with my elder brother and his family at Powai, very close to the Powai Lake,' Malati added. 'The area is very posh and swanky. There is nothing posh or swanky about me, I'm afraid. I'm the original radish chewing, sugarcane juice guzzling rustic from Dilli.'

She giggled.

I live in Halfway House which is a place halfway to despair, halfway to dreams and halfway to reality, thought Bubla to herself.

I live on the periphery of a black hole of personal misery, thought Maltesh silently, in danger of being sucked in any day.

'I live with my brother, sister-in-law and my little nephews Santosh and Subramanium, Sunny and Subi for short. They are the cutest kids in the whole universe,' said Malati proudly. 'And I'm afraid, I am the most spoilt and pampered member of the family.'

I also live with my brother and his family but I'm the odd piece of furniture around that nobody knows what to do with, thought Bubla.

Malto leaned back in his chair and shut his eyes tight. I live with memories, ghosts, doubts, shadows and reptiles as companions, he thought.

Conversation of the general kind followed. Malati got up a little later, glancing at her wristwatch. She beamed at everyone, studiously avoiding looking at Soumitro directly.

'Lovely meeting you, folks. I'll come again. You must come home sometime too. I can promise you a delicious Tam Bram lunch if you do,' she said laughing.

Sketching a smart salute, she was gone.

'Charming girl. So friendly,' breathed Ira.

'Wonderfully effervescent and talkative.'

'Cute. Nice smile.'

There was a chorus of comments after Malati's departure. Soumitro looked up from his crossword. His face was inscrutable as he turned around to face the room once again. His gaze measured every expression in the room; various degrees of interest over the new visitor were on display. Clever actor, knows how to play up to the audience, he thought sourly. He thought of Malati's animated little face and felt a strange, twisted pain knife through him.

22

Malati Iyer sat nibbling her ballpoint pen. Her writing pad lay before her, empty, expectant and waiting. Nothing interesting seemed to be happening in the city these days, she thought dejectedly. No scandals, no juicy extramarital affairs, no cases of adultery, no elopements, no spicy seduction stories and no murders. Nobody jumping off the terraces of skyscrapers or hanging themselves from ceiling fans either and no recent cases of molestations or self-immolation. What was the world coming to, she thought in despair, and how on earth was she supposed to fill up her pages at this rate? Opening the drawer of her desk surreptitiously, she gazed into it with a look of wild longing on her face. Hearing footsteps behind her, she quickly shut the drawer. The footsteps came closer. It was Soumitro.

'Where is the story on the forest bandit ?' he barked out.

'I'm working on it,' replied Malati shortly.

'STILL working on it? Do you think you could have it in by this calendar year?' his words dripped sarcasm.

'Well I might, if there were fewer summons to report to higher authorities,' replied Malati tartly.

Soumitro's blood seemed to rush to his head. No subeditor to date had ever had the nerve to speak to him like this.

'I want the story in fifteen minutes flat. You get it?' he bit out furiously before striding away to his cubicle.

Malati made a rude face behind his back. That man could

really get under her skin, she thought as she banged away at her keyboard furiously. Her face was flushed as she tried to envision ten painful ways of torturing a man. Before killing him outright, of course. In the last week, Soumitro had summoned her to his desk a dozen times, and managed to effectively convey to her that her stories were irrelevant, her mannerisms irritating and her entire wardrobe a disaster. In short, he had made her feel like the lowest possible life form. A worm. She fumed inwardly. She, Malati Iyer, was not the kind of person to take such insults lying down. Setting her chin at a firm, determined angle and narrowing her eyes, she planned Revenge.

Soumitro watched the kaleidoscope of emotions flit across Malati's face with ill-concealed delight. He had managed to needle her again! He felt a sense of unholy triumph at his achievement. Besides, he told himself with amusement, she looked so incredibly pretty when she was angry. She reminded him of a leopard cub he had seen in a zoo as a child.

Almost without realizing it, Soumitro had shifted his desk by inches over the last few weeks. He now kept his window open at an angle of forty-five degrees. He told himself repeatedly that it was partly to let out the stale office air and partly to let in literary inspiration but in his heart of hearts he knew that it was otherwise. The window, thus angled, caught the reflection of Malati's mobile little face clearly, trapping every change of mood and capturing her expressions for hours. It was difficult for Soumitro to look at her directly with all the antagonism and undercurrents running between them and this, he found, was the perfect method of watching her unobtrusively.

Her mood changes were mercurial. Sometimes she wrote like a woman possessed, squinting and scowling at the monitor, her tongue sticking out, wet and pink. Sometimes she looked pensive and abstracted, tearing bits of paper into thin ribbons and watching them flutter away in the breeze. Sometimes, after a tough confrontation with him, she looked like an angry little tigress, muttering venomously under her breath and venting all her fury on the keyboard, and he could barely stop himself from laughing out loud. He couldn't really put his finger on the exact reason, but she bothered him. Bothered him in a strange, inexplicable way that left him feeling vaguely threatened. The sooner she handed in her resignation the better it would be for his peace of mind, Soumitro thought grimly. He leaned back in his seat and sighed at the complexities of life.

'What gives?' asked Maltesh from the next table.

'My greatest dream, you know Malto, is that someday my novel will be a bestseller and filthy little urchins will peddle pirated copies at traffic junctions,' revealed Soumitro with another long, wistful sigh.

'Why that's great! So what's stopping you from reaching your dream?'

'The fact that I haven't even started writing the book I'm talking about. Or thought of a storyline, for that matter. No idea what to write either.' Soumitro sounded morose.

'Yeah, yeah. That's one hell of a problem,' agreed Maltesh sympathetically.

The two bearded men sighed sadly and stared into space for a few moments. Maltesh went back to his sketching presently, leaving the editor to contemplate his literary shortcomings. Julius slithered up to him affectionately. Maltesh ran a caressing finger under Julius' neck. The lizard arched its neck and looked, if it was possible for a reptile to do so, completely ecstatic.

'Are you hungry, little brother?' Maltesh murmured softly to his pet. 'Would you like some juicy cockroaches? Or would you prefer spiders?'

Beatrice who had been passing by stopped, affronted.

'Excuse me! There are no cockroaches or spiders at *Noon Voice*,' she said indignantly. 'We do pest control every three months. Why don't you give your alligator some chips or soft drinks or something? Less messy than insects.'

'For god's sake, Beatrice, geckos don't swig Coke, And Julius is a wall lizard, not an alligator, if you please.'

'Well, whatever,' said Beatrice, indifferent to zoological intricacies, 'just see that the blessed crocodile doesn't mess up the office.'

'Okay, okay, okay,' said Maltesh huffily.

His pets, he thought morosely, were definitely not popular with friends and colleagues.

Noon Voice was at present a hub of activity. The festival season was drawing close as were school vacations. Special weekend supplements on holiday destinations, festival finery and food were being planned. There was an immense amount of work piling up and the sole accountant of the office was down with jaundice. Soumitro, pacing up and down the office floor, ran a harassed hand through his hair. He suddenly stopped short at Maltesh's chair, placing his hands entreatingly on the artist's shoulder.

'Malto, I'm afraid you'll have to pitch in as accountant for a while,' he said.

'Me!' said Maltesh in tones of horror 'No way! My arithmetic is the pits!'

'All you have to do is handle the petty cash and the vouchers...' suggested Soumitro soothingly.

'SB!' groaned Maltesh. 'I'm just not one of these mathematical geniuses. Or is the correct word genii?'

'You're not too hot on languages either, seems like,' muttered Pankaj Bhatt dryly.

'You'll only have to do some simple calculations and remember the office account number...' urged Soumitro.

'I'm an artist! I can't remember my own telephone number for Chrissake, SB!' wailed Maltesh, sounding frantic.

Soumitro threw back his head and laughed. A long, uninhibited laugh. There was stunned silence all around.

'Good god!' muttered Malati, not too softly, 'Ravan actually laughed!'

'Yes?' Soumitro's voice was dangerously silky as he stalked, panther-like, towards her desk. 'You said something?'

Malati swallowed nervously.

'No, nothing. Nothing at all,' she whispered.

'Are you quite sure? I thought I heard something.'

He was looming over her desk now, looking tall and menacing. She looked up at him, her eyes very frank.

'Why don't you laugh more often? You've got such a nice laugh,' she said softly so that only he heard the words.

There was a moment of complete silence. His back hid the rest of the room from her view. It was just him and her and it was an oddly intimate moment.

'I lost the ability to laugh long ago,' said Soumitro quietly, almost to himself. There was no sarcasm in his voice, merely a deep weariness, and Malati felt a sudden twinge of guilt and shame. She must, she decided, be a little less abrasive with him. He stood staring down at her for a long moment. Then, almost as if regretting his momentary lapse in revealing his thoughts, he gave her a curt nod and strode off. Malati found that she could breathe again.

23

Maltesh sat alone in the office of *Noon Voice,* watching Archimedes swim around in circles in a jam jar. It was the goldfish's weekly day out. The tiny orange creature made a welcome splash of colour in the sombre office which stretched before Maltesh, empty and silent. Everybody had left. Except him. Evenings always seemed to affect him in a strange way. A lonely hour when emotions kept leashed through the day came tumbling out, unrestrained and undiluted. An hour of introspection, silences and a long, golden sadness. He glanced out of the window. Office-goers were hurrying home and mothers from the few residential buildings around were coming out, dressed up for the evening and accompanied by small children. A stray balloon-seller had parked himself at the street corner and a bunch of multicoloured gas balloons blazed, iridescent in the light of the setting sun. Birds winged their way home, black specks against the amethyst expanse. All of life, thought Maltesh, seemingly more vital, intense, vivid, vibrant, still and suspended at this sad, edgy hour. What was it about evenings?

Maltesh began to feel his usual fatigue and depression gnaw at his insides. The empty chairs, shrouded computers and silent telephones watched him mockingly. All his colleagues were heading home at this hour. Homes filled with voices, laughter and warm smells of cooking, he thought wistfully, feeling just a little envious. He thought of his own minuscule bachelor pad in a seedy bylane of Santa Cruz. Dark, dingy stairs perennially lined with garbage bins and the all-pervading stench of putrefying garbage. Smells of pickle, defeat and weariness in the dark corridors. He thought of the dreary little room waiting for him. Half a dozen pairs of unwashed socks would be lying around, adding to the mustiness of the closed room. He had forgotten to switch off the tubelight in the kitchen this morning and had in all probability left the pan of instant noodles uncovered. He knew he'd go back to find roaches feasting on the cold, coagulated mess in the pan. Giant-sized, shiny maroon cockroaches that were beginning to multiply and thrive on the unwashed dishes left stacked in the sink all day long.

Every year the rain came down in sheets into the small verandah attached to his living room. Often the water reached the shelf holding his precious art material, leaving his charcoal sticks and expensive cartridge papers a soggy mess. The landlord, after much persuasion, had put up some kind of a thatched extension to the verandah roof. This hardly helped matters, only succeeding in making the place darker and gloomier than before. The thought of home left Maltesh feeling infinitely miserable.

Julius crawled out of his hip pocket, crept up his arm and settled down comfortably in the crook of his elbow.

'Yes, Julius,' sighed Maltesh. 'I'm depressed and I admit it. Freely.'

He missed his guinea pig, but resolutely stopped himself from thinking about what had happened to the creature recently. A murderous rage towards Pankaj Bhatt flared momentarily in his mind, only to be dispelled by an overwhelming feeling of loneliness. A sense of belonging, he thought achingly, wasn't that what everybody searched for? He thought longingly of the drawing room at A-502 Pushpa Milan. Mustafa, Bubla and Dibyendu were sure to be there on this wet, rainy evening. The smell of coffee would suffuse the evening air. Sid would be bent low over his architectural drawing while his twin stuffed hot pakoras into his mouth at intervals. Mishti, Maltesh knew, would be scrupulously cautious about not letting the oily snack fall onto Sid's precious sheets. Noisy arguments would be carried on against the backdrop of retro music, punctuated by some acid comments from Som's grandmother. Maltesh smiled at the thought of the volatile old lady. Neighbours and people passing on the street below would smile indulgently at the usual ruckus at the Banerjees' residence. Lucky Som, thought Maltesh – lucky, lucky Som.

Julius wriggled under his chin restively, having shifted position.

'You guys are not very popular with my human friends, you know,' Maltesh addressed the lizard and the goldfish sadly.

He rigidly tried to keep his mind off Brutus, but failed miserably in his attempts.

This morning at *Noon Voice* had been particularly tense, with everybody frantically trying to meet deadlines.

'Malto, could you keep your relatives under check, please? They're distracting me,' the usually chirpy Malati had sounded snappish.

'Besides,' she added, 'I just might step on them in my hurry.'

'Hey! What's with the wildlife population around?' Soumitro had sounded unusually edgy, finding Julius curled up on his keyboard a minute later.

A week earlier, on his visit to A-502 Pushpa Milan, Maltesh had placed a rescued toad by the doorway and Mishti, coming up the stairs, had mistaken it for a dropped kerchief in the dim light of the landing. Picking it up, she had let out a shrill scream when it had jumped in her hand and had flung it down as hard as possible. The frog had sat still and glowered at Mishti the whole evening, its ego badly bruised.

'Be kind to it, Sharmistha,' Mustafa had admonished her sternly, 'it just might be a prince.'

The advice had only made Mishti shudder and scream again.

No, thought Maltesh despairingly as he remembered the isolated incidents, my pets are not exactly popular. He sighed and sank deeper into his chair. He let his head fall back and shut his eyes. Melancholia swirled around him like a thick mist.

There was a discreet cough behind him suddenly and Maltesh turned around startled. It was Ganesh, the office peon.

'There is someone to see you, sir,' said Ganesh. 'He is waiting for you downstairs.'

'Someone waiting to see ME?' asked Maltesh, his tone incredulous.

Nobody had waited for him in the last twenty odd years. His disinterested relatives having dumped him at the convent in Kodai, had relinquished all ties with him after his parents' death. He disentangled Julius from his shirt collar. Putting him down gently, he followed Ganesh down the staircase. As Ganesh traipsed down the stairs before him whistling merrily, Maltesh felt a sense of curiosity and bewilderment overtake him. Who could be waiting for him downstairs?

Emerging from the darkness of the building, his eyes took a couple of minutes to adjust to the bright light outside. When he gained focus, he saw a tall, swarthy man standing on the pavement and looking in his direction narrowly. Behind him stood an auto rickshaw, its engine rumbling softly and its meter ticking away. Ganesh made a brief introductory gesture to the two men and vanished into the *Noon Voice* building, whistling.

The man smiled at Maltesh. A tight, twisted kind of smile. He motioned Maltesh to get into the waiting rickshaw, obviously wanting to talk. A light drizzle was beginning to fall and it seemed like a good idea to get into the dry interior of the auto rickshaw. What did the man, a complete stranger, want from him? Some message from the Fathers in Kodai, maybe? Maltesh bent low to get into the rickshaw. The tall man followed him in and to Maltesh's surprise the auto rickshaw sprang forward almost immediately. Maltesh then, to his discomfiture, found a second man sitting inside, hardly visible in the darkness of the rickshaw interior. He was, he found to his dismay, sandwiched between two burly men who looked vaguely disturbing and seemed disinclined towards speech. Sheer surprise prevented him from attempting an escape. The drizzle had now turned into a regular downpour, drowning out all sounds save that of the rain. After a few moments, the auto rickshaw began to gather speed with a kind of quiet determination. The men drew down the rain curtains on both sides and plunged the inside of the auto rickshaw into complete darkness.

24

Maltesh and his captors walked single file through the thick Aarey forests at the edge of the city. They had been joined by two other men. Maltesh was at the centre with two men in front and two behind keeping watchful eyes on him. But there was no place he could run to really. They had left all traces of civilization far behind. The underbrush grew dense and thorny on either side of the narrow dirt track, sealing all routes of escape effectively. Besides, he was a complete stranger to these parts and any attempt to escape could prove to be dangerous. And unwise. The four men, on the other hand, seemed to know the terrain like the back of their hands, gauging from their surefootedness and confident body language.

They must have walked for about three hours at a stretch before the tall swarthy man (whom the others addressed as Kali) raised his hand, indicating a break. They had reached a small clearing in the forest and at a signal from Kali, the men flopped down tiredly on the grass. Maltesh, after a brief hesitation, did likewise.

The four men sat in a tight circle, a little distance away from Maltesh. They conversed in low, hushed tones among themselves, glancing at him from time to time. They seemed slightly unsure about how to handle him, keeping social interaction with him to the minimum. A rough leaf bidi was passed from hand to hand presently, from which each man took a long draw. The tall man called Kali pulled out a plastic bottle of water from the tattered rucksack that he was carrying.

'Here,' he said briefly, tossing it over to Maltesh.

His expression was surly. Maltesh drank deeply and greedily, like a child. The water tasted orange-flavoured with a faint smell of plastic. He felt a wave of nostalgia wash over him at the taste. He was suddenly reminded of Malati Iyer (who loved orange fizz) and felt a wild longing to get back to the *Noon Voice* office and to a life that was steady, secure and predictable. The forests above watched him, dark and silent.

He lay back on the grass, his limbs stiff with exhaustion. His legs ached from the long walk as he was not accustomed to so much uphill climbing. What was it that his biology teacher had taught in school? He made an attempt to remember his middle school lessons – oxalic acid crystals formed in the muscles after sudden exercise, causing pain and stiffness. Old Mathai had taught that. Cantankerous and brilliant Mathai, who had taught biology to generations of rowdies before going over the edge, consumed by his own brilliance. He was last heard of doing time at an asylum near Poona. Would he ever see his teachers or his school friends again? Would he ever get a chance to get back to a normal urban life that he had never truly appreciated till today? What were Som, Malati, Bonny, Sid and the others doing at this moment, he wondered hazily. Why had he, an orphan and a complete nonentity, been kidnapped, he thought for the umpteenth time.

The men continued to make desultory conversation among themselves, their low voices accentuating the silence of the forests. They seemed to be waiting for orders from someone, making frequent mention of the name 'Guru'.

Maltesh watched the wind ruffle the feathery fronds of the gulmohur tree overhead. He felt no fear, merely a detached kind of curiosity at the sudden turn his life had taken. Being abducted on an ordinary working weekday was something that he had definitely not bargained for. He felt the wind gently caress his face and his eyelids slowly began to get heavier and heavier...

25

When Maltesh opened his eyes, the four men were gone. In their place sat an older man. He sat a little distance away, smoking a bidi contemplatively. He was watching Maltesh with a faint half-smile playing around his lips. On realizing that Maltesh had woken up and was staring at him, the man came over quickly. Maltesh blinked in sleepy bewilderment as the man bent low over him.

'You look so much like your mother in your sleep,' he murmured softly, almost to himself.

'My mother? You knew her?'

He sat up quickly, jackknifing his body into an upright position. The dregs of sleep vanished from his eyes completely and he stared belligerently at the older man. This man, he knew instinctively, was the one whom the others had waited for.

'Who are you? And why have you got me here?' Maltesh's questions shot out sharp and accusing.

The man sighed, passing a tired hand through his thinning hair. He appeared to be in his late sixties. His build was wiry and compact while his dark, sunburnt complexion indicated an extensively outdoor life. A pair of piercing hazel eyes was the focal point of a lean face that was half-hidden by a salt and pepper beard. The man was dressed simply in a white cotton lungi and kurta.

'I'm sorry,' he said, his tone contrite. 'You have every right to be angry. I had no idea that my men had set off to kidnap the journalist who wrote that derogatory piece about the forest brigand Guru Das.'

'But that was Malati Iyer, the subeditor, and I'm Maltesh Roy, the cartoonist!'

'I know, I know,' the man sounded apologetic and just a little helpless. 'They've picked up the wrong person. It's unpardonable. They are good men but not very intelligent.'

Maltesh sat still, feeling aggrieved and wronged and scowling darkly at the man before him.

'It's all a mistake,' said the man.

Then suddenly he looked up and stared hard at Maltesh. His eyes were searching.

'Or is it?' he murmured.

Maltesh was in no position to answer that nor was he particularly interested in whimsical rhetoric at the moment. He was tired, hungry, disgruntled and needed a wash rather badly. And he looked all of these.

'Come,' said the man in a gentle tone, 'you need to freshen up. Follow me.'

They must have walked close to an hour in complete silence before they emerged onto a grassy clearing close to the edge of a cliff. A tiny rough shack stood under the last line of trees and the man led Maltesh to this makeshift shelter. On entering, Maltesh was surprised to find the interior cool, dry and scrupulously clean. A few rudimentary utility items lay scattered around and Maltesh noticed a kerosene stove, a few cooking utensils and a plastic bucket filled with clean water. A straw mat was spread out in a corner.

'Go ahead. Have a good wash,' said the man pointing towards the bucket of water. 'I'll go and get some food organized.'

26

Soumitro had a penchant for lame ducks. Or rather lame ducks had a tendency to waddle up to him with unerring accuracy. He met old Herman D'Costa while doing his weekly fish buying and it was a bonding that was to last a lifetime. Soumitro was picking up slithery hilsa with inexpert fingers and examining them gingerly when an unknown voice whispered conspiratorially into his ears.

'Look out for red gills,' hissed the deep cracked voice.

Soumitro swung around to see an old man grinning toothlessly at him. He took the fish from Soumitro's hand and prised the gills wide open to reveal ruddy innards.

'Look – red gills. The true sign of freshness. Black gills indicate a day's staleness or more,' he informed Soumitro knowledgeably.

Soumitro bought the fish feeling considerably enlightened in piscean matters.

'I'm a regular here,' said the man, falling in step with Soumitro.

Must be rich to afford the hideously expensive hilsa everyday, thought Soumitro sourly, giving the man a sideways glance, though he did not look it, with his frayed collar and worn-out trousers which had obviously seen happier days.

'My son is terminally ill and undergoing chemotherapy. Needs to eat fish everyday,' said the man quietly, almost as if he had read Soumitro's thoughts.

Soumitro felt anguish and guilt wash over him. Such stories always affected him very deeply. He knew that the man was an artist who lived in the building across from Pushpa Milan. Soumitro had often seen him painting on his third floor verandah. He felt the familiar sense of urgency to do something concrete instead of merely wasting time and energy in agonizing and sympathizing over the man's fate.

'Look,' he began in a rush, 'we badly need an artist at the publication which I handle. Comfortable paste-up jobs, tidy salary, lots of holidays, overtime...'

And Herman D'Costa moved into *Noon Voice*.

Soumitro was deeply embarrassed by these sudden bursts of altruism on his part and to compensate for this deplorable tendency, he barked twice as hard at everybody in office. He sat at his desk now, scowling darkly at a blank sheet of paper.

'Hullo!' said Malati brightly, en route to her cubicle. 'Busy writing your bestseller?'

Soumitro gave her a long, icy look, preferring not to answer. She pulled up a chair and sat down on it. She was very close to him.

'How can you write if you don't know how to live?' she asked conversationally, her eyes very merry.

Soumitro put his pen down slowly, astounded at her audacity.

'You have to love, ache, weep, hurt and exult personally to be able to translate it all into words,' she said 'and you, I'm afraid...'

She paused.

'And me?' prompted Soumitro in a tight voice. 'Don't mind my feelings. Please continue.'

'Well, if you insist, I will,' said Malati shrugging coolly. 'You, I'm afraid are a zombie. You don't live life, you merely make an apology of living.'

She looked supremely satisfied with the character analysis that she had just delivered verbally. Getting up with alacrity before he could think of a rejoinder, she pushed her chair back and was out of his cubicle in a flash.

Soumitro sat still, his mind reeling. Fury lashed at him repeatedly like tsunami waves. In this last fortnight, that infernal girl had called him a tyrant, a slave driver and a prude (when he refused to publish a rather colourful story of hers about a neighbourhood gigolo). And now, to crown matters, she had just called him a zombie! It was really getting to be just too much. Too bloody much!

He threw his papers down, his thoughts in a furious turmoil. There was no point trying to write anything. He would have to take the afternoon off if he wanted to get his mind back to some semblance of order.

The house was dark and quiet when he entered stealthily. The closed doors of the bedrooms indicated that everybody at home was slumbering away at this siesta hour. Soumitro walked into his room and latched the door softly. Walking up to the mirror he looked closely at the man staring back at him. He was surprised to see that he still had a reflection with a definite face and features. And a solid three-dimensional body to boot. Over the years, nihilism, his greatest defence mechanism against a crumbling world had eaten into him so insidiously that sometimes he seriously expected to peer into the mirror and see nothing. A hollow man, he thought, his mouth twisted sardonically, sans emotions, sans dreams, sans achievements, hardened over time.

Soumitro lay down on the bed, watching the slow circular motion of the ceiling fan above him. The rotating movement of the blades along with the rhythmic groan of rusty metal created a soporific effect. He suddenly felt very sleepy and realized that he hadn't touched alcohol for weeks.

His thoughts turned inescapably to Malati Iyer. She haunted his thoughts these days. And a recent habit of hers was sending him around the bend with a kind of frantic curiosity. She frequently and furtively opened her drawer in office, gazed into it with a look of worship on her face and shut it quickly and guiltily the moment she saw someone coming. What was there in that drawer of hers? What was it that she looked at with an expression of such ardent desire? A love letter? Some handsome stud's mugshot? Some celebrity hunk she had developed a crush on? After all, she was interviewing these film star types all the time. Soumitro watched her antics reflected in her glass prison and found himself going quietly crazy. He lay back in bed now, remembering Malati's strange behaviour. An unfamiliar and unpleasant emotion rose in him. Was it jealousy?

Soumitro made up his mind to be even more cutting in his dealings with Malati the next day. She needed to suffer a bit for getting him all worked up, he thought grimly. Malati found her innate good will, good cheer and good intentions towards the world beginning to wane under his whiplash criticism. That man, she told herself through gritted teeth, that man was in for trouble. DEEP TROUBLE. Malati generally harboured a deep-seated sympathy for men, considering them to be a feeble, misguided species with weak, ineffectual intellects, who needed to be assisted and shoved into sensible channels of thought and behaviour by women. She frequently used such forceful methods of coercion on her father and brother with admirable results, but this infuriating unmanageable man really took the cake when it came to perverted behaviour. Not just the cake but the biscuits as well. In fact the entire bakery, oven and all. She snorted inelegantly.

27

'You can call me Guru,' said the old man, leaning back against a tree trunk.

Three of the four men were back again and all of them sat around on the grass, relaxed and expansive after a meagre meal. Maltesh had been given two thick rotis made from ragi, a chunk of raw onion and a piece of jaggery as dessert. Kali and the other men had shed their earlier hostility and lounged close to Maltesh in companionable silence. But for all the apparent air of relaxation, there was a kind of taut tension in the air and the men's eyes met questioningly ever so often. The fourth man was missing.

'My name is Guru Das. Guru could mean a guide, a friend or a mentor,' said the old man.

'I'm a short man, as you can see,' he continued, chewing on a blade of grass. 'And not too many people look up to me. But for those who do, all the three meanings apply.'

The sun was edging towards the horizon, sending strange, long shadows on the grass. Suddenly, one of the shadows seemed to move. It was long, slim and sleek and was heading straight for Maltesh. Kali started to move forward agitatedly when Guru held up a restraining hand.

The long brown snake reached Maltesh in seconds. Its cold, scaly length entwined itself around his ankles before gliding sinuously up his torso. For a second it lay snuggled under his neck and then, almost reluctantly, it glided down Maltesh's back and was gone, vanishing into the tall grass.

'Wow!' breathed Maltesh. 'What a beauty! A rat snake, I think.'

There was silence.

'I think it liked me,' added Maltesh wistfully.

Everybody settled down again, looking relieved and patting the grass around to check for further signs of wildlife. Only Guru sat still and silent. He glanced swiftly across at Maltesh, his eyes intent and searching. Bending low, he made arrangements to light a bidi. His expression was remote and inscrutable as he arranged the loose tobacco with meticulous care on the dry leaf. Rolling the leaf tightly into a thin cigarette, he looked up and met Maltesh's eyes squarely.

'It's time you learnt something about us,' he said.

He took a leisurely pull at his cigarette.

'We,' he began quietly, 'are hunters.'

Maltesh felt a wave of revulsion seep through him. Hunters! Men who maimed, killed, tortured animals for selfish ends. The most vile and contemptible creatures on the face of this earth, thought Maltesh, feeling an agonized sense of kinship with his beloved feathered and furry friends. He averted his face to hide the expression of disgust that he knew he was wearing.

A loud sound shattered the quiet evening. It was a gunshot. Kali and the other two men sprang up animatedly as if they had been eagerly waiting for this interruption. A scream, quickly smothered, rent the air and a flock of sparrows flew out of a tree in alarm.

'Mission accomplished,' said Kali to Guru in a tone of deep satisfaction.

Guru smiled. The three men rose, as if on cue, and melted into the dark forest. Only Guru and Maltesh remained in the gathering dusk. The sun was now a deep crimson crescent at the horizon. Guru took a long satisfied draw at his cigarette again.

'We are hunters,' he repeated conversationally. 'We hunt poachers.'

28

'I did not start life as a hunter of men. I started life as a gentle wandering minstrel, a missionary of peace. I was a traditional baul singer of West Bengal.'

They were sitting on the cliff edge, watching stars begin to appear in the night sky. Light pollution in these lonely mountains was nil and the stars sparkled, brilliant and multicoloured. They appeared almost within touching distance. As was his usual habit, Maltesh looked around searching for the three-star belt of the Orion. It was the first constellation that Father Noronha had taught him to identify as a child and the sight of it still gave him a feeling of inexplicable warmth and security.

Everything is under control, the stars seemed to tell him, winking conspiratorially, and there's no need to take anything too seriously. This moment too, like all of life, they whispered to him, is bound to pass.

Maltesh sat still and attentive. His captor seemed to be suffering from a strange pressing need to unburden himself to him.

'My father, his father and generations of forefathers before that had been traditional baul singers of West Bengal. I did not choose it as a profession for the simple reason that the profession chose me. I was born to it.

'I lost my parents very early in life. Wandering about from village to village and singing songs of peace and spirituality was the only life I knew as a child. I had survived the small pox epidemic that swept through villages and took my parents with it. Maybe, I thought, I had been spared by destiny so that I could carry forth the songs composed by my ancestors. Songs whose music came from the gurgling of streams, from the patter of raindrops on leaves, from the noisy gushing of swollen rivers in the monsoons, from bird cries in the silence of forest mornings and the rustle of the wind in the paddy fields. Lyrics that were created from folklore, simple homespun philosophy, conversation over community cooking fires in winter and the deep cosmic secrets known only to the baul singers.'

Guru took a long drag of his cigarette, narrowing his eyes against the smoke. He seemed to be focussing on some point in the distant past.

'I walked miles over mountains everyday. I took a route from Tarapeeth to Sonarpur via Krishnanagar and came back every few months. I crossed boundaries and barbed wires, hills and valleys, wandering from village to village with my treasury of mystical songs. Sometimes villagers stood, listened, understood my words and tunes and gave me alms at the end of my singing. Some others were plain indifferent and walked away in the middle of a song. Yet some others were hostile and shooed me away like an unwanted stray animal. Some days I got enough rice and fruits to keep me going and on some days I got nothing. Very often, I was rewarded with kicks and curses for my trouble. Sometimes I had a fresh change of clothes and sometimes none. A friendly villager would often offer me shelter and on certain friendless days I shared dry space with goats and dogs. I walked bareheaded and barefoot, come rain, hail or sunshine. I accepted everything philosophically, in the true spirit of the baul.'

The stars were out in all their glory now, twinkling brightly in the dark sky. A shooting star streaked aross the sky, tracing a path of emerald fire as Guru and Maltesh watched.

'And then suddenly one day, when I was around twenty-two years old, my profession turned into passion. I found that I was no longer singing the songs written by my forefathers. I was suddenly writing my own songs, more potent, more lyrical, more relevant to the swiftly changing times. I was putting new meaning, giving new slants to the old family lyrics that I had inherited. Like an alchemist, I was transforming all that I was touching. Poetry seemed to flow in my veins like a raging fever, burning me, igniting me. I left behind all that was time-tested, safe and stereotyped and entered unimagined realms.

'New words, new thoughts seemed to erupt out of me continuously, transforming me. A strange physical metamorphosis was taking place at the same time. I was no longer a mere mortal plagued by hunger, thirst or pain. I became impervious to such sensations. It was almost as if I was becoming an extension of the hills, the forests and the winds that I sang about. I could, I found to my utter amazement, withstand incredible extremes of temperature, thirst and hunger. I had developed a threshold of pain that most humans would find astonishing. My bones seemed to turn into rock and my flesh into wood. I could lie on brambles and thorns and yet sleep the sleep of newborn babies. I had, unwittingly and accidentally, found the secret spiritual path of the ancient sadhus, rishis and fakirs.

'It suddenly felt as if my body was no longer demarcated by cells, membrane or tissues. Or a name. A gender. I seemed to flow into the sunsets, the grass and the creatures which lurked in the forests. Injured animals, young animals abandoned by parents and lost creatures in any kind of misery crawled up to me. I befriended all of them, finding strange, secret healing powers within myself.

'I sat alone every evening, watching the sun set. When the forests around were still, I became still too, holding back breath, blood and heartbeat. When spring came, I rejoiced along with the flowers and the butterflies. I slowly started losing all sense of personal identity, defying the usual manmade parameters of existence. Physically and spiritually, I was morphing into the very elements I sang about. All kinds of creatures crawled over me when I sat still. I was no longer fully human. I was part beast, part human, part mountain and part forest.'

He stopped for a long while, lost in thought. Maltesh waited. Guru suddenly turned towards him, his eyes glittering strangely in the light of the stars.

'Do you understand what I'm talking about, city-slicker?'

Maltesh was silent. He thought of his own lonely childhood jaunts on the misty hills of Kodai, of shivering little creatures who had crept up to him for warmth, of his own strange affinity with nature and animals.

'Yes,' he said softly, 'I understand perfectly.'

There was a long silence. Guru turned away from Maltesh and his face was shadowed.

'This extraordinary phase lasted for about a year, during which I became a total recluse. After that, little by little, I started moving on, beginning to sing once again. I started touring villages once more, meeting all kinds of people on my travels, people who scoffed at me, people who laughed, people who listened and people who wept at my poetry.'

Guru threw the cigarette end, crushing the last burning ember with his bare heel. His expression was remote.

'Your mother belonged to the last group.'

29

There was a flurry of activity as everybody got ready to leave the *Noon Voice* office on Friday evening.

'TGIF, TGIF...' sang Coken loudly and tunelessly.

There was a cacophony of voices and footfalls on the stairs, followed by a hollow silence in the office.

Soumitro leaned back in his chair. He loved these moments when the *Noon Voice* office, charged with activity all day long, suddenly emptied out into a long, resonating silence. He refrained from switching on the electric lights overhead, preferring to watch the fading sunlight cast long shadows over the shabby décor of the office. He cherished these precious moments when the energy of his colleagues still lingered around the place, potent and alive, and yet silences and shadows crept with long, dark fingers around the place. He felt strangely alive and exhausted, stimulated and drained all at the same time. A heady amalgam of pleasurably contradictory emotions besieged Soumitro on Friday evenings.

Worry at Malto's unexplained absence niggled at him on this particular Friday, but he was not unduly disturbed. Malto's precious padres in Kodai must have summoned him on some mission or the other, he thought vaguely, and he expected the cartoonist to get in touch soon. As usual, Soumitro's glance moved around the office, dwelling ruefully on the peeling paint and the chipped furniture. He really needed to renovate the place, he thought for the hundredth time as his gaze came to rest on Malati's desk. His eyes strayed on indifferently and then came back to rest again on her desk. He felt his heart begin to thump loudly. This was the opportunity he had been waiting for. To see what was there in that infernal drawer of hers. What secret lay concealed that caused her to blush and smile to herself as she peeped into the drawer about a dozen times a day? He rose on unsteady feet, hoping that she had left the drawer unlocked. It would save him the trouble of hunting for the duplicate key.

Reaching her desk he felt for the handle of the drawer. The drawer slid open effortlessly at his touch. She hadn't locked it! He dipped his hand into the deep dark recesses of the drawer and felt his fingers close around something hard and rectangular. What *was* it? A framed photograph perhaps? His exploring fingers groped around a bit before dragging out the rectangular object by its corner. It was a bunch of loose papers placed neatly in a cheap plastic file. He switched on the table lamp, feeling curiosity rising within him. The caption was hazily visible through the translucent cover of the file, in Times Roman font. Soumitro flipped open to the first page with curious fingers. Exquisite, urgent, edgy writing filled the page. He flipped to the next page and the next, turning the pages in a frantic hurry. Paragraph after paragraph, page after page of inspired writing stared up at him. A feeling of incredulity rose within him and he let the manuscript fall into his lap in sheer disbelief. He now recognized Malati's precious secret. He was actually holding it in his hands. It was the manuscript of a full length novel. *The Song of the Road* by Malati Iyer.

Soumitro read steadily into the evening. A rumble of distant thunder sounded once in a while, indicating a storm building up over the city, but Soumitro was impervious to everything other than the writing in front of him. Malati's novel traced a young rustic girl's journey across the mountains in search of the mythical kasturi tree. The tree was said to flower only once in ten years and the glimpse of it in full bloom assured a girl everlasting and true love. The men who befriend the girl on her journey, love her, betray her and abandon her, drifted into the narrative which seemed to ring with a thousand mountain sounds. The prose seemed suffused with the smells and colours of the hills of Garhwal. The writing had a kind of leaping vitality to it, and reading it, Soumitro could almost smell the clean mountain air, feel dewdrops on his skin and taste the rain. The songs sung by the girl on her travels reverberated around, spinning a kind of magic in the shabby, silent office of the *Noon Voice*. It was writing at its inspired best. The rustic charm of the mountains and the hopelessness of the girl's search reached out to Soumitro from the pages holding him helplessly captive. Malati must have visited Garhwal to have written so convincingly, thought Soumitro. Towards what must be the penultimate part of the novel, the writing seemed to falter, waver and then petered out completely, as if the author had run into unexpected literary obstacles. Why hadn't Malati finished the story, wondered Soumitro. Why?

Soumitro let the manuscript fall from his hands, feeling a kind of numbing disbelief. The words of the manuscript continued to swirl in his mind. This, he thought in agony, was the kind of novel he, as the editor of a newspaper, should have written, not an inconsequential chit of a subeditor. He sat still in the gathering dusk. The sky was darkening steadily outside as low, heavy clouds gathered in swiftly moving layers. Soumitro sat immobile, his eyes faraway and unfocussed. He now understood why she had always bothered him. It wasn't her unflappable poise, her faultless dress sense or her impeccable grammar. At the very first glance it had been (though he didn't quite recognize the feeling then) an instinctive recognition of one's nemesis.

Soumitro walked to the window and gazed down at the city below. The overcast sky was fast reaching bursting point and a restless wind had sprung out of nowhere. It blew dust and papers all over the sidewalks as pedestrians rushed to reach their homes before the downpour caught them. There was a crackle of menace in the air, a subtle hint of evil. Stealthy insinuations ran thick and deep, keeping pace with the storm clouds. Was that really sulphur and brimstone that he smelt?

Take it, whispered a voice within him, take it, take it, take it. Seize the day. Change the title, change some chapters, give the story a suitable end. Silence those relatives once and for all and sleep the sleep of relief for the first time in your life. *Mountain Echoes* by Soumitro Banerjee. How wonderful it would look on the bookstore shelves. A young, unworldly girl living with relatives in an unfamiliar city was easy to buy off. Money, a promotion, promises… He could offer her many things as compensation. His nightmare debut novel would finally be written, his relatives silenced once and for all, and he would finally sleep in peace for the first time in his life. And his conscience?

Soumitro laughed out loud. A bitter, hollow sound. Did the word 'conscience' exist any more? He couldn't seem to remember ever using it in any of his crosswords. And if he did, would he ever be able to find suitable clues for the word? It was an archaic, near-extinct word, he thought, his mouth twisting, like 'halcyon' and 'sumptuous'. Outdated and out-of-sync words that jarred when used in everyday language.

Somewhere, a window banged hard in the wind and glass shattered with a tinkling sound. The rain burst over the city with a deafening roar as angry streaks of lightning forked across the sky. Soumitro stood outlined against the window, a tall, sinister figure enveloped in a halo of purple light. The city was blotted out by the fierce white spray of rain and he could barely see the cars parked below. He turned away from the window.

Soumitro knew that he could never do it.

His footsteps were weary as he walked back to his chair and flopped down. He was doomed by his chromosomes and his faulty upbringing to always do the right thing at the right time. He could never step off the straight and narrow path even if a gun was held to his head. He was genetically flawed. Unfit to survive in the evolutionary process. Unable to seize the moment. Unable to grab at opportunities even if they lay begging. He was jinxed from his infancy by being born into a family that believed in creating and never destroying, helping and never hindering, bringing things to fruition and never aborting. This is my destiny, he thought grimly, to remain a perennial midwife but never give birth, to be eternally sterile. To aid and assist others in the process of metamorphosis but never take wing myself. So be it, he thought in resignation. He suddenly remembered all those trainee journalists whose skills he had helped hone and who now drove around the city in flashy imported cars while he came to office in a state transport bus.

Sighing to himself, he straightened up in his chair. Switching on the computer, he started surfing the Internet for suitable publishers for Malati's novel. She would need them very soon. The rain beat harder on the windowpanes and the roar over the city grew louder. The claps of thunder came with shorter intervals between them.

30

This was the part Maltesh had waited for all through the narrative. His mother. Any mention of her could still give him goose pimples. At the mention of his mother he seemed to recollect firm, warm arms and the scent of roses. His mother – soft, warm, nurturing. And now dead. Restricted to only a hazy memory. His toddler brain couldn't stretch to anything beyond that.

Guru's voice cut across his thoughts.

'I visited your parents for the first time in basant, the month of spring. The colour yellow was everywhere – yellow blossoms, yellow grains ready for thrashing, women in yellow and orange saris with yellow flowers in their braids... Your parents had been married for just over a year when I first met them and were very much in love.'

Guru paused to roll another one of his leaf cigarettes. Maltesh waited, hardly able to contain his impatience.

'Your father Debashish Roy was a professor of physics in the only college in the district and your mother the acknowledged local beauty. Chitra and Debashish Roy were toasted as the most popular pair in the area and considered an ideal couple. They were wonderfully kind and hospitable to me, a penniless wandering minstrel.' Guru puffed at his cigarette, gazing up at the star-spangled sky and reliving memories.

'I sang for more than three hours in the courtyard of your parents' house on my first visit. The neighbours gathered around, sitting on fences, flowerpots, doorsteps, gateposts and every available nook and cranny. I had never sung to such a large audience and was exultant. Your mother was absolutely enchanted. She reacted to my singing like an excited child, clapping her hands loudly after every song. She was little more than a child, really, hardly sixteen or seventeen.'

'And my father?'

It was the first time Maltesh had spoken during the narrative.

'Ah, your father. Your father escaped politely as soon as he could do so, citing work as an excuse. I could see that my poetry did not quite gel with his physics.'

The sky stretched above them, dark, mysterious and diamond-studded. An airplane flew across the inky expanse, its multi-coloured tail-lights winking merrily. The silhouetted mountains loomed dark and watchful. Maltesh glanced up at the night sky. His eyes lingered again on the three stars of Orion's Belt, aligned almost in a perfectly straight line. As always, they gave him that familiar sense of security. There is geometry, precision, logic and consistency in the universe, the cosmos seemed to tell him reassuringly, and an explanation for everything. Always.

'On your mother's request, I came back month after month to sing for her. She was beginning to write a little poetry herself. Hesitant, timid, girlish poetry. Schoolgirl thoughts unfurling prettily like the petals of some exotic flower. I laughed at the innocence of her poetry and she laughed along with me.'

Guru was silent for a while and then rose abruptly.

'Come,' he said. 'It's getting late. The rest is for tomorrow.'

Sleep eluded Maltesh. He spent the night staring at the stars, falling asleep only at dawn.

'I never had a single relationship in my life as a wanderer. I did not stay long enough at any one place for that. Having lost my family early, I never really learnt how to relate to people. Sometimes, on a repeat tour down familiar routes, some music lover recognized me and came and befriended me. Even ate with me. But for most people, I was a poor, eccentric nomad who surfaced once in months and was easily forgotten.'

Maltesh and Guru were stretched out lazily on their backs in the grass. Speckled sunlight filtered over them through the filigree of leaves overhead. Sometimes, a golden sparkle hit them directly in the eye, blinding them momentarily. Shifting shadows played hide-and-seek on their chests.

'One day,' continued Guru, 'I found an injured squirrel. A giant golden tree squirrel. It was badly hurt, probably mauled by an eagle. It lay weak and limping, bleeding profusely.'

Guru swallowed and for a moment his knuckles gleamed white. He seemed to be having trouble keeping some strong emotion in check and Maltesh glanced at him curiously.

'It was the most gorgeous-looking creature that I had ever seen. With fur that was thick and lush, auburn in some parts and golden in others. Not the usual dirty bronze that one sees in the smaller squirrels. And the tail! It had the most luxuriant, silky tail that I've ever seen. It did not seem to mind my presence as I approached it and tolerated my administrations meekly. Animals have a way of recognizing friends. I treated it as best as I could with my knowledge of plants and herbs. In a week's time the creature was prancing onto my shoulders and nibbling my ears.'

Guru seemed to go into a trance for a short time, shaking himself back to the present with an effort.

'The squirrel became my most loyal and devoted companion. It wouldn't leave me for even a second and followed me like a shadow everywhere. Sometimes, it perched on my shoulders for a joyride and sometimes it snuggled in the pocket of my jacket. When tired, it often took a nap on the back of my neck, and when energetic, it swung from tree to tree keeping pace with me and chattering incessantly,' said Guru.

'It was the only friend I had ever had,' he continued. 'A friend who was willing to put up with my eccentricities, my long silences, my endless treks over hostile terrain without food and water, my crazy singing to the hills and trees and my ever burgeoning poetry. Best of all, the creature understood and responded to my poetry. Good lines had him chattering exuberantly and weak words had him cringing and curling up into a tight ball of protest.'

Guru stared at the branches above, his expression sombre.

'I swear my squirrel was an intellectual,' he said with quiet conviction.

There was a long silence. The wind sighed through the branches, caressing the feathery fronds flirtatiously. The silence grew longer, deep and pregnant in nature.

'And then?' prompted Maltesh impatiently.

Guru gave a long, tired sigh as if the subject suddenly exhausted him.

'It kept me company for months, entertaining me all through the weeks. And then I woke up one morning to find my friend lying dead beside me. The poachers had been at work. Its body had neatly been skinned of its glorious fur. Only the raw flesh remained and the little claws begging for help. The poachers had worked skilfully and silently through the night. I had eaten a lot of the intoxicating mohua berries the evening before and had slept deeply as my friend lay dying beside me.'

Guru looked haunted, as if he was reliving the ordeal.

'Vultures were beginning to circle in the sky above me, waiting impatiently for me to be off on my way so that they could begin their feast.'

Guru got up abruptly, dusting grass off his clothes. His face was deadpan. Maltesh also rose, feeling slightly uncertain about what to say. Guru held his eyes with his own bleak ones for a second.

'And that was the day,' he concluded quietly, 'that my poetry died.'

31

Kali and the other men were busy digging a deep pit. Inside it would be placed long, sharp pikes of wood that were designed to impale any unsuspecting victim who walked into it. Kali's expression was absorbed as he sharpened a stake end with a knife. One of the men was busy gathering twigs, grass and dead leaves to cover the pit with. Effective camouflage was of prime importance in the entire scheme. Kali looked up as Maltesh approached.

'Don't go falling into the pit, boss,' Kali grinned widely. 'That particular honour is reserved only for the poachers.'

'Don't worry,' said Guru watching Maltesh's expression. 'I know what you are thinking. My men take great care to see that animals or innocent villagers don't fall into these pits.'

Guru and Maltesh strolled on companionably, leaving the others to their task. Maltesh wondered fleetingly what his friends were doing in the city. *Noon Voice* seemed so far away at the moment. Geographically and emotionally.

'Poachers, villagers and policeman have always coexisted in these forests,' said Guru, 'each having his own role to play in the scheme of things.'

They were walking down towards the edge of a ravine now. A gushing stream glistened silver far below at the bottom. Woodsmoke from a fire lit by a stray villager hung suspended in the sky like a fuzzy question mark. Guru placed an arm across

Maltesh's shoulders. There was affection as well as a plea for support in the action.

'The police often called me in for interrogation after some major poaching incident. It was a farce as we all knew, a huge joke where every actor played his part, however tiny. A drama being enacted on stage where truth was like the prompter – hidden, whispering and mostly unheeded. Everywhere that I went on my travels, the policemen I found were all the same, smug, lazy and fattened on animal produce. They conducted interrogations in the daytime and barbequed deer in the dark of the night. They walked with the poachers on moonless nights, helping them traffic turtles, leopard skins and rare birds and then made a great show of tracking down these same poachers in daylight.'

Guru stopped and pointed up at the white, fleecy clouds moving languidly across the blue sky.

'You see those clouds up there? Truth was like those clouds, nebulous, shifting, elusive and changing shape every minute.'

They had come to the edge of the ravine now and stood side by side gazing down into the depths below. An eagle glided up in wide sweeping circles below them, catching the fine balance of the valley wind currents in its wings. It spiralled upwards, steadily gaining altitude and coming abreast with them within minutes.

'It was a very amicable arrangement actually. A cordial conspiracy of lies that helped the villagers steer clear of police harassment, left the poachers free to pursue their chosen line of work and kept the policemen happy and well fed. As a wandering baul singer, I did not quite fit into the scheme of things, but as I saw and heard many things on my travels, I made for a very valuable (and musical) witness. The policemen liked to check how much I knew and how much I was willing to reveal. When assured that I was quite safe as a witness, I was even asked to sing at the police stations on certain occasions. I did so very willingly. I remained immersed in my poetry, indifferent to worldly politics and intrigue.' He paused.

'Till I lost the only friend I had ever had.'

Voices echoed in the quiet mountain air. Kali was singing. He sounded happy after a job well done, thought Maltesh. The others joined in and their voices echoed in chorus over the still mountainside. Sounds of laughter floated across. Guru smiled.

'My team is interesting. One is an assassin who was serving a life sentence before breaking out of jail and the other three are also escaped convicts who were doing time for petty crimes. Men who had no place in society, no future and no respect from their fellow beings. But who found a new life in these forests and who now live for a cause.'

Guru laughed aloud and the sound echoed in the valley. There was a touch of irony to his laugh.

'Four criminals and a failed poet bonded together by a love of nature and the urge to protect it from the ravages of mankind.' A strong gust of wind rose out from the valley. Maltesh held out his kerchief and dropped it into the whirlpool of eddying wind currents. The kerchief dipped, for all purposes lost to the ravine. Suddenly, it spun around and lifted. Propelled by the air currents, it fluttered out of the vortex and came back to rest at Maltesh's feet.

'That which is yours comes back to you. Always,' said Maltesh.

Guru smiled. His expression was indulgent.

'Hey that was a great line I came up with! I think I'm getting pretty poetic myself. Must be your influence,' laughed Maltesh, finding it easy to be childish and spontaneous with this strange man.

'Do you think I have the makings of a poet, Guru? Like you?' he asked eagerly.

Guru looked at him very searchingly and then looked away, his expression inscrutable.

'Why should you be like me?' he said under his breath, almost to himself.

There was a moment's silence.

'I knew which path I had to choose after my squirrel died,' continued Guru. 'This was, I realized, not an age for peaceful songs and passive poetry. I had travelled well ahead of all that. My god was too feeble and too overworked to look after the weak, the dumb and the timid and dispense justice. He needed recruits to assist him.'

He paused once again, staring into the valley below. As was his usual habit, he fell into a long, abstracted silence. Maltesh stood, waiting quietly.

'For years I had read about the dreaded forest bandit Veerappan who killed and maimed animals and kidnapped forest officers regularly. Why, I asked myself, why shouldn't I be the mirror image of such a man?'

Guru looked up and stared at the blue sky above.

'Who are we to presume that we are the rightful inheritors of the earth? Who are we to presume that cockroaches and other life forms are less sacred than men?'

There was a long silence.

'And so,' Guru finished simply, 'I became a hunter of men.'

Maltesh and Guru walked a little way till they could see clusters of villages on the banks of the stream far below. Guru stopped and turned around to face Maltesh.

'So now you know my story. Am I sane, a madman or a murderer? You don't have much time to decide. Tomorrow, you go free. Back to your city lights, child.'

He turned and walked away. In these twenty odd years, nobody had ever called him 'child' in that affectionate tone and Maltesh felt oddly disturbed. He sat down on a boulder, trying to sort out his thoughts and put them into a semblance of order. He watched Guru slowly walk away into the distance.

Maltesh glanced down, giving his body a long, hard scrutiny. His feet were callused and his arms tanned a deep brown but he felt rejuvenated and alive as never before.

He tried to blot out the incident that had happened at *Noon Voice* some time back but it kept coming back to haunt him. Brutus the guinea pig had always been a frisky customer if left unchecked and Maltesh blamed himself for not keeping the creature locked up in his drawer that morning. Brutus, on a mid-morning jaunt around the office of *Noon Voice*, had suddenly taken a fancy to Pankaj Bhatt's blue socks. Whether it was the bright colour that attracted him or the soft feel of hosiery nobody was ever destined to know, but Brutus soon started creeping up the owner's ankles with a great deal of interest. There had been a deafening howl as Pankaj Bhatt had leapt to his feet, feeling guinea pig on bare skin, and a moment later a frightened Brutus had gone flying across the floor.

'You filty little twerp, take that and that. *And* that,' Bhatt had screamed, bringing his heavy booted foot down on the shivering little creature again and again till it lay limp and motionless. A sickening squelch had sounded with each stamp of the foot while a pinkish brown fluid had oozed over the floor from the guinea pig's body. Maltesh, caught unawares, had watched the whole scene with a kind of stunned, frozen disbelief. It was all over in seconds.

'But that was my baby,' he had whispered brokenly, hardly audible.

No sound had come from his vocal cords but his vision was suddenly seared with red. A white-hot anger seemed to seize him, crippling all common sense. Picking up a heavy cut glass ashtray, he had sent it spinning at Pankaj's sickening face. Bhatt had ducked swiftly and the ashtray had gone smashing out of the office window. Staffers who had crowded around at the commotion had run to the window to view the damage below.

'Thank god!' breathed Beatrice. 'It's stuck in some branches.'

And Malati had been there, grabbing him by the arm and pulling him into the coffee corner.

'There, there, there Malto. Easy…' she had soothed him as if he was a small child, pushing a mug of hot coffee into his hands. She had been crisp, warm and bracing, he remembered gratefully now, pretending that she hadn't noticed the hot tears scalding his eyes.

The incident recurred as a nightmare every other night and today he was suddenly reminded of it in his waking hours. Maltesh watched Guru's figure retreat into the distance, diminishing in size as he approached the horizon. Guru was climbing a gentle slope now and would disappear from view within seconds. Maltesh felt goose pimples rise on his arms at the memory of Brutus's death.

'No,' whispered Maltesh to the figure in the distance. 'You are no madman. No fanatic. And no murderer either.'

32

The morning dawned crisp and golden, washed squeaky clean by the previous evening's thunderstorm. Birds chirped in the trees, young girls in groups giggled on the pavements, traffic honked and the entire city seemed sunny, cheerful and sane.

Soumitro sat having breakfast at Kumar's. He had resolutely put away all thoughts of Malati's manuscript from his mind but Maltesh's prolonged absence was beginning to worry him. There had been no explanations from the artist's end excepting a strange long distance phone call where an unfamiliar voice informed him that Maltesh Roy would be getting back to office in a day or two. The voice had sounded coarse and uneducated and quite unlike Soumitro's idea of a convent resident or employee. Should he be going to the police, Soumitro wondered uneasily.

Fumes of percolated coffee rose in the air as the busy kitchen clanged with the sounds cooking. Stainless steel utensils gleamed and winked in the bright morning sun. Kumar's, the popular Udipi joint just across the *Noon Voice* office, was a busy place in the mornings. CoKen and Pankaj Bhatt strolled in and Soumitro looked up to see Malati crossing the road. She wore a pretty crimson outfit that set off her tanned skin to perfection and the morning wind was in her hair. Soumitro stood up quickly as she approached and pulled out a chair for her. He suddenly realized that he hadn't performed such a chivalrous act for a lady in years. He felt a strange new respect for Malati.

'Do cutting chai, Thambi,' he turned and told the coffee-skinned little waiter who was squinting into the newspaper over his shoulder.

'How do you cut chai for god's sake?' asked Malati, new to the tea-splitting techniques so popular in Bombay.

'Oh, easy,' drawled CoKen. 'You slice the tea into two symmetrical halves with a kind of exquisite spiritual judgment and then let your guest do the choosing – whether he wants the half which is in the cup or the half which is in the saucer. It's an ancient Indian art practiced from the times of the Harappa and Mohenjodaro civilizations.'

'Aw, shut up!' snapped Malati, irritable with hunger. 'You sound as crazy as Mustafa Saifee.'

'Would you like to eat something, Malati?' asked Soumitro, his voice unusually courteous.

'I'd like to eat EVERYTHING that is available. I'm that famished,' declared Malati, snatching the menu from Soumitro's hands.

Soumitro looked at her for a startled moment and then laughed.

'You know, you're the funniest girl I've ever met, Malati,' he said.

'Why, isn't that just perfect? For a girl to be told first thing in the morning that she is funny? How many girls have you met, by the way?' she asked.

Soumitro was saved from answering that question by Parthasarathy Sharma and Joshua Abraham who came bounding into the hotel. They both looked tremendously excited.

'Hey, guess what, guys?' they asked in unison.

'They've busted the terrorist outfit that was operating from the Powai area,' expanded Parthasarathy excitedly.

'Really?' Soumitro sat up straight.

'Oh,' said Malati disinterestedly.

Terrorist outfits didn't interest her, only promiscuous Page 3 happenings did.

'The cops found a list of targets on the leader. And Malati…' continued Parthasarathy.

'Umm… mmm,' mumbled Malati, her mouth full of idli.

'The Makhijani Foundation School, belonging to the Makhijani builders in Powai, was one of the prime targets,' said Joshua.

'What?' exclaimed Malati, blanching with alarm. 'That's where my nephews study!'

'Precisely. But not to worry,' said Parthasarathy reassuringly. 'The school authorities have been informed and are beefing up security. No dabbawallas, servants, drivers or other visitors to be allowed on the school premises from now on.'

'Let's get the story fast,' said Soumitro standing up quickly and gulping down his coffee.

They all rose, excepting Malati. Soumitro looked down at her, his expression quizzical and amused.

'We'll be gone for a while. Handle the office, will you? Look after yourself and be good, kid.'

And then they were all gone, leaving Malati with three plates of uneaten breakfast.

At the other end of the city, Shreya Banerjee said a special little prayer for her favourite grandson Siddharth as she waited for him to come home with his final examination results. Her prayers included a cosy talk with god and a small matter of amicable bartering which involved good results being exchanged for a big box of motichur laddoos which would be duly delivered to the Ram temple around the corner. She had barely opened her eyes after that bit of celestial bargaining when Mustafa walked in. He was beaming from ear to ear. Shreya waddled up to him eagerly while Ira and Bonny, who had just entered the room, stood waiting for the news with bated breath.

'Mustu,' commanded Bonny. 'Tell all!'

Mustafa settled down on the sofa in a leisurely fashion, enjoying the agitation of the three women around him. He twiddled his toes while gazing at them reflectively.

'How has Siddharth fared?' Ira could barely contain the tremor in her voice.

'Do you know what it is to learn cycling?' asked Mustafa lazily.

Shreya groaned.

'Does that boy ever give straight answers?' she muttered despairingly.

'Mustu! Hurry up or I'll strangle you with my bare hands.' Bonny was more vocal.

But there was no hurrying Mustafa.

'You know how, as a child learning cycling, you pedal with someone holding the bike and running alongside?'

Bonny gave another long tortured groan.

'And that one vital point (and you may not even be aware of it) when you conquer that delicate thing called balance, move out of your guide's arms and surge ahead towards your own horizons? Well, Sid has reached that point. He has surpassed all previous records, outdistanced his professors and scored 87 per cent marks in his exams, which is unheard of in the history of the Sir D.V. College of Architecture. In short Sid has become a celestial cyclist!'

There was stunned silence all around as the three women found themselves utterly speechless with joy. Shreya skipped up to Mustafa and enveloped him in a cologne-scented embrace.

'I'll just have to go and buy those laddoos now,' she whispered incomprehensibly into his hair. Mustafa stood frozen into immobility. He had always suffered from a kind of tactile allergy, having a deep aversion to being hugged or kissed. It probably rose from a lonely childhood and having missed out on cuddling in his formative years. But when Shreya Banerjee engulfed him in her soft, sweet-smelling arms, he had the extraordinary sensation of pure bliss.

Ira turned around to look at Mustafa, her glance slightly guilty. In their extreme excitement, they had forgotten all about Mustafa.

'And what about your results, child?' Ira's tone was gentle.

'Ah, mine,' said Mustafa, in a resigned tone, 'I'm afraid I'm destined to see many more summers in the college campus and indulge in ragging many more batches of freshers.'

He smiled benevolently all around.

'In short, I've failed,' he announced happily.

The three women looked shocked and distressed.

'Why don't you study a little harder, son? You're so good with your poetry,' said Ira in a tone of genuine concern.

'Talking of poetry, I'll quote some lines from…'

'No, no, no,' howled Bonny in anguish.

'Talking of poetry,' repeated Mustafa, unperturbed by her wails of protest, 'I'll quote some lines that are suitable for the occasion.'

He cleared his throat.

Yeh duniya, yeh mehfil, mere kaam ki nahin
Mere kaam ki nahin

And then translated:

This worldly scenario of marks and mark sheets
Is not my cup of tea
And Professor Dilip Dongre can hang himself
From the tallest casuarina tree.

Bonny seemed to be overcome by a fit of coughing at the translation.

'What's a poet like you doing in an architecture college?' she asked archly, when she had recovered.

'Now, then,' Mustafa brought his face very close to Bonny's, his expression aggressive. 'Is there a college exclusively for poets? No? So?'

'Poets infiltrate every profession, buddy,' he continued. 'Poets come disguised as garage mechanics, software engineers, janitors and other things. Poetry is not a profession, it is a medical affliction. Affects the medulla oblongata. Poetry, like paralysis, can strike anytime, anywhere. Be kind to your grocer and the fishmonger, Bonny, they could well be poets in disguise.'

The three women fled out of the house to offer their thanks at the Ram temple just as Soumitro walked in with a bunch of papers tucked under his arm. The two young men were left with each other for company and an uncomfortable silence descended on the room. Soumitro spread out his papers and with a curt nod in Mustafa's direction got down to the serious business of crossword construction.

Mustafa glanced at the older man speculatively. This was one of the few people at A-502 Pushpa Milan whom he had just not succeeded in winning over for some incomprehensible reason. But he, Mustafa Ali Saifee, was a young man with extreme optimism ingrained in his nature. He was not the kind of person who gave up on matters so easily. He leaned forward with what he hoped was a boyishly eager expression.

'Lovely day, isn't it?' he asked brightly.

'Quite.'

'Sun shining, birds chirping, clouds clouding and sky blueing.'

Dead silence.

'Just the day for sitting and making crosswords.'

No answer.

'A day to be outdoors, in the sunshine.'

'Why don't you go out then?' Soumitro looked up finally, his eyes gleaming nastily.

'You know,' said Mustafa, hurriedly changing the topic, 'I really admire people like you who have such a flair for languages.'

Silence.

'I've never been one of these literary types I'm afraid, my reading having begun and ended with *Fun with Dick and Jane* – the class five reader and my eternal favourite.'

Snort.

'However,' said Mustafa magnanimously, 'that does not stop me from appreciating literary talent in others.'

The conversation was neither sparkling with wit nor was it going in the desired direction, decided Mustafa. But he had supreme confidence in his ability to charm and decided to try a fresh angle.

'I may not be the literary kind but I do have a way with words which could help you in your crossword-making,' said Mustafa confidingly.

Soumitro looked up and gave him a long, frosty stare.

'Like,' continued Mustafa unfazed, 'what's one word for a moron who goes deep sea diving without an oxygen mask?'

Silence.

'Oxymoron! Ha, ha, ha, ha…'

Mustafa broke off suddenly, taking a frightened gulp of air and crouching back on the sofa with alarm as Soumitro loomed over him, looking dark and dangerous.

'If you've finished with the literary gymnastics, I'll take my leave of you, sir,' drawled Soumitro with a kind of silky sarcasm.

He crossed the floor with long strides and stormed out of the house. Mustafa was left breathing hard. Shreya Banerjee, entering the house with her puja thali held in her hand, found a disconsolate Mustafa lying on the sofa. She glanced at him with shrewd eyes.

'Has my eldest grandson been bothering you?' she asked gently.

Mustafa nodded, looking unusually crestfallen. Shreya sat down on the sofa and started destringing the marigold garland on her plate. Her expression was guarded and thoughtful, as if she was wondering how to frame her next words. She looked up at Mustafa, her expression grave.

'My eldest grandson wasn't always like this, you know. He was the cutest, bubbliest little toddler that I have ever seen.'

Mustafa looked amazed. Could dour old Som ever have been a toddler? And a bubbly one at that? Honestly, life was full of surprises, he thought. Shreya gave a long sigh.

'Tragedy is a rather cruel sculptor of personality, Mustu. It can mutilate a person out of recognition. My son died when Som was merely a teenager and left him to take complete charge of the family and *Noon Voice*. Do you know what that means? To be the eldest son in a fatherless Bengali household?'

Mustafa shook his head mutely.

'It means educating your siblings, getting your sisters married well and yet being able to afford hilsa when visitors arrive. And never, never breaking down, excepting in solitude. So now you know why Som smiles so rarely.'

Mustafa nodded, looking slightly shamefaced.

'As for his antagonism towards you, Mustu,' Shreya halted fractionally before explaining further. 'You are a poet, he is an atheist, you are a Muslim, while he is a Hindu. You were not meant to be instantaneously compatible. Keep a healthy distance from the Line of Control and all will be fine.'

She smiled at him to take the edge off her words.

'And now,' she said, getting back to her vivacious self and holding out her hands, 'read my fortune. I've been told that you're a good palmist.'

Mustafa took her left hand in one of his and ran the other hand caressingly over her palm. His expression was thoughtful.

'Lovely, lovely hand,' he murmured.

'Hey! Are you trying to make a pass at me, young man?' demanded Shreya archly.

'How I wish I could,' said Mustafa, sighing fervently.

'Naughty boy!' Shreya cackled delightedly, smacking him on the cheek. 'Tell me my future. Now!'

Mustafa claimed her hand again.

'Your life will soon be magically transformed under the influence of an attractive boy hailing from another religion. His name will most probably start with the letter "M"...'

Soumitro walked back into the house to find his grandmother and Mustafa sitting close, holding hands and laughing uproariously. He felt the blood rush to his head. The old hag, after brainwashing him with all kinds of anti-Muslim sentiments, after indoctrinating him with the language of hate and the ideology of revenge, was now holding hands with the enemy. He had been right all along. Women! They were never to be trusted, he told himself cynically for the umpteenth time. All of life seemed like an unfair and wretched affair again.

33

'If you keep your feet very still, fish will come to them,' Guru whispered to Maltesh. They sat side by side on the bank of a stream with their legs dangling in the cool, clear water. Guru had flipped up his lungi to form a hipster skirt of sorts so that his lower legs hung unhindered by garments. Maltesh, likewise, had hitched up his trousers to his knees. They sat in companionable silence, lean, long legs dangling in the flowing waters. At Guru's insistence, Maltesh froze his legs into immobility and right enough, schools of tiny silvery fish soon glided through the crystal waters to investigate and nibble at the four brown bits of mystery. They tickled the soles of Maltesh's feet and he burst out laughing. The fish went scurrying away in fright.

It was Maltesh's last day in the mountains. The next day he would make the long trek back to civilization. Kali and the other men would see him back in just the same manner in which they had got him to the forest.

Guru was looking older, frailer and greyer this morning, Maltesh noticed. He felt a sudden twinge of uneasiness and concern for the older man.

'I've been watching you over these past few weeks,' said Guru thoughtfully, lighting a leaf cigarette.

'I hope you liked what you saw,' replied Maltesh flippantly.

He felt a strange, light-headed boyishness when in the presence of this man, almost a sense of kinship.

'I'm getting tired,' said Guru suddenly.

The usual long, enigmatic silence followed.

'Time to pass on the leadership to fresh blood. But...' Guru's voice trailed off.

'But?'

'But to whom? I need the same kind of lunacy, passion and foolhardiness in my successor that is there in me. I don't see any of these traits in Kali and the others.'

Another enigmatic silence followed. Something lay between them this morning. A thick, urgent swirl of nebulous, unanswered questions. A bird cry sounded somewhere, floating melodiously across the silence of the morning. The sky stretched out above them, a deep cerulean blue with dazzling white cumulonimbus clouds moving languorously across. All around them was the heady smell of wild things growing in the hot sun. It was a bright, clear day and yet, as Maltesh sensed, it was not as innocently bright and clear a day as it appeared. There was something in the air, a mystery, a riddle, a hint of menace...? It was not a day for half-truths, illusions or trickery, as Maltesh guessed instinctively, it was a day for hard, cold and clear facts.

'You must have realized that your parents' marriage ceased to be a happy one, somewhere down the line,' Guru's voice was very quiet.

He took a draw at his cigarette, his gaze abstracted and faraway.

'Your mother was a warm, vivacious woman who lived for the pleasures of the moment. Your father was a cold, calculating and brilliant man who dreamt of being the college principal someday. Theirs was an ill-fated relationship. Your mother did not understand the world of college politics and your father had no patience with her delicate poetry. She waited eagerly for my visits so that she could share notes. My songs, my unworldliness, my lack of roots, possessions and pretences appealed to the romantic in her immensely.'

A butterfly came fluttering and alighted on Maltesh's knee. He sat still, hardly breathing.

'Her poetry, which had started as a light-hearted joke between us, was getting stronger by the day. Pain was giving her verse an edge that had been lacking before. I was stunned by the beauty of her lines.'

Guru's face was inscrutable in the harsh glare of noon.

'There was no loud, overt disagreement between your parents, you must understand. There never is in middle class families, only a quiet drifting, an ever widening chasm with no bridges for crossing.'

There was a moment of complete silence.

'And then came your father's illness that took him away in a year's time. And changed everything forever.'

The sun was high in the sky now. Multicoloured fluorescent dragonflies flitted among the tall grass. An idyllic summer's day. Only, thought Maltesh, feeling a sudden chill, that this is no idyllic summer's day. A shadow seemed to lurk around, waiting to eclipse the sun. Maltesh felt a cold shiver of premonition run through him.

'When I visited your parents' house for the last time, your father was very ill and on his deathbed. His pancreas had failed totally. Your mother had changed beyond recognition, aging almost ten years in ten months' time. She had been given a teaching job at your father's college and taught history. She was wearing reading glasses and poring over thick text books the last time I saw her. She was generous enough to give me a few moments of her time on my farewell visit. She gifted me an anthology of Tagore's poems as a token and told me that I needn't visit her ever again. Poetry and songs, she made it clear, did not fit into her new lifestyle any more. I continued to wander from state to state, singing my songs, but never went back to your mother's village after that visit. Some years later, I heard that she had died.'

Guru seemed to fall into a deep trance that lasted a while.

'I had changed my profession from singing to hunting by then. But through all the changes taking place on all sides and at all levels, I kept track of Chitra Roy's son, the delightful little toddler who had played marbles with me one evening long, long ago. And who was orphaned so tragically and so early. From Kodaikanal to Bombay, I followed you over the years.'

Guru glanced at Maltesh and smiled. An odd, twisted smile. The trees around sighed as a gentle wind blew through them.

'Debashish Roy's health had started deteriorating rapidly more than a year before you were born.'

His voice was deathly quiet now, and the silent afternoon eavesdropped on his words, breathless and intent.

'He was medically unfit to have sired a son as old as you.'

The words spilled out like hard pebbles in silent waters and ripples spread around the quiet statement. Their eyes met in the water. Maltesh's expression was stunned while Guru's watchful. Their gazes held and clung in the clear stream while a school of gleaming fish glided across their reflections. Each of them had the uncanny feeling of looking at himself at a different point in time. The same lush beards, the same hazel eyes, the same love of nature and the same affinity with animals.

'There is no way you can be Debashish Roy's child.'

Guru's voice was so low now that it was almost a whisper.

'Maltesh, are you my son?'

There was an agitated flurry of wings as a flock of parrots flew out of a tree nearby, disturbed by something. They rose up in the air and winged across the sky, forming a brilliant green arc against the deep blue background. Their shrill screeching rent the air for a few seconds and then subsided into silence.

The afternoon stretched on, lazy, golden and questioning.

34

Maltesh, Kali and the three other men walked single file through the forest. This time it was Maltesh who led and not Kali. The men followed Maltesh at a respectful distance. Their bodies were no longer taut with hostility as they were on the first journey undertaken more than a month ago. They now walked with a kind of loose-limbed nonchalance, as if they instinctively realized that they were in the presence of their future leader.

Many thoughts played in Maltesh's mind as he walked silently. Last night he had slept a disturbed sleep, hearing the collective voices of his ancestors whispering in his dreams and telling him which path to choose in life. When he woke up to a golden dawn, he knew with complete conviction which way it was that he had to go. He had risen from sleep feeling a leaping vitality in his veins that he had never experienced before and a strange deep connection with his surroundings. He finally understood the remarkable transformation that Guru had spoken about. His path in life was predetermined by greater forces, acknowledged Maltesh, and it was inevitable that he and Guru should meet.

Maltesh paused in his tracks to glance back. Guru stood on a rocky ledge nearby, watching him depart. They neither smiled nor waved to each other, such gestures seeming childish and superficial at this point in their relationship. A mere exchange of looks sufficed.

Maltesh turned back and continued on his way, his tread firm and sure. He knew that he would never lead the police down this path. The police, who dreamt of capturing the forest brigand Guru Das, dead or alive. He also knew that he would never feel lonely or directionless again. Or agonize over the legitimacy of his parentage. Or hurt at the cruel hints dropped by his relatives.

He made a careful note of landmarks as he walked. He would need them. After all, he would be returning very soon. To these dark, welcoming forests. To claim the leadership that was his. To his mission and to his calling.

He would be returning soon, for sure. Soon. Very soon.

35

Sharmistha Banerjee was waxing and waning like the moon. She alternated between trying to look like Kate Moss and Kate Winslet, depending on the boyfriend of the moment. Her menu switched from salads to salami with disconcerting frequency, alarming her family considerably. If a boyfriend liked the twiggy look, she lived on lettuce and raw cabbage for weeks and if the next one who came along showed a preference for generous curves, she immediately switched over to sweetmeats and cereals. Her skin would wither, her breasts sag, her immunity drop to an all time low and her reproductive system would get shot to pieces if she continued like this, her grandmother admonished her. In answer to which Mishti burst into noisy tears and shut herself in the bedroom shared by the two sisters.

'She's pining for something,' said her mother worriedly.

'Or someone,' said Bonny archly.

'She's malnourished,' snorted Shreya.

'She's in love,' said Siddharth with conviction.

'Shiv, Shiv, Shiv,' muttered Dibyendu frantically with his eyes shut.

But the fact remained that for all the interesting theories being put forward, Mishti continued to behave rather strangely. Advertisements for cosmetics did not enthral her any more as she flipped the pages of magazines disinterestedly. She no longer spent hours before her wardrobe, trying to decide whether to wear blue or green to college and whether her look of the week should be kitsch, chic, ethnic or grunge. It was all very disturbing.

'I'm telling you that idiot is in love,' repeated Siddharth with brotherly shrewdness.

'In love, is she? This gets very, very interesting,' said Mustafa who had just drifted into A-502 Pushpa Milan.

He turned abruptly. The matter needed urgent investigation. He strolled over to the kitchen where Mishti was making toast for herself, her expression wan and tearful.

'Are you in love, sweetie?' demanded Mustafa without preamble.

'Oh, buzz off,' snapped Mishti irritably.

'Because if you are, you should increase your protein intake,' advised Mustafa very seriously.

'Aw, shut up!' snapped Mishti.

'Also drink a lot of fluids. Love dehydrates,' declared Mustafa knowledgeably.

Mishti turned on him exasperatedly.

'Why don't you go and jump off the nearest cliff, Mustu? You'd be doing mankind a great favour.'

'I might, buddy, I just might,' drawled Mustafa slowly and contemplatively. He was staring in a hypnotized manner at the stainless steel containers lined on the open kitchen shelf. Mishti's reflection was trapped in the shining silver metal of the containers. The curved surface distorted her features to a stylized elegance, capturing and distilling secret resonances of her persona that were invisible at other times. Mustafa was suddenly reminded of a priceless painting he had seen at an art exhibition. Why, he thought with a sense of wonder, Sharmistha looks just like a Botticcelli angel. An Indianized version. How come he had never noticed the resemblance before?

Bonny was busy putting finishing touches to her make-up in another part of the house. Dibyendu was taking her to the annual book fair at the far end of the city. Dabbing perfume on her wrists as the last thing, she stared at her reflection in the mirror in consternation. Her eyes seemed languorous, her lips full and her whole body ripe and waiting. What *was* happening to her? Her man-baiting feminist stance was dropping off her like petals off a withered blossom. Her nights now came full of forbidden dreams and she awoke to dawns with her body arching with passionate longing. Where, she asked herself in fright, were all those protective defence mechanisms of a staid middle class upbringing? They had all come crashing down ignominiously. She was changing. And changing fast. Morphing into a near stranger. How textured I am, she thought in despair, how convoluted, complex and layered. With her mind saying one thing, these days, and her body another, and her whole person aching with a million illegitimate yearnings. She was no longer merely a daughter, sister, friend or feminist. For the first time in her life, Bonny felt like a woman. She trod a dangerous razor's edge these days, where all her impulses seemed to be getting totally out of control. It was scary for a person who was always used to being completely in charge of situations. She would have to, she thought nervously, keep a tight check on her emotions at all times.

Dibyendu liked the little pleasures of life. Dipping biscuits into hot tea was one of the things that held a hypnotic fascination for him. It was the perfect exercise to test one's dexterity, reflexes and mental agility. He generally dipped the biscuit halfway through, quickly pulling it out of the tea and popping it into his mouth before the soggy biscuit disintegrated and dropped into the tea. The entire operation was a stern test of one's faculties and he generally managed to garner a pretty high rate of success. But today, he was wearing his new powder blue shirt and taking Bonny out, and he refrained from indulging in his favourite hobby.

Something weird was happening to him these days, he had to admit. Parts of him hardened unexpectedly with desire when Bonny brushed past. He was unaccustomed to such disturbing bodily changes in his thirty odd years of ascetic living and he felt both confused and delighted. Bonny's face haunted his dreams and the smell of her favourite cologne followed him everywhere. He'd have to watch his step, he thought worriedly, guard against revealing his true feelings unwittingly someday.

Bonny took her time in making an appearance. Dibyendu, who had been sipping his tea disinterestedly, felt his face light up like a candle when she entered. Careful, he told himself, careful, careful. He stumbled to his feet, sloshing tea all over the saucer and dropping crumbs down his shirt. After a good deal of mopping and dusting the duo left for the book fair. Shreya Banerjee walked to the door to see them off, giving a string of shrill instructions as they stepped out. She stopped arrested for a moment, as if struck by lightning, after they had left. Her granddaughter's expression seemed to float in her mind and she hurriedly waddled to the window to see her leave. Bonny and Dibyendu's departure seem to hold interesting shades to it and Shreya Banerjee's shrewd eyes were suddenly speculative.

The morning had the kind of perfection that comes just once in a while, when the sunshine, the wind, the mood and the mind seemed to be in perfect sync with each other. When the external and internal worlds met at a perfect tangent, thought Bonny dreamily. Her heart sang as they waited side by side at the crossing, waiting for the never-ending line of traffic to ease.

'Now,' barked Dibyendu as there was a momentary lull in the traffic. 'Run!'

Holding hands they charged across the road, making it to the divider before the stream of cars started again. A gust of strong wind wafted across, lifting Bonny's clothes and her dupatta flew up into the air exuberantly. Bonny blushed, trying to hold down her top from riding up and at the same time capture her truant dupatta. The ordeal left her pink and breathless and she looked up to meet Dibyendu's amused eyes.

'I dream of you every night!' she blurted out without pausing to think.

A truck laden with heavy crates thundered past noisily.

'Bwhat?' bellowed Dibyendu over the din. 'Bwhat did you say?'

An ambulance came screaming next, its whistle rising to a deafening crescendo before fading into the distance as it sped by. There was another lull in the traffic.

'Come on,' said Dibyendu.

They ran again and stood laughing, panting and triumphant, the morning traffic having been dealt with successfully. They still held hands. Office-goers milling around and hurrying to their destinations smiled. They felt both indulgent and irritated with the couple holding hands and smiling idiotically into each other's eyes while blocking the sea of humanity at this rush hour. Bonny glanced beyond Dibyendu's shoulder. A funeral procession was winding down the road, the snow white shroud and orange flowers marking a splash of colour against the moving sea of muted metallic cars. A flea-bitten street dog came limping by and rubbed itself against Bonny's ankles. No, she thought, suddenly feeling cautious and wise, this was not the best of moments to make a declaration of love. And of all people, to a second cousin. Bengali middle class morals were strange things, she thought musingly.

'Bwhat were you saying out there, Bonny?' enquired Dibyendu, 'I couldn't hear because of the noise.'

Bonny smiled.

'There's a South Indian hotel round the corner, I said. Serves wonderful coffee.'

Dibyendu looked enthusiastic.

'I'd love some coffee,' he said.

Bonny let out her breath in a long sigh. Thank god she hadn't blurted out her feelings like some silly schoolgirl, she thought, and risked jeopardizing their easy friendship forever. Her feelings were probably one-sided anyway, and she wouldn't want to scandalize Benuda in any way or shake his ascetic middle class moorings.

'Come on,' she said, leading the way to percolated coffee.

The funeral procession came closer and passed by quietly with muted chants of 'Hey Ram'.

36

Mishti and Bonny were performing their last minute beauty administrations before going to bed. Mishti stared moodily at the starry skies above as she filed her nails.

'What are you thinking about, sweetie?' asked Bonny who was giving her scalp a vigorous massage with warm olive oil.

'Oh, many things,' replied Mishti vaguely.

'Like?'

'Like... like... like meaning something to someone sometime. I'm sick of being a Tinker Bell figure spreading light and sunshine and having boyfriends ditch me every fortnight. I'm tired of being taken lightly by the whole world!' burst out Mishti. She had lately been thinking a lot about how Mustafa's comments on her love life never failed to needle her and was wondering why.

It was a fairly long and intelligent speech by Mishti's standards and Bonny stared at her younger sister in astonishment. Her hands froze on her scalp and oily strands of hair stood up in spikes. Such thoughts, coming from Mishti, were incredibly profound, she thought worriedly.

'Do you... er... have someone specific in mind when you say all this?' Bonny asked fearfully.

But her sister's face became shuttered once again as she bent to file her toenails. Bonny settled into bed feeling vaguely alarmed. She liked life to go as per plans and people around her to behave predictably. Sudden things happening unsettled her as did people behaving out of character. She drifted into an uneasy sleep, deeply worried about her younger sister.

'I'm colouring my hair,' announced Mishti rebelliously at breakfast.

There were varied reactions all around.

'You'll do no such thing,' snapped Soumitro.

'Are you planning to turn blonde? Please give me advance notice. I'm getting on in years and can't take severe shocks any more,' said Siddharth in a discouraging voice.

'She'll look lovely,' said Bonny to her mother.

'She'll look like a tart,' snorted her grandmother.

Mustafa stood up in excitement.

'Go for it, girl! Purple, pink, fuchsia, green, the works! And a tomahawk haircut to go with the colour,'

'Shiv, Shiv, Shiv,' chanted Dibyendu, trying to be safe and neutral.

Mishti sauntered to the front door and down the stairs, followed by her entire family giving her diverse instructions and forbidding her from doing anything drastic. Mustafa and Dibyendu were left with each other for company in the suddenly empty drawing room. Mustafa leaned back languidly, making himself supremely comfortable. He watched Dibyendu with a kind of narrow-eyed, predatory gleam. He had a long decided that Dibyendu, with his pompous, upright air, was to be his next victim. His primness, his deep religious leanings and his antiseptic ascetic beliefs had never found much favour with Mustafa. Such outdated attitudes were inappropriate in these days and times, according to Mustafa, and Dibyendu badly needed to be straightened out. More than anything else, he needed to be shaken, stirred and shocked out of his celibate skin and who could do it better than he, Mustafa Ali Saifee? Mustafa felt a pleasurable sense of anticipation at the task in hand.

Dibyendu suddenly felt slightly hot under the collar, as he always did in Mustafa's presence. He tried to hide his uneasiness at being left alone with the unpredictable youngster. Given half a chance he would have bolted from the scene but his cousins (save one) seemed inordinately fond of Mustafa and it was time he attempted to connect.

'Hi,' he said courteously, for want of a more imaginative beginning.

'Waleikum salaam,' replied Mustafa laconically.

A long silence ensued. Mustafa, lolling back on the sofa, appeared to be fascinated by the circular movements made by the blades of the ceiling fan. He seemed disinclined towards speech.

'I beliebhe you know my colleague's younger brother Anirudh Malgaonkar,' said Dibyendu, seizing the only common contact as a potential topic for communication.

'That schizo?'

'And also his other brother Atul who bwas in your class last year,' continued Dibyendu valiantly.

'That klepto?'

'Atul headed the college cricket team...' said Dibyendu, frantically trying to keep the conversational ball rolling.

'And pansy...'

'... And I was told that he bowled phantastically at the intercollege cricket tournament.'

'Probably transvestite...'

'Atul is said to have a good bowling action. Has a way with the ball, I believe,' continued Dibyendu desperately.

Mustafa snorted.

'Yeah – probably someone else's… the only things he has a way with are lipsticks, rouge and falsies.'

Dibyendu turned a rich shade of maroon. He took a long, deep breath and slowly and silently counted to ten in an attempt to normalize his blood pressure. Mustafa watched him closely with a great deal of interest.

'I met Anirudh Malgaonkar last wheek. You know him whell, don't you?' said Dibyendu making another desperate attempt at connecting.

'Annie? Of course! Who wouldn't know that blighted I-specialist?'

'*Eye* specialist? I thought he was into softwhare,' said Dibyendu.

'Oh, he is. And a consummate I-specialist as well,' said Mustafa.

Strange combination, thought Dibyendu, scratching his head in perplexity, corneas and computers.

'Well, like I said, I met him last week. He was on his way to Hrishikesh,' said Dibyendu.

'Hrishikesh? Annie?' Mustafa sounded dumbstruck.

'He said he was very stressed out and needed a few cathartic sessions up in the mountains,' explained Dibyendu.

'What? I don't believe this! You mean Annie actually uses words like "cathartic" these days?' said Mustafa sounding awestruck.

'Yes. And "metrosexual" too,' said Dibyendu proudly. 'He told me that he was the quintessential metrosexual man of the times, whatever that means.'

It took a moment for the astounding information to sink into Mustafa's brain.

'Good lord!' he exclaimed. 'How he has evolved! The last time I met him, Annie had just three words in his vocabulary – I, me and myself.'

Though not blindingly bright or anything, there suddenly seemed to be a faint glimmer of light at the end of the tunnel.

'Oh,' said Dibyendu in a tone of dawning enlightenment. 'When you said *eye* specialist, you actually meant *I*-specialist.'

Mustafa looked at him strangely. However, the conversation, which had been meandering hopelessly along dark labyrinthine corridors, finally showed happy signs of emerging into the daylight. For the first time in their lives, Dibyendu and Mustafa looked at each other with kindly eyes, bonded momentarily by their common dislike for the absent metrosexual, Anirudh Malgaonkar. Not a bad sort, thought Mustafa, eyeing Dibyendu with friendly eyes, as long as he goes easy on the volume and the grammar.

Not a bad kid, just a little misguided, thought Dibyendu of Mustafa on his way back home, if only he'd go easy on the poetry and the practical jokes. Their relationship, so far volatile, seemed suddenly suffused with the rosy glow of truce.

37

It was the hottest summer in years. The city of Bombay sweated, simmered and swore at the occasional power and water cuts. Tempers were edgy as the sun beat down relentlessly on asphalt and there was the impending feeling that something was going to give way soon.

Malati missed Maltesh. Where *was* Malto, she thought fretfully for the hundredth time. She missed his warm silences when she ranted on about something, his perennial sympathy when the celebrity world let her down and her stories didn't quite click and his eternal moral support when Soumitro behaved like a brute. His strong, silent protectiveness had buffered her against many a blasting from the surly editor.

Malati leaned back and sighed long and hard. Life, she thought feeling unusually profound, was like the movement of heavenly bodies. A celestial pattern where people often collided like asteroids, but then, caught inexorably in the cosmic movement, they drifted away again. If someone had to go out of your life, he just had to go. There was nothing you could do about it. Period.

And now to add to her foul mood, she had lost the story on Guru Das. She rummaged through her drawer muttering irritably as Soumitro walked into the office.

'My hard copy and soft copy have both vanished,' she grumbled.

'Look after your stuff well. Anything can happen in this office,' snapped Soumitro.

'Is this office haunted? Do you have ghosts here?' enquired Malati.

'The only ghost that has ever haunted me is the ghost of mediocrity,' answered Soumitro moodily.

Malati looked up at him in surprise. It was not often that the reticent editor revealed himself to anyone. He was gazing out of the window, his eyes bleak and morose. There was a long pause. As usual, thick undercurrents and a veiled antagonism hung between them, making it difficult for Malati to say anything meaningful. She turned away from him suddenly feeling very young and incapable of handling the complexities lurking around her.

Siddharth Banerjee stood watching summer hit the city from his bedroom window. His mood these days was sombre. His initial euphoria at having secured admission at the prestigious Sir D.V. College of Architecture had evaporated completely. His exceptional results in the recent examinations had been just that, exceptional results on a piece of paper. Reality had been very different. By some strange logic, the secret decision-making mechanism of the college had awarded the prestigious Lokmanya Tilak Award for academic excellence to Medha Dongre, the principal's daughter. Professor Deshmukh's heart had bled for his favourite student, as Siddharth well knew, but he was in no position to refute the decision openly. So that was the way the wind blew, Siddharth thought bitterly – ultimately, his original thinking and his designing expertise came to nothing. Just nothing. He felt a cold rage simmer within him and had a sudden wild urge to physically bust a system that rewarded mediocrity and good connections so profusely and shunned pure talent.

There was no one person whom he could challenge, though. Mass sycophancy was at work here. The panel of selectors had included twelve eminent members who had voted the mousy, mediocre Medha Dongre as the most deserving candidate for the scholarship. Siddharth knew that he faced a very dangerous enemy, an enemy who was nameless, shapeless and worked with lethal stealth.

If Soumitro felt a sense of disappointment at the results, he hid it well from his younger brother. A hefty scholarship at this point would have helped the family finances tremendously. *Noon Voice* was not really sinking, but it was not doing very well either with so many new rival publications suddenly mushrooming all over the city.

'I wish you had got that scholarship, Sid. After all, you deserved it, being the most worthy student in your class,' was all he said mildly.

Mustafa, who was lying on his back with eyes shut tight, rose agitatedly.

'You don't need brilliance to qualify for the Lokmanya Tilak Award, buddy. You need the right contacts, the right genes and the right domicile certificate,' saying which he fell back on the sofa and shut his eyes again.

He rose sphinx-like, a moment later.

'All of which are in the possession of Miss Dongre. She is obedient, prim, proper, docile, a native of this state and the principal's daughter. Can anyone beat that combination?' he asked.

He looked heavenwards with an expression of despair on his face.

'O Kalki, deliver us from this age of darkness and corruption,' he said in a quavering theatrical voice.

'Who's this Kalki, now?' demanded Siddharth.

'Ignorant boy! Don't you know your mythology? Kalki, the last incarnation of god programmed to destroy this cosmic cycle, Kalyug being the last stage of…'

'I'm not bothered about his cosmic missions. All I want this Kalki chap to do for me is get me the Ralph Correa scholarship at the end of the year. And annihilate Medha Dongre,' snapped Siddharth irritably.

'Selfish, egocentric child! A typical product of these modern times. Ah, pathos, pathos,' grieved Mustafa, burying his face in his hands.

Mishti walked in on the scene sporting a new look. Her hair, previously black, was now a rich shade of burgundy. It had been styled and set to frame her face flatteringly and set off her delicate features to perfection. She looked enchanting. Mustafa froze. He gazed at her with a thunderstruck expression for one long moment and then quickly regained his composure.

'Fix me some coffee, will you Mishti? I've got to rush,' Soumitro immediately commanded, completely impervious to his sister's physical makeover.

Mishti proceeded obediently towards the kitchen.

'Your brother Sid believes in socially and environmentally relevant architecture,' Mustafa informed Soumitro, continuing with the interrupted topic of conversation. There was a slightly distracted air about him that hadn't been there a few moments ago.

'So what's wrong with that?' enquired Dibyendu perplexed.

'Everything!' said Mustafa. 'The world belongs to tech savvy, futuristic architecture, brothers. Environmental and socially responsible architecture be blown!'

'And what would *you* know about social responsibilities, you spoilt rich kid?' asked Soumitro nastily.

'What the hell do you mean?' Mustafa sounded insulted. 'My social conscience is alive and kicking. Don't you see me teaching street children every Sunday?'

'You?' exclaimed Soumitro, in disbelief. '*You?*'

'Yep, me. None else. Just this morning I taught them a popular nursery rhyme, somewhat revamped for greater relevance.'

He cleared his throat and began to sing in a high-pitched voice.

Row, row, row your boat
Gently down the stream
Throw your teacher overboard
And then you'll hear her scream

'What!' said Dibyendu scandalized. 'You taught little children that?'

'And why not?' demanded Mustafa aggressively. 'Isn't it the philosophy of our times? I'm also teaching the kids the fine art of distinguishing excellence from mediocrity. So very important in these times, don't you think?'

'And how, may I ask, are you doing that?' Soumitro's voice was dry.

'Well, the first step is how to tell heroes from superheroes,' informed Mustafa.

'How?' asked Siddharth with interest.

'Well, for one thing, heroes wear their underpants under their trousers while superheroes wear them over their pants. That's deeply metaphorical. There is a profound message hidden in this whole business of underpants, but it is eluding me at this moment. Give me a day or two and I'll have it all figured out.'

'Mustu, Mustu, Mustu,' groaned Siddharth in utter despair. 'What is to become of you?'

'Hmmphh!' snorted Soumitro disdainfully. 'Some Sunday teacher these kids have got themselves!'

Mishti was brewing coffee in the kitchen, her head bent low. The rays of the setting sun filtering through the glass windowpane fell on her freshly coloured hair, turning it to a burnished gold. There were footsteps behind her and she turned, kettle in hand. It was Mustafa. For a full minute Mustafa stood and gazed at Mishti's hair. He then cleared his throat and softly quoted lines from an old Hindi movie song.

Tumhare zulf ke saye mein shaam kar loonga
Safar is umr ka
Pal mein tamam kar loonga

There was silence, broken by the tinkle of china as Mishti set the coffee tray.

'Which,' translated for young ladies unfamiliar with the nuances of romantic poetry, means,' he continued:

I shall cast my evening in the shade of your tresses
And live an entire lifetime in these precious moments...

Mishti looked up, surprised. There wasn't the usual sneer in Mustafa's voice and no deliberate distortion in the interpretation either. He was watching her very intently.

'Mustafa,' she said, her voice uncertain. 'Is this supposed to be a proposal?'

'Well, what do you think?'

'I think it's pretty lousy as proposals go,' said Mishti.

'Not if you've been using Lice-Free regularly,' said Mustafa, naming a popular brand of anti-lice lotion.

'Are you ever serious?' asked Mishti crossly.

'I've never been more serious in my life, Sharmistha,' he said, his voice very quiet.

Mishti looked at him, startled. He was watching her very steadily, his expression painfully taut and tense. For a long moment they gazed wordlessly at one another. Then Mishti turned away, blushing deeply. Face averted, she rummaged through the assortment of vegetables lying scattered in colourful abandon on the dining table. Her mother would be coming along presently to chop them for lunch. She found what she was looking for and her hand closed around a medium-sized aubergine. It was purple, slim, curved and seemed to possess all the prerequisites of a mike. Holding it to her mouth with slender fingers, Mishti cleared her throat in a theatrical manner. The occasion called for some drama.

'Here goes,' she muttered. 'I hope I don't sound like Benuda!'

Raising her voice to a loud, dramatic pitch, she launched off.

'To your proposal, Mustafa Ali Saifee, my answer runs thus,' she said:

Aap ki nazaron ne samjha
Pyar ke kaabil mujhe
Dil ki ai dhadkan thhehar ja
Mil gayi manzil mujhe

She took a deep breath.

'Which translated for young men with subzero IQs is,' she said:

I accept, I accept, I accept.

There was a loud burst of applause from the doorway as five people who had been eavesdropping shamelessly tumbled into the room excitedly.

'Allah!' expostulated Mustafa, looking heavenwards. 'Do Bengalis even know the word "privacy"?'

Shreya Banerjee waddled up to Mustafa and commanded him to bend low. When he did so, she planted a resounding kiss on the tip of his nose while Bonny tweaked his hair playfully. Ira met his eyes, her eyes tender and smiling, while Siddharth looked like he had been slugged in the solar plexus with a sledgehammer.

'Mustu for a brother-in-law!' he said, sounding stunned and delighted. 'Yo!'

'Shiv, Shiv, Shiv,' muttered Dibyendu, his voice shaking.

Soumitro, hearing the noise, sauntered in to find out what the din was all about. He stopped transfixed, his horrified eyes fastening on the blushing Mishti. It took a while for the situation to sink in and when it did, he felt a tremor (that would have measured pretty high on the Richter scale) go through him. Mishti and MUSTAFA! MISHTI and Mustafa! MISHTI and MUSTAFA! He felt his brain reel and had a sudden, wild urge to call the police, the fire brigade, the ambulance, the Red Cross, or for that matter, anyone else who dealt in disaster management. Grabbing hold of Mishti's elbow, he dragged her into the quiet corridor.

'Are you feeling quite alright, Mishti?' he asked urgently.

He touched a concerned hand to her forehead.

'No fever,' he muttered frowning. 'Are you sure you're feeling okay? I mean you're not coming down with flu, chicken pox or herpes or something, are you? People in the incubation period have been known to behave very strangely.'

Mishti extricated herself from her elder brother's feverish grasp. For the first time in her young life, she looked at him squarely in the eye. Her gaze was very direct and unflinching.

'No, Dada,' she said, very quietly. 'There's nothing wrong with me. In fact, I've never felt better or happier in my life. And yes, Mustu and I are going to be together.'

Soumitro stood gaping at her, speechless with shock. He felt sheer disbelief wash over him. This couldn't be happening to him. Impossible! It was a nightmare that he would wake up from very soon. He couldn't believe that his adored baby sister, whom he had given piggyback rides to just some years ago, was actually looking him in the eye and talking back to him. Planning to join forces with the enemy. A sense of failure churned within him like bitter bile. All the religious and racial prejudices imbibed over years of ancestral indoctrination spiralled within him, forming a raging, fiery vortex of hatred. For the second time in his life, Soumitro Banerjee watched his world come crashing down.

38

'You're not surprised?'

Mustafa's voice was unnaturally low and serious.

Shreya Banerjee grinned at him, her eyes dancing with mischief behind her glasses.

'I saw it coming long back, Mustu. I wasn't born yesterday, you know,' she chortled with mirth.

'And you don't mind? My religion?'

There was a long, pregnant silence. The dipping sun filled the room with liquid gold.

'Religion is not about your surname, child, nor is it about the direction you face while praying. Or the scriptures you read. It is about perspective. We have always stood at the same altitude and shared the same wavelength. And you Mustu, have always belonged here. From day one,' said Ira softly.

The two women smiled at him, their eyes tender. Mustafa bowed his head, suddenly bereft of speech and his usual wisecracks. Ira and Shreya linked arms with him from either side and drew him gently to the window. Durga Nagar was ablaze with the orange fire of sunset. The sun seemed barely inches above the horizon and the three of them reverently took up positions at the window to watch in silence the sun dip behind the slums.

Siddharth Banerjee watched the same sunset from his bedroom window but with different eyes. He was glad for his twin and his best friend, of course, but there was not much joy left in him any more. The effervescence and enthusiasm of his first year at the college of architecture had vanished completely and in place of the eager, impressionable teenager of earlier years there now stood a hollow, bitter boy on the brink of manhood. His boyish squeak was now a deep baritone though adolescent acne still spotted his greasy cheeks. The eyes were still fine and sparkling behind the spectacles but the expression in them was sombre and brooding. He viewed the city of Bombay through different eyes these days, the rose-coloured lenses smashed beyond repair. Forever. He no longer felt hunger and a desperate urgency to resculpt the skyline. He only felt black despair. Melancholic music played behind him on his music system, the lyrics reaching out to his tortured thoughts.

Summer has come and passed
The innocence can never last
Wake me up
When September ends

The sad, haunting lines reverberated around his bedroom. Green Day. The collective favourite of the entire batch of final year architecture students.

Like my father's come to pass
Seven years has gone so fast
Wake me up
When September ends

Summer. A time for aestivation, Siddharth thought. A time to be in the cool, dark indoors. Recuperate. Revitalize. Put one's thoughts and objectives into neat little pigeonholes of good sense. So why did good sense continue to elude him?

Here comes the rain again
Falling from the stars
Drenched in my pain again
Becoming who we are

As my memory rests
But never forgets what I lost
Wake me up
When September ends

Ring out the bells again
Like we did when spring began
Wake me up
When September ends

How apt, thought Siddharth. Only, I don't want to be woken up. Ever. The haze of heat reached out to him through the window.

Summer.

A time to suspend all physical activities. Clean out the mind. Lick ices, walk on the beach, run with puppies. If only. If only he hadn't grown up quite so quickly in these last few months. Siddharth shut his eyes, feeling pain in his temples. There was no innocence left in him any more. He had lost the ability to be carefree. His ice-cream licking days, he had to admit to himself, were gone forever.

The building site that he had visited the evening before swam before his eyes. The topic of his college project dealt with ideal urban architecture in the upcoming colonies that were still under construction. Siddharth had stood amidst a half-built colony, clicking pictures for his submission. The buildings, set at angles to one another, formed a giant atrium where gardeners were working diligently on landscaped gardens. The windows unadorned by signs of human habitation echoed with the sounds of carpenters at work. There was an eerie sense of waiting about the place, as if the silent, sterile spaces were just yearning to be filled with the sounds of human voices and children's laughter. Smells of fresh paint and varnish hung in the air. The construction was solid, the aesthetics exquisite and the colony could easily qualify for the position of ideal urban architecture and he could quickly and conveniently fold up his project.

And yet.

Siddharth knew that the colony had been built on land stealthily claimed by deliberately destroying the mangroves that had existed for decades in these parts of the suburb. Land acquired illegally by land sharks who were masters at destroying the ecology in an unobtrusive, almost invisible manner. The mangroves had been steadily vanishing under Siddharth's anguished eyes. A lot of talk about preservation came up once in a while, making headlines and then dying a quick death with environmental questions being hastily swept under the carpet. Housing colonies had sprung up almost overnight and what had once been a wide expanse of green teeming with microorganisms that kept floodwaters at bay now suddenly appeared as a multitude of snazzy buildings one fine morning. Siddharth felt physically ill when he thought of the constant rape of natural surroundings by avaricious builders in different parts of the city – when he saw malls and multiplexes move in slyly, inching their way towards a complete takeover.

He had stopped voicing his protest and concern to his professors. Builders and environmentalists were old enemies, he was told callously, and it was wiser for a student of architecture to have sympathies with the former group. There was a lot he kept silent about these days. The haphazard vertical growth of the city with its burgeoning populace sickened him. The thought of natural resources stretched to bursting point frightened him. A city of lights, he thought bitterly. Sure. But built on rotting, precarious foundations of greed, corruption and adulteration. The quality of materials was suspect in even the best of the city's constructions, as he well knew now, and all those exalted beings residing in their glass towers stood in imminent danger of crashing down to ground reality someday soon. Indiscriminate structural changes brought about by residents contemptuous of blueprint regulations completed the picture. He felt a sense of revulsion at having chosen such a profession. A career of malpractice, avariciousness and a compulsory disregard for one's environment if one wanted to survive and prosper, he thought in despair.

He could foresee the future pretty clearly. Vanishing mangroves, rivers interrupted, trees chopped indiscriminately, lakes dying and being encouraged to fill up with silt, buildings mushrooming in rightful zones for greenery, all of life a concretized nightmare... The rise in temperatures resulting from an excessive use of asphalt, weather fluctuations, the clogging of drains in the absence of mangroves, the noise, the dust, the pollution without trees to absorb and buffer it, the implications of city rivers perpetually interrupted by encroachers, vanishing flora and fauna, a city without crows, vultures and other natural scavengers...

He was reminded of the school biology lessons that he had never paid much attention to. Of mangroves being an entire ecological world that supported minute organisms which played a vital role in stabilizing the environment. Of vultures which disposed of the dead in the Parsi-owned Towers of Silence in the city. Of global warming and the endangered ozone layer to which each Bombay resident was callously adding his precious destructive bit. His childhood lessons, read so casually and forgotten, were reaching out from the past and coming right back at him like furious waves lashing out at high tide. Trees, he thought wretchedly, that besides giving out oxygen absorbed noise and dust, rendering the atmosphere cleaner and quieter, these vital old trees were now being hacked regularly in the city to make hoardings more visible. He felt a pressing sense of despair. Conservationists could shout themselves hoarse and stage a million protests but in the end it was always the destroyers who won, he thought cynically.

Unfortunately, no architect was an island and could work in the insulated spaces of his own beliefs, he realized rather late in the day. An architect came as a package deal with builders, contractors, municipal authorities, goons, land sharks and other partners in crime, he was told by his seniors, and to expect integrity to run through the entire chain was idiocy, as he well knew. 'If you can't beat them, join them' was the motto followed by most of his colleagues. So why couldn't he just join this brigade with their conveniently shifting ethics? Because he was doomed by his chromosomes, he thought, unwittingly echoing his elder brother's sentiments. Genetically geared to protect and preserve rather than harm and mutilate.

Siddharth Banerjee had no illusions about himself. No matter how grand his ideals, he was all too conscious of the physical limitations of his personality. He could be assertive but never aggressive, he would simmer in the face of injustice but was hardly likely to stand up and confront. He was undoubtedly good at his work but he lacked the strength to fight for his beliefs and take a tough stand in the face of tough opposition. In short, he was doomed.

Watching the sun set over Durga Nagar, in his last term of his final year at the Sir D.V. College of Architecture and with his entire family waiting expectantly for him to graduate, Siddharth Banerjee realized that he was not really cut out for mainstream architecture.

39

'I really admire people who have extramarital affairs,' said Malati in a tone of deep reverence. 'Imagine, what wonderful time management skills! My poor brother can't seem to manage even one spouse!'

'Silence!' bellowed Dibyendu deafeningly. 'No non-bhej topic in phamily room!'

'What's non-vegetarian about it, for Chrissake? These are facts of life. And whose family are you referring to? Yours or mine?' retorted Malati perplexed.

Dibyendu looked far from pleased to have his orders overruled so irreverently. The smell of cappuccino wafted in from the kitchen as Mishti fixed the evening coffee. Thank god Mishti is not in the room, thought Dibyendu in relief, such topics were most unsuitable for her young, maidenly ears. He looked at Malati surreptitiously, with acute distaste writ large on his face. The chirpy young subeditor with her constant thirst for drama never failed to get on his nerves.

There was palpable excitement in the air at A-502 Pushpa Milan that evening. Bubla Basu was applying for a teacher's job at a local school. It was the first time that the chronic asthmatic was stepping out of her house to make a career for herself and the Banerjees and their friends and cousin were in a state of high excitement. A visibly nervous Bubla sat in the centre of the room, being bombarded with advice from all quarters.

'Wear a sari. A cotton one,' advised Malati. 'It always makes an impression.'

'I'll give you one of mine,' offered Bonny.

'I'll do up your hair before the interview. A smart chignon,' promised Mishti who had come in with the coffee.

'You'll need teaching aids. I'll make cutouts in thermocol for you. Continents, islands, isthmus, peninsula and estuary-shaped models. You'll be teaching geography, won't you?' asked Siddharth.

'Which class will you teach?' asked Dibyendu.

'Sixth graders. If I get the job, that is,' replied Bubla nervously.

Soumitro glanced at Bubla from his crossword-making corner. Strange how they had all developed a fiercely protective streak towards the frail spinster in these few months, he thought wonderingly. The 'Lame Duck Syndrome' was how Soumitro labelled this feeling of proprietorship over a less fortunate person. And Bubla was a perfectly suitable example. A woman who, besides being besieged by chronic ill-health, received extremely shabby treatment from her brother and sister-in-law, if the local grapevine was to be believed. He'd dig up some impressive words that she could use during her job interview, he decided, flipping through the dictionary at his side.

'I'll supply some suitable poetry for the occasion. Just give me a minute or two,' offered Mustafa enthusiastically.

'Mustu,' said Bonny decisively, 'I don't think geography and poetry go very well together.'

'They do, buddy, they do. Poetry gels with everything. Birth, death, weddings, divorces, heartbreak, history, geography, astronomy, nutrition, gynaecology, palaeontology…'

'That's quite enough in my opinion,' snapped Soumitro. 'No point confusing Bubla. We stand hugely enlightened by your views, though.'

Bubla leaned back in her chair contentedly. The Banerjees' drawing room was the only place where she felt cherished, pampered and respected, all three being long forgotten emotions since her parents' death. She got up to leave, suddenly feeling optimistic about the job interview. Mishti walked up, and putting her arms around Bubla, kissed her gently on both cheeks.

'You'll do fine, Bubladi,' she whispered encouragingly.

'Cheers. And all the best,' Soumitro gave her a vigorous thumbs up signal.

'Go for it, girl!' Mustafa stood up on the sofa with excitement. 'Axe them, fell them, jump on them, stab them, annihilate them and floor your interviewers with your deadly charms!'

'Mustu, I think that is quite enough,' said Mishti, placing a restraining hand on her boyfriend's arm before his enthusiasm ran away with him.

Bubla walked back to Halfway House. Opening the front door quietly with her latch key, she entered the house stealthily. She still felt warm and nurtured from her visit to the Banerjees. She trod softly, taking immense care not to disturb her sister-in-law who liked to sleep late into the evenings. Boudi's siesta time was sacred in the house as nobody around was brave enough to face the wrath that the slightest disturbance was sure to unleash. Bubla tiptoed to the tiny cubicle down the corridor that she had to herself and crept in soundlessly. It was the end of the corridor partitioned off and not a room really but it afforded Bubla a few square feet of intensely private space and she was supremely happy with it. It had a rickety bed and a minuscule dressing table, but most important, it held her tin trunk which was pushed under the single bed and pulled out only on special occasions.

The tin trunk held memories.

The memories were visual, olfactory and tactile in nature. Moth-eaten greeting cards yellow with age, empty perfume bottles that still held the whiff of childhood, treasured cosmetics well past their expiry dates, snuffboxes that reminded her of her father's tight hugs and soft muslin saris belonging to her dead mother and still smelling of lavender water lay snuggled alongside dainty embroidered handkerchiefs and potpourri. Old, sepia photographs of times gone by showed a very young Bubla posing in a Kashmiri dress and flanked by houseboats, receiving a trophy in school, and riding a horse. An old-fashioned studio picture of her parents posing self-consciously against a satin curtain took pride of place, but strangely, there were no pictures of her brothers anywhere.

The tin trunk was very precious to Bubla. It held in its depth smells, textures, memories, joys and sorrows of a much loved part of her life that had vanished forever. She drew it out gently and unlocked it. A million memories leapt out at her along with the perfume of lavender and sandalwood. Bubla breathed in the amalgam of scents ecstatically, finding herself transported to other, happier times. Within minutes her suddenly flagging self-confidence had reasserted itself and she felt ready for her first job interview. She loved her tin trunk to a point that was almost pathological in nature. If at the back of her mind she realized that she was perpetually trying to escape from the reality of being shackled to a loveless household, she tried hard not to admit it to herself.

Sitting down on her narrow bed, she started cutting a picture from the previous day's newspaper using a pair of kitchen scissors. She would add it to her vast collection held in a tattered folder. Bubla had been collecting pictures for years. Pictures of rainwashed paths leading towards unknown horizons, yellow fields of mustard dancing in the wind, children chasing butterflies, coloured kites flying in blue skies, birds caught mid-air, their flight trapped forever, and other such things. They gave her a deliciously happy feeling. She used a stick of glue borrowed from her little niece who often helped when her mother was not at home and filed the pictures in a folder discarded by her brother. At other times, Bubla's sister-in-law made sure that the girls didn't get anywhere close to their aunt.

Bubla gazed at the picture that she had just cut out. It showed a tree-lined forest path disappearing into the mysterious green depths of the forest. After a while, almost effortlessly, she found herself lifted out of her bodily limitations and transported to the shady, beckoning path in the picture. She could almost feel the squelch of wet mud between her toes and the sting of cold raindrops on her face and limbs. Her mind became calm and serene. The world she escaped to was so much more alluring – the grass greener, the air cleaner, the raindrops sparkling and the people so much nicer. Besides, like a shimmering silver curtain in the background hung the possibility of something wonderful happening someday, sudden physical beauty, a miraculous cure for her asthma, an unexpected friendship, even love…? This trance-like experience happened very often when she gazed at one of her beloved pictures, and they were coming with greater frequency in the last few months. Boudi, with her constant screeching and complaining about the expenses of having to look after an asthmatic sister-in-law, seemed very far away at such times as did the rest of the wretched real world around her. She seemed to transmogrify on such occasions, entering other times and other places portrayed in the pictures. The walk down these strange, magical realms, however, invariably left her shaken and confused and she emerged from these trances feeling exhausted and sleepy. Coming back to the hostile world where she was regarded as a burden was always something of an ordeal.

Bubla put down the picture and walked to her tiny dressing table. She stared at her emaciated, bespectacled reflection. Her eyes appeared dreamy and faraway, still in the grip of her tin trunk magic. They misted over now with some nameless emotion. Very soon, she thought in resignation, her sister-in-law would wake up and rend the air with her screams of discontent. The servants were sloppy, the evening tea brewed by Bubla too strong, Bubla really was hopeless at every job, and why couldn't she take up a job and contribute to the family finances, after all her asthma medicines cost a packet... Evenings were never quite right for Boudi, thought Bubla wryly. Neither were mornings. Nor afternoons. Nor nights, for that matter.

40

The gulmohur trees were ablaze with their red-orange blossoms. Siddharth, watching summer advance from his bedroom window, noticed that while some trees sported bright vermilion blossoms, some others were laden with flowers that were orange in hue and in yet some others trees, the bloom had lightened to a pale lemon-yellow. The rain trees that interspersed the gulmohur trees were heavy with their pink powderpuff blossoms, and coupled with the deep green foliage of trees the blossoms created a riot of hectic colours that would have looked positively gaudy had the sober grey of asphalt not broken the madness of summer's picturesqueness. How long would these exuberant trees survive, wondered Siddharth, before concrete and tar took over completely?

He avoided looking at the skyscrapers that loomed behind the Durga Nagar slums. Suddenly, almost overnight, he found himself repelled by chrome, glass and landscaped gardens, the very things he had sworn by some years ago. He felt revolted and sickened by steel, concrete and the tortured-looking artificial city gardens that did more harm than good, as he now understood, the beautiful thick, waxy-leaved plants depleting the soil more than cement could have ever done. Architecture sans good sense, city planning sans sensibility, he thought viciously, environmentally responsible growth, a term left to be used by jokers and morons.

Siddharth felt a wild craving for all things old-fashioned and simple. For earth covered architecture, for kitchen gardens that grew the day's vegetables, for the clip-clop of horses' hooves, cobbled pathways, lantern light at dusk, homely conversation in place of uncommunicative television viewing and smells of cooking and baking at every doorway. Grass, flowers, birds, butterflies left to their precious life cycles, uninterrupted by man, he thought achingly. A slow, frightening anger was beginning to take shape within him, a deep-seated hatred for the superficial, shallow and the glitzy. The neon lights, once so very entrancing, seemed to scorch and scar his skin, while the hoardings screaming their lies to gullible consumers seemed to rip through his sense of integrity, disfiguring him. He realized with a sinking heart that he had fallen out of love with Bombay.

Siddharth had been doing a lot of reading lately, concentrating on topics like rainwater harvesting and low-cost hollow brick housing techniques. The final year presentation loomed before him ominously, the dreaded presentation, the results of which could make or break a student's career. There were two months to go before each student officially declared his chosen topic before a panel of professors and he did not have much time on his hands to get cracking on the job.

'I'm thinking of choosing eco-friendly architecture as my topic for the presentation,' said Siddharth, trying to bounce his ideas off Xavier.

Xavier stopped dead in his tracks.

'Are you out of your mind, man? You want to commit harakiri? Everybody is trying to outdo each other in futuristic themes and you want to go backwards? Have you been smoking pot or something?' Xavier sounded distressed and horrified.

But the thought stayed with Siddharth. He failed to see any future in the march of metal and cement. The only solution was to go back to one's roots. He put forth the idea hesitantly to his family and friends during the evening coffee session.

'Eco-friendly architecture? Bravo, Sid!' cheered Mustafa. 'And we'll all wear leaves to your convocation ceremony. No fancy dress code please, the invite shall insist, only flowers and grass skirts allowed. Women permitted to go topless.'

Siddharth took no notice of his best friend, his eyes fixed on some imaginary city. He sat in a trance, visualizing a city with earth covered low buildings, patches of greenery compulsory with every colony, rainwater harvesting facilities built in every residential zone – a city that grew graciously and horizontally, without being a vertical nightmare. A city where flora, fauna and man coexisted with dignity and for every tree felled, a dozen were immediately planted as compensation. Impossible dreams, he told himself, as the aroma of coffee and conversation washed over him.

He sauntered over to the window and gazed out. Some distance down the road, a tea-seller stood in the shade of an old gulmohur tree brewing tea for his evening customers. There was a brief lull in business and the man sat chewing tobacco and ruminating. Siddharth watched him with a wistful expression. A slab of concrete measuring about four feet in length and two feet in breadth had been cleverly placed across an unused gutter to make the floor of the tea shop. A rickety little table held a kerosene stove, large aluminium pans, cups and saucers, packets of pasteurized milk and glass jars filled with biscuits. The hip-high wall next to the gutter formed a convenient seating arrangement for the customers who could be seen sitting in a line and discussing a wide range of topics ranging from cricket to politics and Hindi movies to crime. In summer, when the tree was in bloom, it was not unusual for a flame-coloured blossom to fall into the tea. On windy days, the feathery leaves drifted down in the breeze, often coming to rest on the tea-sippers' heads. The customers did not mind such happy accidents. On the contrary, many of them liked to have their tea spiked with the flavour of the season.

The entire tea shop resting precariously on the gutter was nothing short of an architectural marvel, thought Siddharth admiringly. The tea-seller was a good listener and emanated an air of warm sympathy. This, along with the excellent liquor that he brewed, ensured that he was never short of business. A pan of tea liquor sat boiling at all times and he stirred the brew from time to time with a steel ladle, his ear cocked at the prevailing conversation. Occasionally, he lifted a ladle full of tea and poured a thin jet of brown liquid down into the pan where it hit the parent body of liquor with a joyous froth of chocolate coloured bubbles.

Elderly couples, fitness freaks, youngsters, lovers, friends and acquaintances sat in a line sipping while the tea-seller served tea, listened, empathized and in case of awkward silences even supplied some intelligent conversation. He was highly innovative. In winter, he spiced up the tea with ginger, cardamom and pepper while in summer he served tea dusted with rock salt and a dash of lime juice. Conversation, secrets, seasons and trends had washed over him for years, giving him a rock-like quality. To Siddharth's envious eyes, he exhibited all the admirable traits of a winner and showed every sign of surviving in the evolutionary race, even in the age of colas and cocktails.

Siddharth sighed. There was a weariness in him these days that permeated his very bones. His head throbbed with the pressures building up. The irrationally high expectations held by his mother and elder brother and his professors in college (especially Professor Deshmukh) left him shaken at times. Would he be able to live up to those grand expectations? He looked at the tea-seller wistfully again. What a wonderfully well-ordered and predictable existence the man had. Like a compact, knife-edged glass prism holding all of life's securities and bliss. The hard trunk of a tree to lean on, the soothing murmur of generations of tea drinkers, flowers raining on the head all day long, no challenges, no fears, no cut-throat competition and no dirty politics. All that was required was that the tea should be steaming hot and should taste good. Siddharth felt a wild urge to chuck his portfolio out of the window and request the man for a partnership in his tea stall, trade T-squares for teapots, so to speak. He laughed at himself. He took one long last look at the tea shop before turning away to join the others. Feathery fronds from the gulmohur tree outside the window drifted down in the gentle evening breeze. They rained on the scene with their specks of green and to Siddharth it seemed as if his vision was suddenly showered with green confetti.

41

Malati Iyer gazed out of her office window with unseeing eyes. Her mood was unusually contemplative.

Maltesh had come in for a few days and disappeared again. He had been strangely abstracted and bursting with some kind of secret excitement. For the few days that he was back, Maltesh worked in a kind of frenzied hurry to finish all his pending work after which, inexplicably, he vanished again.

Malati missed him. She missed the warmth that had made words unnecessary between them. She felt just a little lost and vulnerable without his strong, silent support.

Soumitro leaned back in his chair lazily, his hands clasped behind his head. He watched Malati's expressive little face reflected in the glass pane with amusement. What ailed the girl, he wondered in concern, noting her distracted frown. Malati suddenly rose from her seat and made her way towards his desk. Soumitro swung around on his swivelling chair, quickly shutting the glass window with its mirror-like face.

'SB,' Malati began hesitantly, 'could I take the evening off? I've got to attend my nephews' school annual award ceremony. They're both getting general proficiency medals this year.'

'Of course! Go ahead,' said Soumitro readily. 'Great news about your nephews getting medals. They're smart kids. They study at the Makhijani Foundation School in Powai, don't they?'

Malati nodded. Soumitro was gazing at her with a hint of a smile on his face and she flushed, suddenly feeling flustered. The new Soumitro, polite almost to the point of tenderness, alarmed her considerably. She found herself wishing for the curt, rude editor of earlier times. At least she had known where she stood with him.

'Okay then.' There didn't seem much else to say.

Turning around, she made her way back to her table, acutely conscious of his eyes on her back.

'And don't forget to put on your shoes,' he called out, laughter in his voice.

Malati blushed. Her habit of walking around the office on bare feet was well known to all. On a few occasions, in a distracted frame of mind, she had walked all the way to the bus stop without footwear and Ganesh, the peon, was never tired of relating the incident to everybody. It never failed to raise laughs.

'Thanks for reminding me,' Malati muttered embarrassed. 'I won't.'

The Makhijani Foundation School grounds were ablaze with floodlights and activity as the school geared up for the most important ceremony of the academic year. Chairs were laid out for parents over the lush, immaculate lawns which were beginning to fill up rapidly as evening advanced.

Malati, who had been held up in traffic, made her way to the rear of the crowd and selecting a corner chair, settled down comfortably. She was just in time as the principal and the senior teachers were coming in to take their places on the dais. From her place at the back, she could clearly see her brother and sister-in-law a few rows ahead of her. Her brother, in an attempt to hide his receding hairline, had side-swept his hair across his shiny pate while her sister-in-law's salon-set hair gleamed elegantly in the floodlights. Both of them strained painfully to catch a glimpse of their two little sons. The students, neatly brushed and squeaky clean, stood in queue. They could be seen fidgeting restlessly as they waited for their moment of glory when their names would be announced and they would go up on stage to receive the medals.

There was an oppressive feel to the evening. Malati shifted in her seat as the principal's opening speech progressed. She felt oddly restless and uneasy and unable to concentrate on the happenings around her. Leaning forward, she tapped her brother on the shoulder, taking care to bend out of view of the teachers on the dais. Mutely she signalled for the car keys which he handed over equally stealthily. Slipping out of her seat unobtrusively, Malati walked out of the school premises, the principal's voice echoing behind her. Finding the family car parked close by, she unlocked it and slipped into the driver's seat.

For a few moments she sat still, drumming her fingers on the steering wheel. The award ceremony progressed steadily with the names of the awardees being called over the mike. The list began with the youngest lot of students.

There was an odd pensiveness in Malati. The idyllic scene on her right with fresh-faced students, eager parents, stiffly starched teachers and lush lawns bathed in golden floodlights seemed unreal somehow. Almost dream-like in quality. And that soft, steady ticking sound... was that her heart beating? And whom did that unpredictable organ beat for so desperately, she thought feeling whimsical. Soumitro? Or Malto?

She sat lost in thought, her mind meandering aimlessly. Would her manuscript be accepted by any publisher, she wondered, would her novel see the light of day? Would it grace the shelves of bookstores some day? Would Maltesh ever come back to *Noon Voice* from wherever it was that he had disappeared to? Was there even a remote chance a of her having a normal and cordial relationship with Soumitro in the near future?

Her thoughts were sad when they dwelled on Maltesh, her one true friend, who had accepted her so unconditionally, with all her eccentricities. The ticking grew louder. She frowned. The sound was too loud to be that of her heart beating. It seemed to be coming from the back of the car. Twisting around, she glanced at the rear seat. A bundle of napkins lay on the seat along with a couple of empty water bottles carelessly strewn around. The ticking seemed to be coming from the pile of cloth napkins. Turning awkwardly in the driver's seat, she reached out and rummaged among the napkins, feeling her fingers close over something that was twisted, cold and plastic in texture. It seemed like a wire. She tugged at it with her outstretched arm, curiosity rising within her. She gave a hard yank and her hand emerged with a bright yellow wire. It seemed to be attached to a box of sorts which was partially hidden under the napkins. A warning bell seemed to go off in her head. Graphic illustrations seen in the newspapers recently flashed through her mind in quick succession. Something stirred in her brain, a premonition of danger. She flung off the napkins with urgent fingers to see what lay beneath.

It was a detonator.

42

For an entire minute Malati sat there in stunned silence. If she hadn't been quite so frightened she would have laughed at the irony of the situation. She, Malati Iyer, who had always thirsted for drama was now actually holding it in her bare, trembling hands. Could life get more ironic?

Suddenly a hundred thoughts poured into her mind without coherence, without sequence and without grammar. The list of targets found on the terrorist outfit busted recently... the Makhijani Foundation School belonging to the Makhijani builders on top of the list... security beefed up in the school... but not enough, as it appeared now... not enough... the ticking in her ears... a timer... seconds ticking by... precious seconds...

Malati felt a wild, hysterical urge to laugh out loud and she tried to still the trembling of her hands. How on earth was one supposed to defuse a bomb? Jump on it, stamp it, hold it under a tap, splash it with Coca Cola (there was a bottle of Coke lying somewhere in the car), yank out the wires? The newspapers gave one extensive information on how to spot a bomb but they rarely told you what to do if you found one, she thought desperately. Hysteria welled up within her, threatening to swamp all intelligent thought, and her skin prickled with sweat. Her hands felt cold and clammy.

She looked at the detonator and quickly glanced away again, focussing on the award ceremony that was in progress on her right. If the bomb exploded now, as it was meant to, it would take half the audience with it, which included her brother, her sister-in-law and her two little nephews. Something gleamed ahead of her, almost begging to catch her eye. It was the Powai Lake, visible through gaps in the tall buildings and merely at a distance of a few hundred yards.

Something snapped into place in her mind with an almost audible click. Common sense, her most vital asset, reasserted itself with a vengeance. There was really no time for histrionics or hysteria now, she told herself sternly, suddenly feeling cool and composed. There was merely time for quick, intelligent action. Her mind worked furiously. The Powai Lake was only two to three minutes driving distance from where her car was parked, if she drove really fast. The main road skirted the lake and was divided from the water body by a wide stretch of marsh which was choked with water hyacinth. There was no wall in between, with the road giving way to the marshy bank almost seamlessly. If she could drive at top speed now, go off the main road and plough the car into the marshy bank of the lake, the bomb might explode in relative safety in the lake. If there was time left of course, she thought in panic, the timer ticking in her ears urgently. The lake area, urgently in need of desilting, was uninhabited, being unsuitable for both boating and fishing. If she drove the car into the lake in time, nobody would be hurt. Only her brother's precious new car would blow up. And she, Malati Iyer, with it in all probability, if she didn't have time to flee. For an anguished moment, visions of her manuscript and Soumitro's bearded face swam into her head. Then, resolutely putting all thoughts away from her mind and setting her chin at a determined angle, she switched on the ignition. With one hand steadying the steering wheel, she reached out for her mobile phone and called a familiar number.

Soumitro sat lounging in his favourite office chair, his relaxed limbs stretched out before him. His shirt buttons lay open carelessly, his hair was tousled and he looked younger than his years and very vulnerable. A half-finished crossword lay before him on the table along with Malati's manuscript. A nebulous idea on how to end the novel was beginning to form in Soumitro's mind as he lay sprawled in the empty office. Strange how his imagination, which never got started when it came to his own book, was working overtime in the case of Malati's book, he thought wonderingly.

The phone rang shrilly, startling him out of his reverie. He reached for it, irritated. It was Malati at the other end.

'Listen,' she began without preamble. 'There's a bomb in my car and I'm driving it into the Powai Lake.'

Soumitro jerked to an upright position.

'What!' he exclaimed. 'What the hell are you talking about?'

'No time to explain. I'm just outside my nephews' school, the Makhijani Foundation School, and there's a bomb in my car.'

'Get off,' ordered Soumitro, his voice clipped. 'Get off and run. As fast as you can.'

'If it explodes here, it kills my family and half the school with it.'

'Now don't try to be melodramatic,' snapped Soumitro, his hands icy on the receiver. 'Get off and run. Do you hear me?'

'SB?' her voice was very soft and tremulous.

'Yes. Go on, go on,' his voice sounded hoarse even to his own ears.

'If anything happens to me... the manuscript, well, it's yours.'

'What manuscript?'

'Oh, come off it!' Even at this incredible moment her voice seemed to hold a laugh. 'You've been reading my manuscript on the sly and leaving cigarette ash all over it.'

Soumitro seemed to be having trouble breathing and his skin felt cold.

'I don't want your goddamned manuscript, understand? Just get out and run, like a good girl,' snapped Soumitro, his voice hard and urgent.

'Som?'

It was the first time she had called him that and his heart skipped a beat.

'Yes, yes?'

'I love you.'

Soumitro felt the breath knocked out of his lungs. He shut his eyes. The three trembling words seemed to travel like a lamp down a long, dark tunnel of self-denial deep within him. He sat speechless, the receiver shaking in his trembling hand. Come back Malati, he wanted to shout out loud, come back to me. I've thought of an ending to your novel. He opened his mouth to say something, anything, he wasn't sure what, when a deafening crack ripped through the telephone line. There was a wild crackle of static before the line hissed and went completely dead. Soumitro sat as if turned to stone and the telephone receiver slipped in slow motion from his nerveless fingers. It hit the edge of the table, went sliding down the side and hung swinging from side to side like an ominous black pendulum marking time.

A gentle breeze blew in from the window. It rustled among the papers, blowing cigarette ash out of ashtrays. It wafted over to Soumitro sitting immobile and expressionless and gently caressed his face. Suddenly, without warning, the breeze seemed to gather strength, turning hostile. It blew around the room, knocking stationery off tabletops. It hovered with malevolence around Malati's manuscript, circling it and tugging at the cover with a perverted persistence. The cover of the manuscript suddenly flew open and a hundred odd pages of *The Song of the Road* flew jeering into Soumitro's stricken face.

43

Professor Anant Deshmukh walked down the corridor of the Sir D.V. College of Architecture, his footsteps echoing over the old stone floors. He had an ear cocked to the tune of the winds in the casuarina trees. They had been whispering secrets into his ears for decades. Watching evening fall on the college campus, Professor Deshmukh felt the usual sense of bliss wash over him. He loved the daytime hours when the campus was bustling with noise and activity, but he also loved the evening hours when the old, sprawling stone building fell into a dreamy silence, recuperating and replenishing its spent energies.

He knew what the wind in the trees was telling him of course. He had known for years without being in a position to do anything about matters as they stood. Supernatural powers and cosmic warnings were not required to point out what was going horribly wrong at Sir D.V. College of Architecture. Plebeian sensibilities, nurtured and encouraged by the current principal Professor Dongre and half a dozen of his predecessors, had taken over the reputed college almost entirely. The doors had been flung open to the classes oppressed for centuries and who now held the upper hand in all things. Long denied of rightful power, they were now hungry to compensate for decades of deprivation as they went about setting standards of performance that pushed daring originality off the map and established the supremacy of uniform mediocrity. Professor

Deshmukh's recessive paternal genes seemed to suddenly rear up, becoming sharply dominant as he simmered at the turn of events at the Sir D.V. College of Architecture.

Professor Deshmukh took serious heed of the warnings that the doleful casuarina trees were giving him. Though he could not openly voice his protest, the presently falling standards of the college appalled him. Such trends were not good news for the future of the college, he thought shaking his head, not good news at all. He sincerely believed in helping friends, relatives and the underprivileged, but to an extent that was within the limits of sanity. To sacrifice quality at the altar of social justice and nepotism did a college no good.

If he got elected to the post of principal next year... He felt a surge of excitement at the prospect. There was no end to the changes and reforms he could bring about as principal. Revamp the ailing syllabus, nurture and promote pure talent, cut out all present malpractices from the system and put the college back on the city's success map. In an effort to uplift his entire clique of cronies, Professor Dongre had downgraded the image of the college over the years in the most abysmal manner, in Professor Deshmukh's critical eyes. Having the college teem with children, relatives, friends and sycophants was not conducive to the progress of the college. Now, if he were principal... He fell to the pleasurable task of indulging in his favourite fantasy.

His thoughts suddenly switched to his protégé Siddharth Banerjee and he felt his spirits lift buoyantly. Siddharth was his ticket to success. Professor Deshmukh had nurtured, moulded and backed Siddharth right from his first year in college, as if he was a much favoured racehorse. Only Siddharth, like a thoroughbred stallion, was capable of galloping to the finishing line in a spectacular fashion, taking his mentor, Professor Deshmukh, along with him. Three major events were looming before the college in the remaining academic year. The final year examination results which determined the job placement of a student (the topper being a prize catch for top-notch companies), the coveted Srimati Kamala Bai Trophy (accompanied by a hefty cash prize) to be given to the best outgoing student and the Ralph Correa Trophy that entitled the winner admission and funding to a prestigious college in the U.S. Professor Deshmukh knew in his heart of hearts that Siddharth Banerjee would easily qualify for all three, being head and shoulders above everybody else. But the point was, would he win any of them? Medha Dongre's vacuous face swam into Professor Deshmukh's thoughts and he felt frustration tug at his insides. It was Professor Dongre's Medha versus his beloved Siddharth, as he well knew. He suddenly felt fanciful, likening himself to Krishna with Siddharth in the role of Arjun. The timid, pigtailed Medha Dongre made for a rather unlikely Duryodhan and Professor Deshmukh stifled a laugh. If only, he thought desperately, if only his protégé could pull off a hat trick and bag all three awards, as his mentor his position as future principal would be assured. As a professor, he had nothing personal against the unexceptional Medha. If only she had a little more personality in standing up to her father and his wily ways, thought Professor Deshmukh with irritation.

Professor Dongre's lean, cunning face loomed before Professor Deshmukh menacingly. His cut-throat manipulative ways were well known in the college. His habit of flattering and wheedling before the college trustees had influenced many an administrative decision in his favour. The forces working within the college were dangerous and they could tilt decisions any way they wanted. The only thing left to do was to ensure that Siddharth came up with an outstanding final year project that no one could pin a flaw on. A topic that symbolized speed, progress, technology and aesthetics blended in perfect proportion and where towers, skyscrapers, metal, glass, metro rails, flyovers, multiplexes, waterways, skywalks, hovercrafts and other fantastic things defined a sleek city of the future. Yes, thought Professor Anant Deshmukh, the future of the college undoubtedly lay in Siddharth Banerjee's capable hands.

44

The hottest topic of discussion in the Sir D.V. College of Architecture was the thesis subjects to be presented by the final year students before a panel of senior professors. The principal, Professor Dilip Dongre, looked forward to the event. His precious darling Medha would be participating. He could hardly believe that his little girl was on the verge of graduating. Medha's topic had already been chosen by one of the faculty members while the others were busy giving concrete shape to the concept before presentation day. Later on, his colleagues and juniors would set to work on making an elaborately detailed thesis while a professional commercial artist would design a suitably impressive cover for it. His little baby Medha would assist in fleshing out cosmetic details with her slender, incompetent fingers but his colleagues would make sure that she was not unnecessarily pressurized in any way. And when the time came, Medha would bag the Srimati Kamala Bai Trophy for the best outgoing student, ensuring that the hefty scholarship remained within the college clique. Professor Dongre leaned back feeling satisfied and complacent at his foresight and planning. A niggling worry troubled him though, which when inspected closely took the shape of Anant Deshmukh. They were old enemies with a healthy fear of each other's danger quotient but being the principal, Professor Dongre had always had the upper hand. If only that infernal maverick Siddharth Banerjee hadn't joined the college. If there was one person who had the ability to queer Medha's pitch, it was the undoubtedly brilliant Siddharth Banerjee. Professor Dongre was reminded of his instinctive dislike for Siddharth from his very first year. For years as an academician, Dilip Dongre had trod on safe and time-tested paths of teaching and thinking, being acutely averse to experimentation and extremism in designing methods. And then the diminutive Siddharth had come along and turned all his working methods upside down with his mind-boggling ideas and futuristic concepts. Pioneers did not find favour with Professor Dongre, sticklers for stereotyped methods did. Students hailing from cramped homes and thinking low-budget mediocre thoughts were Professor Dongre's prime concern, as were the children, nieces and nephews of his colleagues who were always there right behind him, supporting him in all his nefarious activities. Herd mentality when insidiously ingrained into youngsters was such a wonderful thing, he thought, with everybody behaving so very predictably and batches of clones graduating year after year in comfortably established uniformity under his able guidance. So why did the world throw up such horrible irritants like Siddharth Banerjee and Anant Deshmukh who seemed hellbent on putting a spoke into the well-oiled wheel of the college? He'd have to do something about the two of them, he thought coldly, something very drastic.

Presentation day was moving closer. Siddharth Banerjee felt the tension straining at his nerves. He had to perform. He was well aware that he was caught in the crossfire of college politics that ran between Professor Dongre and Professor Deshmukh and this only added to the stress he was under.

'I don't want to witness the death of this college, Siddharth. Don't let Sir D.V. College gather mould and birdshit like the other heritage buildings of this city. It is all in your hands now. Prepare well for Friday's presentation. There is so much at stake,' Professor Deshmukh told him, his elderly figure stooped with worry.

'Don't hold yourself back, son. Give full steam to your ideas,' he added as a parting shot.

If there was anyone who could push the envelope, break new ground, shock and jolt the panel out of their blinkered inertia with his innovative designs, it was Siddharth, he thought for the thousandth time. He more than made up for the dozens of students indifferent to the magic of architectural studies and who lolled about in the canteen in a pink haze of hashish all day long. The professor looked on with unconcealed affection.

Siddharth looked morose as he crossed the college grounds. Professor Deshmukh's pep talks were anything but stimulating in his present frame of mind. The colour of his dreams had changed, he wanted to proclaim to all and sundry, going from silver and glass to green and earth brown. He had no wish to add to the chaos and confusion that went on in the name of Bombay nor did he have the will to try and redesign a city that was beginning to decay at the roots. His mind was made up in the matter of his thesis topic but he wished he could feel happier about his decision.

The college hall was filled to the last inch on the day of the topic presentation by the final year students. The expressions on the faces of the students ranged from nervous to cocky and Siddharth Banerjee fell somewhere in the middle on the scale of confidence.

Professor Deshmukh sat at the back of the hall, watching his protégé proudly. For a split second his eyes met those of Professor Dongre at the other end of the hall. They did not acknowledge each other. This was the moment of truth, as they both knew, the confrontation that years of politely concealed animosity had been leading to. Like gladiators they sized each other up as they waited for the arena to open. This was not just Medha Dongre versus Siddharth Banerjee as they both knew – it was safety, security and predictability against brilliance, originality and vision. They leaned back in their chairs, their bodies tense, as students started stepping up to the dais to present their topics. The panelists sat up, looking more alert.

Modernism seemed the order of the day, thought Professor Deshmukh as the event advanced, with each student trying to outrace the other in speed architecture involving advanced technology. His students had done their homework well, he thought smiling as he waited impatiently for Siddharth's turn. And Medha's. There was a feeling of strain evident in the air with the entire lot of students being well aware of the undercurrents that ran deep and dangerous in the hall. College politics was never a confidential affair.

Siddharth rose slowly as his name was announced and walked to the podium. Straightening himself, he faced his audience defiantly, his eyes glittering strangely in his white face.

'A very good afternoon to everybody,' he began. 'For my final year thesis, I go back to the era of mud houses, cow-dung flooring, gobar-gas fuel, lantern light and kitchen farming. My selected thesis topic is "Eco-friendly architecture..."'

There was stunned silence all around as his voice rose in volume, warming up to his chosen subject. To the hundred odd students watching, Professor Deshmukh seemed to wilt, wither and disintegrate totally like an Egyptian mummy left out too long in the sun. His skin paled, taking on the texture of parchment, and his eyes sank deeper into their sockets in horrified defeat. His thin frame seemed to stoop further, condense, shrivel and fold up completely. He shrank, losing body fluid, willpower and form under their very eyes, turning into a parody of his earlier self.

Across the room, Professor Dongre smiled, showing nicotine-stained teeth. A smug, polite sneer. Leaning back, he crossed his long legs with lazy, elaborate grace, bringing the tips of his fingers together stylishly. His smile lingered on his lips as he watched Professor Deshmukh slowly begin to crumble. Satisfaction was writ large in his body language. There was nothing left to fear now. The battle had been won before it even began.

45

The vast hall lay empty and silent, the only sound being that of the ancient ceiling fans creaking. Professor Deshmukh sat still on one of the students' benches and stared blankly into space. Siddharth walked up to him, his tread heavy and slow. For the first time since his squeaky adolescent voice had cracked to an uneven baritone he felt close to tears. He knelt before the shrivelled figure of his mentor and placed a hand on the old, knobbly ones of his beloved teacher. Hands, he thought wretchedly, that had taught flawless architectural rendering to generations of students.

'Forget the final year thesis, Sir,' he said softly. 'I'll get you the Ralph Correa Trophy. I swear I will.'

But Professor Deshmukh did not answer. He did not seem to hear the words either. His gaunt cheeks only sank further and his vacant eyes focussed on a point somewhere behind Siddharth's head. He seemed to be watching the fading of a much loved dream towards some distant horizon.

When Siddharth returned home, his footsteps on the stairs were leaden and defeated and he felt strangely reluctant to cross the threshold of his home. His mother looked up as he entered the kitchen, glancing at him from the top of her glasses.

'How was your presentation, Siddharth?' she asked.

She was cleaning rice spread out on a big steel platter, he noticed absent-mindedly, a task for which she needed reading glasses.

'Oh, pretty good,' said Siddharth, his tone offhand.

A long silence followed. Ira took off her glasses with a slow, thoughtful air and placed them on the kitchen platform.

'Babla, come here,' she said softly. When she uttered this particular term of endearment, Siddharth knew it was a matter of concern. 'Look at me.'

He walked up to his mother, feeling perplexed. It was not often that his mother looked at anyone directly. His mother's eyes, he found, were now anxious.

'You will have to win the scholarship if you want to continue with further studies, Babla. *Noon Voice* is sinking and your elder brother...'

There was a moment of pregnant silence.

'Well, Som is going through a serious personal crisis. I hope you realize that,' she finished lamely.

Her glance at Siddharth's face was tense and controlled. Siddharth felt shaken. He had no idea things were so bad financially. Yes, Dada did seem very withdrawn and silent lately, but he had not paid undue attention to it, thinking it was the usual effect of his crossword-making pressures. He heard voices coming from the drawing room. Soumitro seemed to have come home with a visitor in tow. Siddharth turned swiftly, making his way to the drawing room. He needed to talk to his brother urgently.

CoKen sat alone on the sofa in the drawing room, puffing away at a cigarette.

He was worried. Something seemed to be seriously wrong with old Som. Almost overnight he had turned grey, silent and haggard, a ghost of his original self. He appeared perpetually weighed down with worry and a secret grief seemed to be gnawing away at his insides. He barely spoke to his colleagues these days, maintaining an unnatural, deathly silence. He was inexplicably absent-minded and blundered into furniture and tripped at doorways constantly. CoKen watched him narrowly for a few weeks and then came to a firm decision. His friend needed a chaperone at all times. To protect him from imminent disaster and to protect him from himself. With the loyalty of a fierce watchdog, CoKen appointed himself Soumitro's permanent bodyguard.

He now sat smoking contemplatively and waiting for Soumitro to emerge from the inner quarters of the house. His bloodshot eyes were thoughtful and he looked up as Siddharth entered the room.

'Ah! The architect I presume?' he drawled, holding out a cool hand.

'Not yet,' said Siddharth shortly, taking the proffered hand.

'But of course! The little matter of a convocation ceremony and a certificate still remains, I believe,' said CoKen, leaning back again, 'What's your topic for the final year thesis?'

'Eco-friendly architecture,' replied Siddharth.

There was a short silence. Suddenly, without warning, CoKen leaned forward, thrusting his face so close to Siddharth's that their noses almost touched. The pupils of his light-coloured eyes were dilated and his irises appeared enormous.

'Environment, huh? You one of these idealistic blokes who want to restore the earth to its past glory?'

'In fact...' began Siddharth.

'Negate the filthy smog of industrialization and grow roses and brinjals all over the place?'

'I...' stammered Siddharth.

'Get people to walk or cycle and throw all petrol-fuelled vehicles off clifftops?'

'Well…'

'Well, grow up!' snapped CoKen tersely.

'What do mean?' Siddharth's voice sounded hurt and confused.

'People like you jump off cliffs pretty early in life. Or sip pesticide as a nightcap. Or switch over to chicken farming, animation or teaching aboriginal kids,' drawled CoKen.

'Now look here…' began Siddharth heatedly.

'Now, *you* look here, kid,' bit out CoKen. 'It's no use, son. Wake up and smell the coffee. Don't get all idealistic and try to save the world. We've moved beyond all that juvenile rubbish. It's much safer to be Walt Disney than Howard Roark these days. Definitely more practical. Choose a nice, safe, non-threatening career that will pay you well. Let sleeping dogs lie. Let the environment go to hell.'

Siddharth felt himself beginning to shake all over. He was having trouble formulating words for an answer.

'This city stinks, kid. Don't go building your mansions on rotting foundations,' said CoKen.

He glanced at Siddharth searchingly.

'Your brother is very, very ill, pal,' he said softly, 'I hope you realize that.'

Footsteps sounded in the corridor. Soumitro was coming back. Siddharth suddenly found that he couldn't face his brother. He sprang up to escape, casting a venomous look at CoKen. Shut up you half-blown junkie, he wanted to scream, shut up, shut up, shut up… No sound came from his lips.

Siddharth staggered to the door and slammed out of the house just as Soumitro entered the drawing room. He raced out of the building and onto the road. His lungs screamed for expression and hot tears scalded his eyelids. He would show everybody what eco-friendly architecture was all about, he vowed to himself. Architecture that did not maim, deform or rape the environment but moved with the flow of nature. Architecture that did not shred or uproot greenery and sculpt tortured, artificial gardens in its place but moved gracefully around existing flora, enhancing it further. City planning that did not interrupt water bodies and obstruct sea breezes from reaching their distant destinations but left channels free for easy movement. Architecture that did not allow rainwater to go to waste on one hand while citizens suffered from chronic water shortage on the other but tapped and harnessed the full potential of rain.

Siddharth felt red-hot anger welling up within him. He'd show the whole bloody world what sensible architecture was all about, he thought, feeling close to hysteria. His frantic feet tripped over the edges of gutters as he walked faster. He'd show them, he thought with teeth gritted tight, he'd show the whole bunch of bastards that he was no bloody loser.

46

'If you are going to be a part of this family, it's time you got acquainted with Bengali culture,' said Shreya Banerjee to Mustafa Saifee.

'Let me start by blowing the auspicious conch shell,' said Mustafa enthusiastically, picking it up from Shreya's puja platter.

He tapped it with the flat of his palm, the way he had seen Shreya do it and holding it to his lips, blew long and hard. A loud, ugly, unmelodious sound ensued. Shreya threw her head back and laughed.

'It's not so easy, son. Blowing the conch shell is a fine art. It needs strong lungs, good technique and a finely tuned spirituality. Let's start with something simpler. Have you ever done the dhunuchi naach?'

'What's that?'

'It's an age old traditional trance dance done holding live coals,' explained Shreya. 'And is mainly performed by men and women to invoke the blessings of the goddess Durga.'

She stood up and gave Mustafa a smart chop in the waist with the side of her hand.

'Oww!' yelped Mustafa.

'Get up! And follow my steps,' she ordered.

Shreya spread out her sari anchol into a fan. Twisting the end slightly, she gathered up a corner and tucked it in at her waist and out of the way of her feet. Holding an imaginary holder with live coals high up in the air, she started swaying her hips hypnotically. Mustafa, after a couple of false starts, followed her movements inexpertly. The two of them stood swaying to imaginary dhaak beats, their expressions absorbed. The door opened and Soumitro came in. He stopped short at the scene before him.

'Hell! What's going on here? A pantomime?'

'Som!' reprimanded his mother shocked. 'That's your grandmother you're talking about!'

'Don't I know it?' retorted Soumitro callously.

Ira felt an inordinate wave of relief wash over her. Her eldest born was back to normal! Soumitro's congenital knack for sarcasm was emerging again as was his antipathy towards his grandmother. It was a sure sign of recovery. She shuddered to think of his condition these past few weeks when he had lain like a corpse in the darkness of his room, without eating, saying nothing. Bouts of shivering came and went, leaving him further drained. His eyes, empty and shocked, had been the most frightening part of his breakdown. What had caused it, she wondered for the umpteenth time. The popular opinion among friends and colleagues was that the sudden dip in the *Noon Voice* sales and the disappearance of his best friend Maltesh Roy had something to do with Som's illness but Ira's instinct said that the reason was something altogether different. Her mother's intuition was strongly convinced that the brutal death of Malati Iyer had more to do with Soumitro's nervous breakdown than anything else. The newspapers had been full of the bomb blast at Powai that had so tragically claimed the life of the pretty young journalist Malati Iyer but Soumitro had refused to even glance at the news items for some strange reason.

Soumitro stalked out of the drawing room now, muttering uncomplimentary things under his breath and the dhunuchi naach resumed. Mishti seemed very happy this morning, humming soft tunes to herself.

Pagla hawa badol dine
Pagol amar mon metey othe

She glanced at Mustafa sternly.

'You might as well get to know Tagore. The lines that I just sang are vintage Tagore and when translated go,' she said:

O wild wind
On this cloudy morning
You make my mad heart
Dance with sheer joy

'You don't need anybody or anything to make you mad, you already have a couple of screws coming loose,' informed Siddharth with brotherly candour, 'to accept Mustu as a suitor. Pppfff! And don't tell me you've caught the bug from him and are planning to converse through songs, henceforth?'

Siddharth sounded dismayed at the prospect and his twin ignored him.

'My all time favourite Tagore number is,' said Bonny joining in:

Tomar holo shooru
Amar holo shaara
Tomay amay meele
Emni bohe dhara

'What does that mean?' demanded Mustafa pulling out a blue diary from his pocket to jot down notes.

He appeared to be very serious about getting Bengali culture right and waited eagerly for the response.

'It means,' Bonny said:

You now begin
As I end
You and me both
Make up the stream of time

'Hmmm,' said Mustafa scribbling furiously. 'One generation handing the baton to the other. Not bad. Not bad at all. Uncle had a way with words, to be sure.'

He had always harboured the belief that only Muslims were capable of true shayari, the others being just fakes, but now he was getting a fresh perspective on things.

'Uncle was pretty good, I must say,' he repeated admiringly.

'You bet he was,' said Bonny proudly. 'And by the way nobody calls Rabindranath Tagore "Uncle". Not even his own nephews and nieces, I'm sure. Not respectful enough.'

'What does one call him, then?'

'Gurudev,' said Bonny, 'guru as in mentor and dev as in god. The mentor as god.'

'You Bengalis!' exclaimed Mustafa. 'You are the biggest lot of cultists going around, making gods of mere mortals.'

Bonny stood up, beginning to morph into Xena the Warrior Princess, and Shreya intervened hurriedly.

'Poetry is unaffected by caste, religion or colour, children. Poetry is a non-competitive and universal language,' she said firmly, nipping all arguments in the bud.

Peace descended once more in the drawing room. There was an unmistakable heaviness in the air, though. Siddharth seemed unusually subdued and Malati and Maltesh were conspicuous by their absence. Shreya sat still watching the room lit by the usual gold of sunset. Dusk, she thought, was a strange hour, its long shadows showing up things that were otherwise invisible. Twitches, insecurities, fears, warts, vulnerability, viciousness… Things that were kept hidden safely in the bright light of the day showed up so very unexpectedly at this dangerous hour preceding night. An hour when the body and mind were tired, unguarded, naked and incapable of holding on to secrets.

'Where's Benuda?' asked Mishti. 'Isn't it time for his father's phone call?'

Sunday evening was the time for the weekly phone call from Dibyendu's widowed father who lived in Asansol. The long distance call had everyone falling in queue to speak to Pinaki Ganguly who judiciously divided his talk time between his sister-in-law, aunt, nephews, nieces and his only son. Dibyendu generally was the last in the queue, winding up the telephonic conversation with repeated assurances about his well-being in the city of Bombay. Sometimes it was Ira who concluded the call, with fervent promises to find a suitable bride for her nephew. Dibyendu turned very red on these occasions as Ira's side of the conversation was clearly audible to all. He studiously avoided meeting Bonny's eyes at such times.

Dibyendu walked in looking grimmer than usual.

'Bubla didn't make it to the teacher's post,' he announced quietly. 'There was hell at Halfway House.'

Dibyendu's windows at home directly faced Halfway House, giving him a bird's eye view of the flats below. When voices were raised (as Bubla's boudi's often was) he could even hear snatches of conversation. There was very little at Halfway House that was hidden from Dibyendu Ganguly.

There was a long moment of distressed silence.

'Poor Bubla!' sighed Bonny.

Bubla stood at the tiny window of her poky little cubicle. A full moon was rising in the sky. She knew that the huge orange orb at the horizon would soon rise high up in the sky and turn into the same unexceptional silver little moon that she saw at nights. Her mind skittered away nervously from the evening's happenings. The phone call from the school conveying regrets that Bubla Basu had not been selected for the post of geography teacher and the huge ugly display of histrionics by her sister-in-law when the news came through were thoughts that she wanted to blot out from her memory. Bubla wondered whether a few thousand rupees in the way of a teacher's salary were truly capable of changing Boudi's attitude towards her. She walked disconsolately around the house which was comprised two adjacent flats joined together by knocking down the dividing wall in between. A long corridor ran down the length of the house, with a series of bedrooms off the corridor. The doors of the bedrooms were generally kept shut, each room forming a separate isolated island. Bubla crept into the corridor in her shapeless gown, looking like a wraith. A gentle wind blew down the dark corridor, tugging at her clothes. Her reflection in the mirror at the end of the corridor was shadowy, ephemeral and ever changing. Who was she, what was she doing here and what was her objective in life, she asked herself softly, the cool wind tangling her hair. Her role as a cherished daughter had ended the moment her parents died, she did not seem to be particularly competent or well-liked as a sister and sister-in-law and now she had ignominiously failed in her first job interview.

The only role that she excelled in was that of an aunt and her heart warmed at the thought of her two adorable nieces who loved her so fiercely. She stood quietly in the twilit corridor, listening to the sounds filtering out of the bedroom doors. Television dialogues emanated from her brother's room interspersed with snatches of her sister-in-law's voice raised in shrill monologue.

'We're stuck with her forever, do you hear me? *Forever.* She'll outlive us, I tell you. Asthmatics have strong hearts. Our daughters will be landed with your sister then. She'll ruin us, you understand, ruin us completely...'

A part of Bubla's mind quickly drew down shutters. She walked a few steps ahead. Her nieces were studying for their terminal examinations. They insisted on being in the same room and were perpetually trying to shout each other down.

'Life is possible on earth due to the presence of water and air on it,' chanted Nina.

'Matter is anything that occupies space, has mass and can be perceived by the senses,' chanted Tina.

'The only permanent source of heat for the earth is the sun,' Nina raised her voice a few decibels higher.

'Matter exists in three states – solids, liquids and gases,' Tina raised her voice too.

'The radiation from the sun reaching the earth is called INSOLATION,' Nina was nearly shrieking now.

'Solids have a definite MASS, solids have VOLUME and solids have SHAPE,' snapped Tina curtly, her voice ringing with deep conviction.

The shouting match continued. Bubla stood outside the closed doors, listening intently. How wonderfully uncomplicated childhood is, she thought wistfully, how utterly blessed. She sighed a long, deep sigh of resignation into the gathering darkness.

47

Bubla had got herself a new computer. Or rather, an old one discarded by her elder brother. It had been dumped in a dusty, unused bathroom and lay awaiting its fate. Bubla, who knew a little about computers, fiddled around with it in her spare time, eventually gathering up courage to call a local boy to come and arrange an internet connection. A million tantalizing possibilities seemed to explode before her as Bubla suddenly discovered the exciting world of virtual reality.

Her skills developed fast. She no longer lay in bed on quiet afternoons wrapped in her mother's old saris and enveloped in scents and memories. The cotton saris softened with frequent handling had never failed to conjure up reassuring memories of her mother's cooking, her father's absent-minded concern for her health problems and the feeling of being cherished, pampered and loved, but all that changed with the coming of the computer. Afternoons became secret hours filled with a kind of delicious pleasure. So many people were reaching out to her, so many hands wanted to touch her, so many hearts wanted to love her…

The computer with its iridescent blue light held her a willing captive. Sometimes she retreated into the past, searching Google for events gone by, and sometimes she jumped into the future with exciting queries. Bubla studiously avoided the present.

Her special friend erupted on the monitor unexpectedly one evening when she was beginning to feel rather drowsy and was thinking of disconnecting.

'Hi!' he said brightly. 'Lonely?'

At times she was frightened at the speed in which the relationship developed. Her virtual friend was truly wonderful. He seemed to understand her in a way that nobody ever had so far. He instinctively understood her mood swings and appeared to know her darkest fears and secrets. He extended unstinting sympathy to her day to day problems and he was really the most wonderful friend any girl could have. She hugged the secret tightly to her breast, feeling a delicious thrill go through her everytime she thought of him.

They chatted for hours on the net but he never once asked to meet her. She felt disappointed. Would their friendship remain a virtual one forever, she thought in despair, sensing a wild urge to take the relationship further and to a physical plane. He hadn't sent any pictures of his and so she refrained from sending any of hers. An allure of mystery hung around the whole thing. She was thankful that he hadn't asked for her photograph, she didn't want him to be put off by her appearance at this stage. She desperately wanted him to know what a wonderful person she was before he saw her. Looks did not really matter in the important journey called life, she told herself firmly.

It was a night of the full moon again. She stood watching the moon rise for a while as it went from a gigantic golden orb to a diminutive silver one. Suddenly, somebody whistled below. After a few moments, the whistling stopped. She raised her arm to pull the curtains when the whistling came again. She froze at the window, listening intently to the tune. It was one of her favourite childhood tunes. Then again there was silence. She sighed, feeling nostalgic, and got ready to get into bed. The whistling sounded again. Another one of her pet tunes. It stopped and then started again. Yet another one of her best loved songs. And another and another and another... She clapped her hands to her ears, the hair on her skin prickling with fear. There was silence. She leaned out of the window. Was there anyone in the bushes below? There was no movement in the shadows. It was her imagination playing tricks on her, she thought frantically. Switching off the lights, she got into bed. Fear, excitement and a strange desire welled up within her. Who was it who knew her taste in music so well? The whistling below started again. She pulled the bedclothes over her head.

When Bubla woke up, the morning seemed surprisingly normal. Her sister-in-law was screeching at the maid, the children's feet scurried noisily as they got ready for school and somewhere outside a dog yelped. Bubla looked at herself in the mirror wonderingly. Who was it who had whistled so hauntingly last night? Who was it who knew her favourite tunes? Who was it who watched and waited for her in the darkness? Was he a friend? A foe? A well-wisher?

She went through the day feeling a warm sense of excitement all over. She was no longer alone. Somebody was out there. A secret admirer.

'I'm being stalked,' she announced to her friends at A-502 Pushpa Milan, a delicious blend of desire and danger whipping through her body as she related the sequence of recent happenings.

The Banerjees, Dibyendu and Mustafa looked astonished. They listened to her story with varying degrees of incredulity.

Shock, horror and anger followed in quick succession. Who could have the nerve to harass their precious, fragile Bubla?

'This is very, very interesting. Don't panic Bubla. Just give all the details to Uncle Mustu like a good girl and I'll have him in the hospital with a broken jaw,' said Mustafa grimly.

'What's his name?' asked Dibyendu.

'I don't know his name. He signs himself Z,' said Bubla.

'This is serious Bubla, he could be a sex maniac or something,' said Bonny worriedly.

'How do you know that he is male?' asked Mishti.

Bubla was silent. Because, she wanted to tell them, because there is a kind of caressing in the whistling, a flirtatousness to the emails and a strange alchemy that generally happened between lovers and not friends.

'Describe him and I'll try and do a sketch as per your description,' said Siddharth, holding his favourite Rotring pen with the 0.3mm nib poised in his hand.

Bubla sat still, a glazed, faraway look in her eyes.

'I don't know whether he is tall or short, fair or dark, slim or well-built. The physical description eludes me. But he haunts my nights with his whistling and my days with his emails. I don't know what he wants from me,' said Bubla softly.

'Has he proposed to you?' asked Mishti eagerly. 'Is he in love with you?'

'Mishti, please! Bubla can do without the love of such a pervert, thank you,' said Soumitro crisply.

He frowned, looking worried. Bubla rose to leave, her face appearing strangely tranquil and composed. She went down the stairs slowly, her footsteps echoing eerily in the silence that followed. There was a wild blabber of voices on her departure.

'This is serious!'

'Should we go to the police?'

'Or maybe try and nab him ourselves?'

'He could harm Bubla.'

'Yes. There's no saying what a stalker is capable of.'

Shreya Banerjee, who had been strangely silent all through the visit, suddenly sat up straight on the sofa.

'There is no stalker,' her voice rang out crisp and cold.

Everybody turned to stare at her in amazement.

'There is no stalker. He exists only in Bubla's mind.'

Shreya rose, her painful arthritic feet unstable.

'Can't you see that Bubla is a very, very sick woman? She desperately needs to see a psychiatrist,' she said.

She hobbled unsteadily out of the room after a sharp backward glance at the assembled company. There was stunned silence all around.

'If it wasn't enough for the old hag to be a political traitor, she now has to go and turn psychoanalyst!'

'Som,' rapped out Ira. 'That's your grandmother you're talking about.'

Soumitro grinned devilishly, looking momentarily like his old self.

'Don't I know it?'

48

Siddharth's classmates were beginning to get their portfolios ready. The best portfolio ran the highest chances of bagging the Ralph Correa Trophy which funded a whole year of studies abroad. As was the usual practice, the affluent students unhindered by work ethics were getting their portfolio covers designed by professional commercial artists. Some others were going to the extent of having their architectural renderings done by professional draughtsmen. If such practices came to the notice of Professor Dongre, he conveniently chose to look the other way. After all, why draw attention to such matters when his own colleagues were busy working on his daughter's portfolio?

Siddharth felt his apprehension growing in inverse proportion to the dwindling number of days left for project submission. Getting out of bed every morning seemed an unmanageable ordeal these days and each day at college seemed to pose impossible challenges. He felt incredibly old and weary. It was true that he had complete confidence in his academic calibre and he was aware that he possessed a fair sense of aesthetics but in his heart he knew that he could never match the polish of a job done by a professional. His personal ethics and the state of his family's finances could never afford him the help of a professional and he only had his own faculties to fall back on. Siddharth's insides smouldered as he watched the others, cursing a system that made winners of cheats, but hadn't that always been the way with the world, he asked himself cynically.

He would have to think of an extraordinary cover concept if he wanted to hold his own, he thought dejectedly. A cover idea that no one had ever thought of before and which would stand out by virtue of its originality. Surrealistic graphics were being done to death as were stylized camera angles of the city's architectural high points. Interesting interiors, heritage sites and pictures of landscaped gardens were being done by nearly a dozen students. Siddharth racked his brains for inspiration but all creative thought seemed to have deserted him temporarily.

Voices rose from the drawing room and Siddharth schooled his face into an expression of cheerful nonchalance. There was no point in revealing his insecurities to his family. His elder brother seemed to be recuperating from whatever ailment he had been down with and Siddharth had no wish to rock the domestic boat right now. Deliberately whistling a gay tune under his breath, Siddharth strolled into the drawing room.

Obituaries were being written. A passionate discussion was on about how the words should be framed for the different candidates. Three sets of obituaries had to be written, one for old Mr Herman D'Costa's son who had succumbed to thalassemia, another for Malati Iyer who had died in the recent bomb blast and the third one for Dibyendu's colleague who had suffered a fatal heart attack while in office. The text for each dead person was being custom made by the people on the job.

'We'll need something crisp and short for Malati. After all, she was such a peppy little soul,' said Bonny to the others.

They all bent their heads and applied their minds to the task in hand. Mustafa looked up presently.

'How about "I came, I saw, I blew up"?' he enquired.

'Mustu!' said Dibyendu sternly. 'That was atrocious! Death is no joking matter!'

'You mean to say life is?' Mustafa said belligerently, bringing his face close to Dibyendu's. 'You know, there are definitely more jokers surrounding one in life than in death!'

Bonny groaned.

'Okay, okay, okay,' she said wearily. 'Could we cut out the metaphysics and get on with the job, please?'

'You know Sid, speaking of death, I really like your method of cremating the dead,' said Mustafa in a conversational tone. 'Flesh, bones and blood unto wind, water and air. Back to the basics, so to speak.'

'On the contrary, I like your burial methods, Mustu,' said Bonny. 'Almost as if the person is just sleeping deeply and hasn't gone away too far.'

'Phew! Spooky!' Mishti shuddered.

'This is a completely inappropriate conversation for a middle class Bengali household,' Ira Banerjee's plaintive voice rose in protest.

Nobody took the slightest notice of her.

'Electric crematoria are the order of the times,' stated Mutafa admiringly. 'No fuss and no delay, with the dead reduced to a compact little urn of ashes in merely a few hours. Neat. Very neat.'

'This is the most shocking, disgusting, morbid conversation...' Ira's scandalized voice rose a few more decibels.

'Electric cremation?' Shreya shuddered, interrupting Ira. 'Never, never put me into one of those things. I've always had a horror of electric shocks!'

She looked perplexed as everybody howled with laughter. The company suddenly sobered down, glancing guiltily in Soumitro's direction.

Soumiro sat in his father's chair, gazing at the sky above with unseeing eyes. He held a plastic-bound manuscript tightly clutched in his arms and seemed completely oblivious to the conversation around him. Mustafa threw a speculative glance in his direction and cleared his throat noisily. Raising his voice to a theatrical pitch, he broke into poetry.

Chhod de sari duniya kisi ke liye
Yeh munasib nahin aadmi ke liye
Pyar se bhi zaroori kai kaam hain
Pyar sub kuch nahin zindagi ke liye

He cleared his throat once more.
'Which translated for dimwits is,' he went on:

Love sucks, love hurts, love stinks,
Do not make a career of love,
Opt for software engineering instead,
Finito.

Mishti cast a nervous glance in her elder brother's direction.
'I'd cut out the corny verse if I were you, Mustu. And that, by the way, was a pretty ghastly translation,' she said.
'Ah!' lamented Mustafa. 'The trouble with the whole lot of you is that none of you know how to grasp the soul of poetry. I had best construct my own epitaph seeing that I'm surrounded by literary disasters. And what with people popping

off left, right and centre, one never knows when it might be one's turn next.'

'Oh, for such splendid luck,' muttered Bonny with a wicked gleam in her eye.

'Tell me Mustu,' Siddharth leaned forward interestedly, 'what kind of an obituary would you like for yourself?'

'Siddharth!' Ira's voice sounded positively hysterical. 'That is no question to be asking a good friend...'

'Me? Well...' Mustafa seemed fascinated by the idea, giving it long and serious thought.

He straightened up in a while.

'Considering how disillusioned I am with the world, I would like to fade out of the scene on the famous words of the actor Guru Dutt. To quote some lines of his which express my feelings beautifully,' Mustafa said:

Yeh mahalon, yeh takhton, yeh taajon ki duniya
Yeh insaan ke dushman samaajon ki duniya
Yeh duniya agar mil bhi jaye to kya hai?
Yeh duniya agar mil bhi jaye to kya hai?

Dibyendu looked coldly disapproving. He did not like such frivolity in matters of death. While it was true that the Hindu scriptures proclaimed death to be merely a casual punctuation in the long journey of existence, the occasion demanded respect and reverence. This cheery, chatty attitude towards obituaries was in extremely bad taste to his mind. The telephone rang shrilly and Ira ran to answer it, thankful to have escaped the unhappy trend of conversation. Mustafa paused contemplatively. 'Guru Dutt's lines interpreted for the contemporary mind is,' he continued:

This world of casinos, derbies and dodgy portfolios
This world of perverts, slime and sleaze
Bloody hell!
Even if I did get this screwball life
I'd kick it in the butt
And so I bid you goodbye!

There was a moment of silence during which Mustafa looked hugely impressed with his own translation skills.

'Don't you think that the ending was slightly abrupt? And the meaning slightly convoluted?' asked Siddharth dispassionately.

'I think the lines were just perfect!' said Mustafa.

He stood up suddenly, looking excited and overawed at his own literary brilliance.

'What lines! What utterly brilliant lines! It's an obituary worth dying for! I must put it down on paper. I must!'

He raced out of the room and clattered down the stairs muttering to himself.

'That boy is mad. Bonkers. Crackers. Insane!' exclaimed Bonny in disgust.

She rose and stomped out of the room holding a hand to her throbbing head. A migraine seemed to be coming on. Really, she thought in irritation, that Mustafa was really too much! As if it wasn't bad enough having so many deaths in quick succession without having Mustafa turn the whole obituary writing session into some kind of farce. At the end of the corridor her feet stopped and she froze. Her mother was talking on the phone. Whispering, rather. Ira giggled. She was talking to Dibyendu's widower father.

'Yes Pinakida, yes, of course. I've been listening to a lot of Rabindrasangeet and Nazrul's songs. Do you remember that other song…'

There was a reply from the other end and Ira gave a low, husky laugh. She blushed like a rose. In the dim light of the corridor, she looked beautiful.

Feminine. Sensuous. Mysterious.

Bonny stood immobile, her mental faculties frozen in a state of shock.

The telephone was placed on a wrought iron stand at the end of the corridor. Mishti, in an effort to beautify the corner, had placed a potted plant and a vase of fresh flowers next to the phone. A low cane seat was cleverly placed to ensure that the person talking on the phone did so in utmost comfort. Telephonic conversations, as the Banerjees were well aware, were vital, life-changing things and to be treated with utmost respect. A window at the end of the corridor let in muted sunlight throught translucent glass panes and right now the late evening sunlight bathed Ira in dull gold.

Ira laughed again. A low, happy, satiated laugh. Bonny's mind reeled in shock. Her mother. Her gaunt, bony and absent-minded mother who needed her spectacles to talk on the phone and who frequently put the alarm clock in the refrigerator at night, her muddle-headed, ineffectual mother was looking ravishing right now.

Desirable.

In love.

And why not, argued the feminist in her. Why ever not? Why do we always make the mistake of boxing mothers (especially widowed ones) into cardboard cartons of duty, selflessness and an antiseptic sterility? Mothers were not just mothers, they were women too, she told herself quietly, feeling suddenly older and wiser than Ira. With flesh, blood and desires.

Her mother was singing now, in a soft tremulous voice.

Tora je ja bolish bhai
Amar sonar horeen chai
Monohoron, chopolchoron
Sonar horeen chai
Amar sonar horeen chai
Tora je ja bolish bhai
Amar sonar horeen chai

Bonny continued to stare at her mother in a bemused manner while a sense of panic welled up within her. God help us, she thought, what is happening to the whole lot of us? Ma, Benuda, Pinaki Mesho and me, the whole lot of us caught in a treacherous quicksand of desires. Straining at invisible leashes and dreaming prohibited dreams, willing and unwilling prisoners to snares of illicit emotions. Blurting out things that are best left unsaid and not saying things that were waiting to be expressed. What tangled webs we are caught in, Bonny thought in despair. She suddenly remembered her mother's dreamy expression as she dozed in the afternoon, her book of poems held close to her breast and her thighs tightly crossed. Ma and me, she thought in a kind of terror, separated by thirty years of existence, aching with the same desires and dreaming the same impossible dreams. Propriety and time-tested codes of conduct seemed to be falling apart in the house, along with well-learnt mores and morals. Like a pack of cards balanced in a particularly fragile formation. Trying hard to suppress the turmoil rising within her, Bonny quietly dragged herself back to the drawing room on slow, heavy feet.

Soumitro sat gazing out of the drawing room window with blank eyes. He was completely oblivious to the din and chatter around him. An eagle flew high up in the air, circling the murky Bombay skies languidly. Far below, the urchins of the Durga Nagar slums flew colourful kites. To Soumitro it seemed as if the eagle and the kites ran the danger of colliding at some delicate point but he knew it was all an illusion. Like the rest of life, he thought wearily. In reality, the eagle and kites were separated by more than a distance of fifteen feet. Soumitro wanted to retreat into himself the way he had done as a child when hurt. Go into a dark, private space and lick his wounds. Consolidate his pain. Confront it, acknowledge it and face it head on. Like a bear preparing to go into long hibernation, he wanted to squeeze himself into a tight, insulated ball and break all ties with the external world.

Malati and he had been heading for something. A cataclysmic inevitability had always loomed over their relationship from the very beginning. Soumitro had gone so far as to visualize a golden, melting climax to their love-hate equation. That the end would come in crushed, shattered and bloody fragments with trailing strings of ruptured emotions was something that he could never have foreseen. Malati's vivid little face with its mercurial changes in expression continued to haunt his waking hours and his dreams. Everything else had ceased to matter to him these days other than the memory of her face. Even Maltesh and his strange disappearance, the shaky future of *Noon Voice*, his family and the obnoxious Mustafa Saifee seemed to recede into some hazy background.

A stray whiff of breeze wafted into the room through the window. It ruffled the pages of Malati's manuscript, drawing Soumitro's attention to it. He slowly bent down to look at it, an arrested expression on his face. Suddenly, almost in an instant, he realized what his next step should be. Wallowing in grief would really lead to nothing. In a trance-like state, he had a vision. A vision of Malati's novel gracing the shelves of the bookstores in its finished state. With a smart dust jacket, a crisply worded blurb and a superb cover picture. But of course! He got up abruptly, startling the others. Soumitro now knew exactly what he was going to do with his life. He should have known long back. He would turn Malati's unfinished dream into reality. It was the best homage he could pay to her memory. Edit the text, give the novel the ending that he had thought of, start approaching publishers, set the ball rolling. *The Song of the Road* by... His thoughts clamped down hard. Never mind. He could decide all that later on. While Malati had written the bulk of the novel, he would be penning the crucial ending. The main thing was to get the best possible publisher. He felt a sense of purpose sweep through him. Suddenly it did not seem to matter that his younger sister was planning to sleep with the enemy while the older one made eyes at a second cousin. That his best friend had vanished into thin air and the only girl he had come close to falling in love with had gone up in a puff of smoke. All that mattered to him was the precious manuscript held tightly in his trembling hands. His mission in life was clearly outlined, Malati's novel being the fulcrum on which his whole existence would now rest. He would finally have that novel that he had never managed to write in years. He walked to the door on frantic feet and slammed out of the house, ignoring the surprised looks of his family. His footsteps on the quiet sun-baked afternoon road were unsteady and hurried. The vision of the slick published copy of the novel seemed to lure him on, beckoning enticingly. His footsteps got faster. There was a publisher he knew very well who lived in Bandra and who might agree to look at the first hundred pages. His footsteps echoed faster and faster. The hot afternoon sun beat down on his head but he was impervious to all bodily discomfort. His feet nearly flew over the hot tar road as a kind of sweeping madness overtook him.

49

Bubla opened her eyes to hear sparrows chirping on the windowsill. There was a bright stillness to the moment. She lay in bed for a while in her minuscule cabin while her childhood came tumbling out of the tin trunk lying open on the floor. Vague memories of a nightmare clung to her consciousness and she breathed in the comforting scents of musk and rose emanating from her mother's crumpled sari. The old, familiar and much loved smells soon sent all unpleasant shreds of her nightmare scurrying away in the bright light of morning. She would write a long, cathartic email to her special friend today, she thought ecstatically. She would tell him how lonely she was, how much she depended on his warm empathy and how wonderful it would be if he jumped out of the monitor and into her life!

An angry screech rent the peace of the morning. Her sister-in-law was building up a domestic storm again. Bubla sighed in resignation. The screaming continued, rising steadily in volume and venom. It sounded more serious than other days. Bubla got out of bed and walked over to the door of her room. Bending and putting her ear to the keyhole, she listened intently. She straightened up a moment later, her face deathly white. Her peacock blue sari worn for the job interview had bled colour, it appeared, and ruined the children's white school uniforms. Bubla stood shaking, her back to the door and her hands balled into tight fists. Her knuckles showed white. Hot, hurtful words washed over her.

'Two sets of expensive uniforms ruined!' shrieked her sister-in-law. 'She will drain our finances with her inhalers and her medicines and her irresponsible behaviour… the girls will be of marriageable age before you know it… YOU had better explain your spinster sister's presence… she'll ruin our daughters' lives the way she is ruining ours… she'll outlive us, I tell you, she'll outlive us all…'

Bubla pressed her fists hard to her ears in an attempt to drown out all sound. The harsh and searing tirade continued on the other side of the door. She stood trembling, trying to think of distracting things like rain on mountaintops and valleys full of fluttering butterflies. But today, when she needed it most, her favourite defence mechanism seemed to be failing her completely.

'I must put all this behind me,' she whispered desperately, 'I must.'

But the words echoed around the tiny room, shattering the fragile peace of the morning beyond repair. The sunshine outside suddenly seemed a cheap yellow and not the sparkling gold it had appeared just a few moments back. The bird calls sounded harsh and jarring and not sweet any more. She felt a wave of giddiness and reached out for the cold tea and biscuits lying on her dressing table. She took a bite of biscuit and a sip of tea from a cup that wobbled in her hand. But nothing was quite right this morning and the tea and biscuits turned to ashes in her mouth.

Suddenly, almost on cue, she could hear the whistle. A sweet, haunting tune, well-remembered from her kindergarten days.

'Here we go round the mulberry bush, the mulberry bush, the mulberry bush…'

Visions of a beautiful English countryside at winter flooded her mind. Sunshine, warmth, flowers bobbing in the breeze.

Children's laughter sounded in her ears. She rushed to the window and leaned out. There was no one below. The road and the footpath were completely empty. The whistling came again. Another well-loved tune.

'Sing a song of sixpence, a pocket full of rye...'

For a moment she relived the happy days spent as a student at the convent. There was someone down there trying to reassure her at this moment of crisis. She struggled out of her nightdress and threw on some presentable clothes. Stealing out of the door on soundless feet, she walked sideways like a crab, keeping out of view of the drawing room. Within seconds she was at the side entrance of the house and with a gentle, soundless click of the latch she was out of the house. She ran down the stairs on urgent feet and was out of Halfway House in a flash. Her scurrying feet took her to the wide, open stretch behind the building that ended in a cliff edge and had shantytowns sprawling for miles below.

Out in the open and safe from her family she paused for breath. She stood gasping and uncertain for a long moment. The whistling sounded a little further down now, the hauntingly familiar tunes luring her on. The whistler was going further back in time, picking lullabies sung by her grandmother and the beloved K.L. Saigal songs that her grandfather had listened to in the mornings. Bubla's skin prickled with excitement and apprehension. How did he know her grandfather's favourite tunes? She stood in the open, vulnerable and unsure, wondering which way to go. Before her was the aptly named Halfway House where everybody was doomed to be perennially halfway to happiness. A house which held hate engraved in its very woodwork, where she was unwanted, unappreciated, even wished dead at times... The whistling sounded again, sweet and enchanting, behind her. On the other side was a secret sharer who waited patiently with acceptance, sympathy, balm for a bruised heart, maybe even love…? The choice was really not difficult. Swinging on her heels and turning her back to Halfway House, she walked resolutely towards the cliff edge.

50

The October heat lay in a thick haze over the city of Bombay. Durga puja was fast approaching, to be followed closely by Diwali and Christmas. The window dressing in the big shops got brighter while clothes took on glitter and bling. Beauticians worked double shift to get their clients groomed to perfection in time for the coming celebrations.

Bonny was having trouble with her hair which insisted on taking on an Afro frizz in the hot, humid climate. A dozen broken combs were relegated to the dustbin after a spirited tug-of-war with Bonny's unruly hair. Mishti sighed in despair.

'You've got to go puja shopping with Benuda, Didi. You can't go looking like *that*! For god's sake, go to a salon and get your hair done professionally!' she told her elder sister.

Bonny had never seen the inside of a beauty salon as it went against her feminist ideals. But her feelings for Dibyendu were slowly changing her perspective towards most things in life and she realized the wisdom of revising her old habits.

Ira Banerjee hummed happily to herself as she fixed breakfast for the family. She was unfazed by the heat. A lot of shopping had to be done for the approaching festival. A big-sized rohu fish had to be bought (a three kilo one would suffice) she thought dreamily, fresh flowers for the urn, incense, coconuts, sweet potatoes, extra sugar and milk... She mentally made a neat list of things and decided that she would send Bonny and Dibyendu to do the shopping. Both of them were so very sane, dull and dependable, she thought gratefully, and were unlikely to get distracted from the job in hand. They would probably talk about mundane matters like religion, the weather or feminism on the way and such discussions were unlikely to disrupt the shopping list.

Ira felt a wave of guilt wash over her as she hugged her delicious secret tight to her shrivelled bosom. Pinakida had promised to ring up in the afternoon when her children would be out and she could talk freely and without fear. She glanced at herself in the mirror fleetingly. It should be my daughters and not me who should be feeling this way, she thought uneasily, mulling over the incongruity of the situation before a wave of breathless anticipation cast all guilt aside.

As a mother she had always led a hyphenated existence, all her adult emotions flavoured with a dash of infantile ones. It was like eating caviar with caramel popcorn, she thought whimsically, laughing out loud at the simile. On the one hand, her womanly sensibilities had sharpened in these years of widowhood, maturing like rich red wine and on the other, she often regressed to a childlike state in a desperate attempt to connect with her complex brood of children. She had been embarrassed in the past when words like 'nosey' for nose had slipped out in adult company and adolescent slang like 'cool', 'hip' and 'chilled out' had rattled effortlessly off her middle-aged tongue. But now things were different. And wonderfully so! Her children were slowly and surely taking definite shape, form and substance. They did not really need her emotionally any more – maybe it was she who needed them more than they did? The appendages of her hyphenated existence were falling off, proving superfluous at this point in time and she was once again emerging as her own woman. A real woman and not just a mother, daughter-in-law or a widow. A second life beckoned, so to speak, and she rose to greet it gladly. This was a different life from planning menus and tackling laundry. It was about chasing literature and poetry on quiet noons, of long, magical telephone conversations, of hugging pillows tight to a body aflame with lust and longing. A new life was taking shape within her. A new beginning.

Scaffolding was coming up in the neighbouring building as the entire area around the Durga Nagar slums readied itself for the most festive trimester of the year. The building was going to be given a fresh coat of paint in time for the annual festival of lights and the colour chosen for the exterior was lilac. Shreya watched the proceedings from her balcony with trepidation and deep misgiving. She remembered an old family story where her grandmother (a noted singer of her days) had been trilling away merrily in the bath without a stitch on when she had suddenly found herself face to face with a horrified painter at the open window. Needless to say, the lady's musical prowess had suffered a severe setback. Be careful, Shreya repeatedly warned Bonny, Mishti and Ira, there are MASONS around.

The October heat intensified steadily over the city. People got lethargic, preferring to stay in the cool indoors. Dark-skinned Bengali sari-sellers from West Bengal moved from one area to the other, glistening with sweat and carrying their big white bundles of new saris. When spread open in rainbow ribbons on the drawing room floors, the saris got quickly lapped up by the probasi Bengali womenfolk who had been exiled from their native state for years and the crisp cotton saris smelling of starch and newness brought back nostalgia for times gone by.

The sari-sellers pocketed the crisp notes and dreamt of going back home laden with gifts for their wives and children. But they well knew, in their heart of hearts, that dreams were mere dreams. Living in the expensive city of Bombay, they could never amass enough money for train tickets and gifts for the family. They were good psychologists when it came to their trade, playing on the ladies' emotions with skill and finesse, convincing the darker women that they were actually wheatish-complexioned and filling the wheatish ones with the conviction that they were dazzlingly fair. The ladies laughed coquettishly, half-believing and wholly amused at the clever psychological sales pitches, and along with the mandatory bargaining, the entire sari buying session turned into a hugely entertaining experience. A hot cup of tea and some light snacks rewarded the sari-seller at the end of a hard bargain and over tea they spoke of faraway things like the fish farms of rural Bengal and the violent summer storms called kaalboisakhi that destroyed their crops and cattle. They spoke of crippling poverty, sick elderly parents waiting endlessly for their sons and the inability to repay loans in years. They filled the posh Bombay sitting rooms with the sad and beautiful smells and sounds of West Bengal and the well-heeled Bombay women, running caressing hands over their new saris, were often left with tears in their eyes. How unfortunate were these men, Ira Banerjee thought on many a sari buying occasion, shackled to their professions in alien cities and dreaming of home every waking moment. Living in poky dormitories in the dingy streets of Parel or Byculla, walking endless miles laden with their heavy bundles, their only hour of comfort and camaraderie coming at night while chopping onions and draining rice during the group cooking done with other sari-sellers. Conversation flowed at such times and songs were sung as a deep, sad, collective homesickness gnawed at their tired bones after dinner.

How wonderful were all Indian festivals, thought Shreya, watching the city come alive. Of course, the fervour of Durga puja back home in Calcutta was so much more spectacular and ubiquitous. But there was a personalized comfort in the Bombay pujas that could never be found in Calcutta, as if the Bengali communities of each area were snuggling up annually to reassure each other of their communal connectivity. Festivals, as Shreya now knew in her ripe old age, were less to do with godliness and more about adding crucial punctuations to the long, lonely journey called life. Nobobdy talked about it openly but every Bengali in Bombay knew that the Durga puja coming in the hot month of October was a lofty attempt to dispel the weariness and the introspection that the long months of the monsoons brought with them. A reunion with sunshine and nature at harvest time, so to speak. Festivals, reflected Shreya, were things that built happy boundaries between seasons, made people come out of themselves and mingle with fellow beings and forced them to look around at the marvels of the cosmos. Women cooked elaborate sweetmeats together, enjoying the gregarious tediousness of the job more than the finished products, new garments were bought over giggles and endless discussions, jewellery admired and coveted and colour schemes for clothes planned well in advance. Life, thought Shreya astutely, broken into welcome little paragraphs of hectic activity after the long, dreary chapter of the rains. What supreme intellectuals were those men who started it all, she thought, what wonderful psychologists.

Bonny was getting her arms waxed and her hair done at a Chinese beauty parlour down the road while Dibyendu waited outside patiently. It was the first time Bonny had entered a beauty parlour and her debut visit was creating a minor storm in the little salon.

'Don't scalp me or fry my hair. Careful with that hair dryer, idiot! Owww!' she bellowed as the wax strips came off her arms.

The cute Chinese girls were beginning to look severely stressed and stood in danger of losing their famous good humour any moment. Bonny emerged out of the frosted glass door half an hour later and a pleased looking beautician accompanied her.

'Xxcuizze me,' she lisped, smiling up at the waiting Dibyendu.

'SQUEEZE you?' repeated Dibyendu in a tone of horror.

'She means "Excuse me",' explained Bonny dryly.

'Xxcuizze me, how duth you'll gull-friend look?' asked the beautician grinning delightedly.

Bonny blushed a beetroot red. Dibyendu turned to looked at Bonny. He stared and stared, completely mesmerized. Bonny's hair was like a sheet of black silk, her skin glowed and her eyebrows shaped in wings no longer resembled the rainforests of the Amazon.

'Beauthifull!' said Dibyendu, looking and sounding as if he was lost to this world and losing grammar and pronunciation once again. 'My gull-friend look justh beauthifull!'

A-502 Pushpa Milan was bustling with frenzied activity. The brass glistened, fresh flowers spilled out of vases and smells of special cooking wafted through the air. Dinner was going to be served early as the youngsters were all planning to go trooping in a truck to get the neighbourhood puja idols from the idol-makers across the city. Mustafa was already practicing the dance steps which he would perform atop the truck while Mishti got the conch shell and other paraphernalia ready as they waited for Bonny and Dibyendu to return. Only Siddharth sat sullen and withdrawn from all activity. His overnight bag packed for the college excursion lay in readiness next to the main door. He would miss the first two days of Durga puja, he thought glumly, but it was unavoidable as joining the final year excursion was considered mandatory in college.

Many worries plagued Siddharth. Shreya watched a procession of disturbing expressions flit across her youngest grandson's face. Of all her grandchildren, she loved Siddharth the most. She did not understand the intricacies of the present day education system but all she was bothered about was that it made her beloved grandson unhappy. Siddharth was deeply disturbed at the moment, as she could clearly see, but he was concealing his emotions pretty well before the others. She walked up to him and placed a gentle hand on his head.

'Trust in God, Babla. He will do the needful,' she whispered softly and walked on to join the others.

Siddharth looked up startled. Trust Thamma to see what the others hadn't. He had a sudden urge to hug his grandmother and bury his face in her bosom the way he had done as a child. No Thamma, he told the retreating figure silently, my god is incapable of doing the needful. My god has Alzheimer's disease. He neither sees, nor hears, nor responds. My god is sterile, impotent, old and withered. He forgets and messes things up all the time.

Mustafa sauntered up to his friend.

'We'll miss you Sid. Anyway, don't ever let the long shadows of failure and disappointment get you rattled. Realize that rewards and success invariably come from the direction in which you are not looking and enjoy your excursion, kid,' said Mustafa magnanimously.

'Are you turning into some kind of a soothsayer, Mustu? Please give me advance notice if you are so that I can get myself into the correct receptive frame of mind,' said Siddharth caustically.

'I don't have to turn into anything, buddy. I AM the original seer,' stated Mustafa with supreme confidence.

'Good. Great. In short, the original piece of work. I'm quite sure they broke the mould after making you, Mustu. Don't see too many people like you around,' Siddharth's tone dripped sarcasm.

Mustafa looked at his friend searchingly. It wasn't like old Sid to be so caustic. He sounded just like his elder brother. The pressure of the approaching project seemed to be telling on Siddharth. Mustafa had a wild urge to tell his friend that academic results were utter bullshit in the entire scheme of things and he should learn to live life only for the moment.

'They've come back!' shouted Mishti from the window, curbing Mustafa's intentions.

Everybody rushed to the window and stood watching Dibyendu and Bonny as they got out of a taxi laden with packages. They looked flushed and happy and wore slightly idiotic expressions. Why, thought Ira with a sense of wonder, watching Bonny from above, my baby looks just like a bride! Shreya, standing next to her at the window, wore an inscrutable expression. The taxi driver came up to help as the duo descended with a great deal of fanfare.

How lucky were people who possessed the ability to be happy, thought Siddharth watching them, pure happiness being a scalar quantity bestowed on only a chosen few. But love and ambition were vector quantities. They came warped, complex and twisted in all kinds of directions and people like Dada and me, he thought in resignation, are neither destined for peace nor happiness.

Here comes the sun… tra la la la

Mustafa sang happily at the window, making a rare switch from Ghalib to the Beatles.

Aloker ei jhorna dharaye dhuiye dao

Ira hummed one of her favourite Rabindrasangeet tunes.

Roshni hogi itni kise thi khabar
Mere man ka yeh darpan gaya hain nikhar

Mishti softly sang a snatch of a retro Hindi number, watching her elder sister's expression all the while.

Shreya quietly watched the others as they watched Dibyendu and Bonny's slow progress into the building. Strange, she thought, very strange. Strange that on this day full of shadows, everybody should be singing of light…

51

There was dancing at night. A bonfire crackled merrily, sending glowing embers up into the cold mountain air. The firelight glittered on the vibrant-hued mirrorwork skirts of the girls and turned their fresh adolescent skin to gold. The shifting tongues of fire caught the highlights in their silky, swinging hair.

Siddharth sat a little distance away from the others, lost in thought. He hugged his Windcheater close to him. The little hill station of Matheran was cool at this time of the year. He watched his classmates dancing for a while but there was no answering music in his soul. Only a great, unquenchable thirst and a desperate quest. The unfinished portfolio cover loomed in his mind. Sighing, he heaved himself up from his comfortable position on the bench. The music was getting on his nerves and he could do with a spot of solitude. Unnoticed by the others, he sauntered out of the holiday resort's gates and slipped out into the dark, waiting woods. He chose a dirt track that vanished into mysterious-looking depths between the trees. Echoes of laughter and music rang in his ears for a while before they petered out completely and a heavy stillness overtook all human sounds. Nothing moved in the forests. Not a leaf stirred and not a bird chirped in the silence. Siddharth's feet, crunching over dry leaves, made the only sound that broke the silence.

He must have walked steadily for an hour and a half before he came to a clearing at the edge of a cliff. Good heavens, he thought in amazement, I've walked all the way to Sunset Point!

This was a favourite tourist spot as was evident from the number of little cold drink stalls that lined the mountain edge and the empty wafer packets strewn around. From previous visits, Siddharth remembered the cliff edge as milling with horses and tourists in the evenings. The city lights of Bombay could be seen far below as could blue flashes of the Arabian Sea, both being visible only on clear, unclouded days. But now, at night, the place stretched out lonely and eerie, the stalls shuttered and the cliff edge devoid of noisy tourists. The flat expanse of mountainside stretched before Siddharth, silent, moonwashed and faintly hostile.

And then he saw it.

His heart leapt into his mouth and his blood froze. He felt momentarily suffocated. The tree rose from somewhere below the cliff edge and appeared to be suspended in space. An awesome tree, nude, majestic and timeless. The gaunt, agonized trunk with the rippled branches caught the silver moonlight while the long, furrowed grooves in the trunk lay in inky shadows. Tinier leafless tertiary branches fanned out from the main ones, creating a silver filigree design against the darkness of the sky. A couple of stars winked throught the meshwork of the branches. They looked like exquisitely ethereal embellishments and added mystery and allure to the white skeleton of the long dead tree. A fossil, thought Siddharth in excitement, a near fossil. He inched closer to the cliff edge. A rare, exquisite remnant of a once proud living tree full of sap and stories, he thought with his heart beating hard. He went closer. Traces of stories were visible still in the smears of ashes and vermilion on the tree trunk. The tree had probably been worshipped by villagers in the distant past. Women, pilgrims, sadhus and fakirs must have trodden these mountain paths and done obeisance to the once regal tree, thought Siddharth in excitement, trying to conjure up the past. Deep, cruel, manmade cuts split the bark in places. A crude heart with an arrow passing through it had been engraved on the trunk. Two names, 'Pinky' and 'Bunty', were etched on either side of the heart. Cigarette butts and empty packets of popcorn lay scattered at the base of the tree. There was tragedy, comedy, tales of worship, torture and abuse etched in every ridge of the tree's surface. A million untold stories lay trapped in the now frozen sap. The roots stood half pulled out of the soil and frozen like claws.

There was something almost human about the tree. A sense of waiting. A kind of hunger in its stance. And an almost tangible feeling of hatred towards mankind for allowing the cliff edge to get eroded and bringing about its death. Its branches rising like arms ended in talons, as if making a prophecy. A small section of root clung hard to the slope of the cliff edge even in death. Its only visitors now, as Siddharth could guess, were wild goats, birds, squirrels and monkeys, where earlier it had seen a procession of worshipping humans. It had survived wind, rain and soil erosion for decades, maybe for a specific reason...? It stood majestic and proud even now, gazing into the ravines below. What did it contemplate, thought Siddharth bemusedly, what kind of hunger was it suffering from and what did it want in order to appease this hunger? It must have seen a million sunrises and would probably survive to see a million more. The branches reaching upwards towards the sky seemed raised in deep, silent prayer. What was it waiting for, wondered Siddharth again, and what were in its prayers?

It appeared to be a sandalwood tree. *Santalum album*, most probably, thought Siddharth, recollecting his botany lessons in a hazy fashion. The tree might have been dead a good many years but its defiance still stood out clearly. Insults, trash and hurt had been heaped on it over decades but hate, pride and the spirit to survive were still visible in its contorted branches. The moonlight falling on it gave it an almost predatory look and for a terrifying second Siddharth had the feeling that the tree was waiting to pounce on him, thirsty for warm, fresh human blood to appease its hunger. He stepped back in alarm and then laughed out loud at the astonishing turn his imagination was taking.

Siddharth felt exultation sweep over him.

He had found his portfolio cover.

His fingers closed over his camera. It was an old Nikon model gifted to him by his elder brother on his tenth birthday. With complete clarity, he saw the cover picture in his mind's eye. The splendid fossilized tree bathed in silver thrown into relief against a black night sky with a silent ring of mountain ranges at the horizon paying homage to the scene. An extraordinary cover idea, never conceptualized by anybody at the Sir D.V. College of Architecture before. This is what architecture is all about, thought Siddharth – beauty, tenacity and the will to survive against rapidly changing conditions in the resolute march of evolution. Good architecture was the ability to be relevant at all times and in all circumstances, like the dead tree. In life, the tree had given shade and sap to hundreds of living creatures and also provided a place and reason for worship.

In death, it stood proud, reminding creatures of the frailty of life and destiny. The tree epitomized all that he believed in, thought Siddharth, feeling waves of some nameless emotion sweep over him. It symbolized the triumph of nature over man and the timeless role of aesthetics, symmetry and poetry in all things. It would be a cover that would create a sensation in college, he thought happily, the examiners being used to repetitive factory line concepts for years, where each cover appeared so like the others.

His pulse was racing. He would have to edge down the cliff and kneel at the tree's base to get that perfect picture. Genuflect, so to speak. Siddharth started walking crabwise down the slope of the cliff edge, taking care to keep a good grip on his camera. His steps were hesitant and his feet angled to reduce the chances of slipping. His eyes were glued to the ground. He tried to keep a check on his speed which was proving to be difficult with a kind of madness creeping up on him with every passing second. The portfolio cover swam before his eyes tantalizingly. Was this what Mustu meant by the word junoon? Yeah, he thought, so be it. I'm crazy. *Junoon, junoon, junoon.* He looked up at the tree in a state of hypnosis and his breath quickened. The tree seemed to be smiling at him. Faster, whispered the tree, its claws stretched out invitingly, come on, you can do better than that, faster, faster, faster... Siddharth's footsteps fell awry in their haste as he raced to obey the tree.

And slipped.

For a split second, the universe swung around and the moon and the stars came rushing at him. Siddharth's feet lost grip as they went rolling over loose stones and he made a wild grab at the bushes growing on the mountainside. They came out in tufts in his hands. He was losing whatever balance he had and he made an instinctive move to save his camera with one hand while the other clawed at the air for support. He was twisting, slithering, sliding and tripping towards the perilous edge of the bottomless ravine, trying to stall himself frantically. Quicker, whispered the tree, quicker, quicker, quicker… Siddharth made a last grab for support, any support, before his body spun into a wild, spiralling mass of tangled limbs.

One by one, his belongings dropped from him as if denouncing all ties with the owner. His pocket pad drifted lazily down the abyss, scattering white pages over the moonlit mountainside. His beloved Rotring pen with the 0.3mm nib followed next, bouncing from boulder to boulder and then shattering into fragments. The only thing that continued to cling to him loyally was his camera slung around his neck. This is it, thought Siddharth in agony, the end. An ignominious end to the idealistic architect. Despite the involuntary thrashing of his limbs in a frantic attempt to regain balance, his mind blanked into nothingness. An entire procession of images floated before his anguished eyes in quick succession: beautifully designed eco-friendly cottages set amidst greenery, Professor Deshmukh's anxious gaze, his mother's careworn, tired face and Medha Dongre's cow-like placidity. The last face to swim into his vision was that of his ever gentle, all-knowing grandmother. Have faith in the powers above Siddharth, she seemed to be whispering to him urgently, her voice almost audible in the stillness of the night, have faith in yourself…

Miraculously, almost by some sort of divine intervention, his flailing hand closed over something hard. He swung perilously by one hand for a long, tortured moment before his second hand managed to reach and grip the thing. Slowly, almost sobbing with pain and desperation, he levered himself over the edge of the cliff.

Siddharth lay on his stomach on firm ground for a long time, weak with exhaustion and relief. It had been touch and go. His mind swirled round and round, mulling over the details of the near tragedy. What had he grabbed in his moment of desperation? What was it that had saved him from sure death?

Getting up shakily, he made his way to the cliff edge to investigate. Peering down at the shadows, he found his answer. It was a gnarled bit of projecting root belonging to the dead tree, firmly embedded in the mountain.

A gust of wind blew across the mountaintop and the branches of the tree rustled. In the dead of the night it sounded like a low chuckle. Siddharth glanced up at the tree in gratitude and reverence. The tree no longer looked hostile and hungry. To Siddharth's bemused eyes, it appeared warm, amused, almost human. Go for it kid, the tree seemed to be whispering softly, fight for your dreams and your ideals. Assert yourself. Show those bastards what you're all about, once and for all!

Siddharth smiled weakly up at the tree, his sheepish grin luminous in the moonlight. He turned his back to the treacherous cliff edge, his back straight and resolute. All the latent optimism that he had recently buried under despair and cynicism seemed to explode in a glorious celebration. There was a very definite message in tonight's near-death experience, he thought. It was almost uncanny how he had been given a second chance to live by the very things he believed in. It was as if the entire universe was conspiring to propel him towards fulfilling his destiny. He had learnt a lesson this night. He would not give up or run away from his responsibilities ever again.

He glanced back at the cliff edge once again. So many living things must have gone down the drop, he mused, some of them accidentally and some of them deliberately. Picnickers, lovers, children, animals, men with dreams, men without dreams and many others must have gone plunging to their death over the years. Well, he, Siddharth Banerjee, was damned if he was going to be just another statistic. He would justify the new lease of life just granted to him. He would find a way to prove his mettle. He would beat his detractors at their own game. He refused to be annihilated or intimidated.

His hand closed over the camera nestling on his chest. It was time to take that perfect portfolio shot of the tree. From a safer angle, of course. Just like his entire perspective of life which had shifted angle in a major way.

A feeling of intense excitement for the future spun through him. His family, with great faith in his abilities, was waiting out there. The Bombay skyline was waiting for him. Professor Deshmukh's credibility and pride had to be restored to him somehow or the other. He had work to do.

Siddharth's future beckoned and he rose to meet it. Gladly.

52

Dibyendu Ganguly stood before the bathroom mirror, lathering his chin. He looked deep into his own eyes in the mirror as if he was having a long, private conversation with his reflection. He used an old-fashioned stainless steel razor, the kind that opened when unscrewed and one neatly dropped in the blade, holding it gingerly between forefinger and thumb. And then one screwed on the razor tight again. Among the many other things that bothered him, Dibyendu had a deep distrust of electrical gadgets. A cousin who had come down from the U.S. had gifted him a snazzy electric razor but on switching it on, the little gadget had leapt in his hand and lunged straight for his jugular, startling him out of his wits. Dibyendu, very politely and hastily, had returned the gift to the cousin, confessing that he was just not tech savvy enough for such advanced gadgetry.

Shaving done, Dibyendu mopped his chin with a towel and headed for the balcony. With elbows hooked on the railing, he leaned forward to watch the Durga Nagar slums wake up below. It was his favourite early morning ritual and one that he refused to miss at any cost. Almost against his will, his glance skittered in the direction of A-502 Pushpa Milan. A lot had changed in the last seven months. There was no music, no laughter and no noisy arguments to be heard from the family on the first floor any more. No smells of cappuccino drifted out into the air at dusk. Passers-by glanced up curiously once in a while, missing the din of earlier days, but shrugging philosophically, they walked on again. The baby birds must have grown wings and flown the nest, they mused. An inevitable step in life.

The lives that had entwined so intimately at A-502 Pushpa Milan had suddenly taken such diverse paths, thought Dibyendu. Siddharth, losing out to Medha Dongre in the thesis (in a predictable manner), had more than compensated by bagging the Ralph Correa Trophy and the scholarship. He had torn through the crippling mesh of favouritism and dirty college politics to make a stupendous impact on a panel of external jurists. It was a moment of quiet triumph and vindication for Siddharth and a cause for intense jubilation in the family. The shores of a foreign land now beckoned enticingly as Siddharth ran from pillar to post, getting his final documents ready for departure.

Dibyendu sighed. So many friends had vanished abruptly from their lives. His thoughts turned to Maltesh and Malati. Maltesh was last spotted in the forests near Karjat by city trekkers who ran into him pretty frequently. He always wore white and was unfailingly courteous to picknickers as long as they left his beloved trees and animals alone. On the few occasions when some rowdy tourists had started shooting birds and squirrels with an air gun for fun, he was said to have turned pretty violent and aggressive. It was rumoured that the city artist with an affinity for animals had joined the infamous forest brigand Guru Das but again it was all hearsay and nobody knew the facts for certain. Not even Soumitro, Maltesh's closest friend at one time.

And Malati.

Dibyendu sighed long and hard at the thought of a young life snuffed out so tragically. But Malati lived on miraculously in her manuscript which was being jealously guarded by Soumitro and which was finally beginning to take the shape of a novel in the hands of a well-known publishing house. Dibyendu thought of *Noon Voice* which was steadily going downhill and Soumitro who seemed to be living for the sole purpose of seeing Malati's manuscript in print. He trod a dangerous shadow line between illusion and reality as they all knew, living his literary aspirations through Malati's work. They could only watch him, feeling helpless and apprehensive, but were unable to summon up enough courage to burst his golden bubble of illusions. Let him be, their eyes told each other mutely, let him exist in his intoxicating mirage as long as possible – tacit silence was the greatest language in this conspiracy of love.

The Banerjees had tried hard to transcend tragedies in this past year and had broken through so many existing moral fences, acknowledged Dibyendu. They had risen above religious prejudices and lost and found direction a dozen times. Lines of demarcation between the accepted and the prohibited had been diffused forever, catapulting them in unexpected directions. Dibyendu thought of his widower father in faraway Asansol. He and Ira Mashi had a strange thing going. Based purely on the melodies of Rabindrasangeet, it was an inexplicable magic that crackled over miles of telephone cable, bringing comfort to two lonely, ageing hearts. Dibyendu was not at all sure whether he approved of such inappropriate behaviour in the senior members of his family, but one look at Ira Mashi's tragic face made him hold his tongue. With one son living a life far removed from reality and another headed for a distant land, this was a tricky time for Ira Mashi. The look of fragile hope at this time of crisis told him that it was wisest to keep silent. He realized that he, along with the others, had taken a quantum leap in beliefs and attitude.

Shreya and Ira were now closer than mother and daughter, glued together by personal tragedies and reconciliation. Secrets that the others would never know about lay thick and shared between them. Shreya wore an inscrutable expression when Pinaki's call came through but she always left the room for Ira to talk and sing in privacy.

Dibyendu found himself looking forward to the weekend when he would drive Bonny over to Poona in his battered old Ambassador. His trusted jalopy had taken him all over the country and he refused to trade it for any of these newfangled fancy models. He would drive Bonny over the scenic Sahyadri range as he always did once a month. They would drive through long, dark tunnels lit up with rows of lights like golden crystal balls and stop for coffee at a mountain café. They would soak in the silences and bird calls while sipping sweet coffee and think about Bubla whom they religiously visited once a month. Bubla still heard voices and held imaginary conversations with invisible people but was otherwise comfortably ensconced in the schizophrenic ward of the Yerawada Lunatic Asylum on the outskirts of Poona. Dibyendu still shuddered to think of what may have happened many months back if an alert slumdweller had not stopped Bubla from jumping off the cliff. Bubla's brother and sister-in-law had been questioned extensively by the police for aiding and abetting suicide on grounds of mental torture but nothing conclusive had come of it. However, it was immensely satisfying for the Banerjees and their friends to see the couple completely ostracized by society and being forced to leave Halfway House and move to another part of Bombay.

Bubla, whose days and nights often tunnelled into one another without any kind of clear-cut time demarcation, truly looked forward to her friends' monthly visits, Dibyendu and Bonny's visits standing out like green oases in the barren wasteland of her unhinged mind. She sat in the sun with other schizophrenics and knitted little scarves to gift to her visitors, humming nursery rhymes all the while.

Dibyendu's thoughts turned to Bonny and he felt the blood rush to his face as he felt warm and happy all over. Of course, there were many things a well brought up Bengali Brahmin boy was never supposed to do and professing love to a second cousin was one of them. Their relationship had weathered a dozen storms in these few months, merely strengthening with every knock. They could not formalize their feelings or be open and demonstrative with each other even now. But they would continue to meet over coffee and long drives, their fingers brushing over teacups and gazes clinging across the room. Such leashed emotions suited his Shaivite mentality admirably. He suddenly wondered what Mustafa would say if he ever came to know about how things stood between him and Bonny.

'Aaah! Non-tactile, long distance love! How wonderfully charming and medieval,' he would probably drawl with his inimitable sneer.

Thank god for Mustu, thought Dibyendu, feeling a sudden rush of warm affection for the absent Mustafa who had become such a close friend. Mustafa was doing all that was humanly possible to help tide the Banerjees over Siddharth's impending departure. I'll gift him a set of Tagore's poems to translate, thought Dibyendu in a burst of generosity, let's see what he makes of those! Rabindranath remixed by Mustafa Ali Saifee. Dibyendu laughed long and hard.

'Insupherable Muslim brat!' he muttered, feeling overcome by affection and gratitude for Mustafa.

He leaned over the balcony railing. The area was fast waking up with unkempt looking delivery boys beginning their morning rounds on their bicycles. Old Mr D'Costa, wearing striped pyjamas and a nightshirt, was out looking for early morning crabs and prawns. His bent, bony body was stooped low and showed defeat in every limb. He had still not got over the death of his only son. Urchins were coming out to play from the hutment area. They were brown and barebodied, their lower limbs clad in tattered shorts. Their eyes gleamed with excitement at the new day beginning and made a farce of the pity aimed at them by the dwellers of the tall buildings around. They settled down to their roadside games as their mothers bathed in the open, close by.

The youngest and filthiest urchin started building a castle with trash cans and discarded cardboard boxes. Dibyendu watched fascinated. The boy's grubby fingers were ingenious and his method of working undoubtedly brilliant. Curves fitted into grooves and corners into angular spaces with precision. The beautifully proportioned castle rose higher and higher. It finally stood poised and upright in an exquisite state of completion before coming down crashing. The little boy started all over again. Dibyendu felt a nameless emotion wash over him and ran an agitated hand through his hair. The little urchin made him suddenly think of Siddharth. He felt excitement and hope surge through him. In the responsible and rooted world, like the one envisaged by his cousin, surely there would be a niche and a bright future for talented little boys like this one?

He had seen the boy before and heard the others addressing him as Mani. His mother was a slim, dark, coquettish woman who had a number of male admirers visiting her in the evenings with garlands of flowers. The father was a mystery, not seen in the locality so far. The woman seemed more interested in her men friends than her little son, if he remembered right. Dibyendu felt a sense of purpose churning within him. I'll take that filthy twerp, bathe him, feed him, educate him and make him an architect someday, he thought in excitement. After all, what would he, a bachelor, do with all that money that he had accumulated over the years? A sense of urgency built up within him. He could hardly wait to reveal his plans to Bonny. She would approve heartily of them for sure. He warmed to the idea, feeling as pleased as a child and making elaborate plans in his head. He gazed down at the road below. Old Mr D'Costa was trudging homewards tiredly while the urchin was near to completing his second attempt at building a castle, a differently structured one this time. Life is strange, thought Dibyendu reflectively. Your only son could die a slow, painful death and you still had to buy the fish for dinner. And pay the grocery bills. Feign a life of normalcy. And snotty little kids without any kind of formal training but with impeccable physics would rise to build castles out of cola cans and shoeboxes. I'll make that little blighter an architect, I swear I will, Dibyendu promised himself. He'd dip into his savings and discreetly try and help his relatives who were going through a rough patch due to the failing fortunes of *Noon Voice*. A strictly RETURNABLE loan, he'd bellow threateningly at his cousins when they all knew that he didn't mean a word of it. He'd do all that was physically possible to get the music, the laughter and the coffee sessions back to A-502 Pushpa Milan, he vowed to himself.

It was time for his bath and Dibyendu slowly unhooked his elbows from the railing, reluctant to move. Inertia had settled over him thickly this morning. He would start running the hot water in a minute. He insisted on bathing out of a bucket in an old-fashioned manner, having developed a deep distrust of showers after seeing a busty blonde getting electrocuted under a shower come alive in an electric storm. The incident, watched on the National Geographic channel on television, had left a lasting impression on him, steering him firmly towards traditional bathing methods. Besides, he told himself defensively, all that bending with a mug was good for a man's waistline.

He threw open his wardrobe. He'd wear the new dusty pink shirt that he had been saving for a special occasion, he decided. It would do all kinds of happy things to his already ruddy complexion and get Bonny's mind momentarily off Sidharth's leaving. At the thought of Bonny, he felt the usual rush of adrenalin and he blushed. Life seemed to beckon with all kinds of exciting possibilities. He might remain a celibate Shaivite and then he might not. He might confess his feelings to Bonny someday and then he might not. He might practice a dignified restraint at all times and then again he might not. There was no saying what life had in store for a bloke with an open mind. He ran a hand through his hair, feeling nervous, excited and just a little stupid, all at the same time. He glanced back for a last look before heading for the bathroom. The air outside seemed to shimmer with all kinds of promises and was shot with a strange sense of anticipation.

Temple bells somewhere close by pealed into the morning air.

Acknowledgments

This novel would not have taken shape without the contribution of certain people. My heartfelt thanks

to my husband Sandip, the eternal cheerleader
to my mother, siblings and extended family for being there for me
to my father for the constructive criticism and helpful suggestions
to C.P. Surendran and Balaji Venkateswaran for their invaluable feedback
to Albina Sharma for explaining to me the finer nuances of Urdu poetry (and sacrificing many a siesta in the process)
to Arun Meshomoshai, Deepakda, Maladi, Pukkulda and Tutludi for their immense encouragement and moral support
to my sons Syamantak and Supratim for rescuing me from every computer related crisis (and there were so many of them!)
to Harpreet A.D. Singh, G. Sampath, Padma Vaswani, Aliefya Vahanvaty and Janhavi Acharekar for rising above the call of friendship at all times
to my editor Saugata Mukherjee for sharing the same lexicon of words and vision and for believing in my novel
to a certain literary critic who, in a rather backhanded manner, got me to write this book. I can never thank him enough.